THE BIG BOOK
OF SUBMISSION

VOLUME 2

THE BIG BOOK OF SUBMISSION

VOLUME 2

69 KINKY TALES

EDITED BY
RACHEL KRAMER BUSSEL

CLEiS
PRESS

Published in the United States by Cleis Press, an imprint of Start Midnight, LLC, 101 Hudson St, Suite 3705, Jersey City, NJ 07302.

Printed in the United States.
Cover design: Scott Idleman/Blink
Cover photograph: iStock
Text design: Frank Wiedemann
First Edition.
10 9 8 7 6 5 4 3 2 1

Trade paper ISBN: 978-1-62778-222-7
E-book ISBN: 978-1-62778-223-4

Contents

INTRODUCTION: SO MANY WAYS TO BE SUBMISSIVE

When I approached the process of editing sixty-nine more BDSM erotica stories for *The Big Book of Submission, Volume 2*, a small part of me wondered: How many ways are there to be submissive?

I knew from personal experience and reading and editing lots of kinky sex stories that there were numerous approaches to submission, but still, this question lingered in my mind: Could this volume hold up to the hotness of the first?

Well, I'm here to tell you that I learned a lot about the thrill subs get from taking orders, absorbing pain, giving service, playing with power, getting spanked, being bound, and so much more by editing this book. These authors, who hail from around the world, have unlocked the beauty of submission in so many of its forms.

With an anthology of very short fiction (each story that follows is 1,200 words or less), writers have to do many things at once: take us into the minds of the characters, give context for the BDSM relationship, and turn readers on.

You should know before you start reading that this book puts a premium on variety—there's not one type of Dominant or one type of submissive in these pages. There are men, women, and nonbinary characters. There are 24/7 lifestyle couples and newcomers to kink. There are those who get off on being stuffed with two cocks at once, those who enjoy being given orders—some easy, some close to impossible—and those who simply want a respite from decision making. Some live for bondage, for being bound and "helpless," while others put a premium on the rush of pain delivered by the person they trust the most to deliver it.

Others like to live on the edge of public humiliation, of being "found out," such as the protagonist of "Grocery Run," in which Rose P. Lethe writes, "Jess did hide her face this time, covering it with her free hand while humiliation and—god help her—the stirrings of arousal poured over her like hot wax. Squeezing her thighs was how she liked to come."

In a more private but no less delicious form of being humiliated, the narrator of "Way of Life," by Selena Kitt, experiences a "surge of shame," the kind that for some submissives provides the ultimate arousal. They may protest that they don't want the shame, but deep inside they know they do, know it turns them on like nothing else. Kitt writes, "I didn't stop sucking as he reached into his shirt pocket but I did cry out when he attached a clamp to my throbbing nipples, first one, then the other. They bit into my flesh, a sharp sting that built to a slow, steady burn. He watched me writhe on the machine." It's the physical acts, the body's reactions to that throb and sting, expertly combined with the reason she's submitting in the first place. In other words, the mental aspect of submission and all it symbolizes is just as meaningful to her as the "punishments" he provides.

Other stories take ritual acts and turn them into sexual wonderlands. In "*Twelve*," R. A. Buckley takes the act of counting and turns it into one that's undeniably erotic as the narrator recounts a hard spanking. "He makes my body sing and react in ways that I never thought would be possible. I've orgasmed from His bare-handed spankings many times in the past, and other ways as well. It's part of our dynamic and why I love Him so."

While there are numerous committed kinky couples here, there are also strangers who meet and instantly connect, finding their counterpart who will say those words that are music to their ears, that put them into a mind-set that makes them want to obey (or deliberately disobey, brat style). I welcome readers who've known for a long time about their kinks, as well as those who, like some of these characters, are exploring them for the first time.

From rope to role-playing, exhibitionism and multiple partners, sex toys and spankings, and so much more, these characters meet their naughtiest fantasies head on, with some help from the Dominants who give them a push (or in some cases, a not-so-gentle shove) in the right direction. They highlight the symbiotic relationship between top and bottom, where one needs to control and the other thrives on surrendering.

Rachel Kramer Bussel
Atlantic City, New Jersey

WORDS

Jo Henny Wolf

Words are enough to start a fire between her pelvic bones.

She never dares to speak them out loud, but she thinks them over and over, and sometimes mouths them to herself. They lie on her tongue, soft as rosebuds, and fill her skull with their taste. Gerard has to know this. He smiles as if he does when he whispers into her ear before he leaves that morning.

"I want you to write down exactly how you want me to fuck you tonight, darling."

For the rest of her day off, Audrey's veins surge with heat. A constant flutter tugs at her loins. She presses her thighs together and rolls her hips when she sits down to write, after a morning spent doing chores while her thoughts circled around this task. It's the most important one, the one she dreaded and thirsted for at the same time. Her writing slants more than usual on the page, the words an almost unintelligible scribble. She isn't forbidden to touch herself, and she longs to take the edge off, longs to quell the dread and want. She doesn't. Audrey tasks herself to stay chaste and let the words do their wicked magic inside her.

Her palms are damp, and the page crumples with the humidity of her skin. Maybe it's cringing from the crudeness of her words. Her fingertips prickle as she takes a wooden ruler to underline the title: *How I want you to fuck me.*

Audrey slides her fingertips along the edge of the ruler, feeling the little incisions that mark the distance. Centimeters, millimeters. A throb between her legs answers her imagination as she thinks of the ruler in use against her skin.

She cannot look at her words once she's done writing. The thought of reading them to her husband has her short of breath.

Gerard kisses her temple when she opens the door for him that night. A fleeting touch of his lips against her skin, hardly a touch at all, and yet it sows anticipation inside her. Will he ask her to undo his shoes for him? Audrey waits with bated breath and pounding heart, longing to sink to her knees to pull at the laces of his smooth Oxfords.

"Want to help me with the shoes?"

Audrey wishes he wouldn't ask. She wishes he would

order and demand. As she kneels, pink tints her cheeks and her heart swells. She longs for more. When she pulls at the bow that ties his Oxfords, she wishes he would order her to bend low and pull the laces open with her mouth. She wishes he would let her kiss the tip of his shoe. Her mouth floods with saliva and her tongue turns heavy. She doesn't dare to voice this longing that dwells between her ribs and chokes her.

"Hungry?" she asks. Gerard takes her hand and helps her to her feet again.

"For you, yes. Did you do what I asked of you?"

Her cheeks grow even warmer. "Yes," she whispers. For a word so little, it feels big in her mouth, like a cotton ball that tickles her palate and slips fuzzy tendrils down her throat.

"Then read it to me."

Audrey's hands tremble and she chokes on her shyness. Gerard leans against his desk and watches her, his gaze hot and heavy on her, caressing her inside and out as she sits before him, her back straight and not touching her chair. She wets her lips. Clears her throat.

"How I want you to fuck me." Her voice breaks around the last two words. They roll around in her mouth like pebbles.

"Go on," Gerard rasps when the pause stretches on. His own voice is hoarse. Its promise ripples through her and pools between her hips.

"I want you to ask a list of me. 'Write down what you want to be for me; write what you want me to make of you.' I *besmirch* the page for you with the filthiest words I know." Audrey has to lick her lips again. They're parched. And how short of breath she is!

"More. Read on." There's urgency in his voice now. He waits for her words like a starved beast in a cage. Audrey longs to open the door and let it out to devour her.

"You make me bend over the desk; you order me to spread my legs apart; you lift my skirt and bare my panties. And you make me read my list. You wait, your wooden ruler in your hand. For every word I say, you slap my…crotch."

He notices the pause. "Is that what you wrote there? Be honest."

Audrey lowers her head, cheeks aflame. Her scribbles could say *crotch*, with a mighty portion of goodwill. "Cunt," she whispers.

"Ah." Gerard curls his hands around the edge of his desk for a moment. The wooden ruler lies close to his hand, and he picks it up, turning it between his fingers. "Go on."

"For every crude word I say, you give me another slap, until all I feel is my cunt. My panties are soaked through, and I keep reading until I can take no more. I want to be your…"

Oh, it's hard. Her voice cracks.

"My what?" Gerard asks, and Audrey groans in shame.

"Your bitch. Your pussy. Slut. Come slut." Her heart beats like a drum.

Gerard doesn't laugh. His gaze turns heavy lidded, lewd in a way that makes it hard to look at yet at the same time breathtaking and exciting. Her skin tingles.

"Read on."

"At last, when I can't keep going, you stop, and you pull down my panties and make me step out of them. I'm still bent over the desk, now exposed to you, and you drag your fingers through my dripping cunt. Then you pull at my shirt and expose my tits. You squeeze them, and pinch my nipples, and when I squirm and moan, you stuff my panties into my mouth and gag me."

She has to close her eyes for a long moment when she imagines this. She presses her thighs together and swallows heavily. Gerard's knuckles are white, so hard is his grip around the ruler, and his pants bulge at the front. Audrey forces herself to look away and read on.

"You grab my hair and fuck me from behind, bent over your desk, hard and merciless, until we both scream. And after you've come, you take my panties out of my mouth, make me kneel, then make me clean you with my mouth."

Audrey lets the page sink down and forces herself to look up. Her blood sings with want. Gerard bites his lip, extends his hand for her to take. Audrey's knees are weak as he pulls her to her feet.

"Thank you, sweetheart," he says, and his tone sends a shiver down her spine. "And now, bend over the desk."

With a needy groan swelling up in her throat, Audrey obeys.

THE ASSISTANT

Malin James

Y ou have ten minutes. Make me come."

Her tone is flat. Matter-of-fact. The man inclines his head.

"Of course, Ms. Page. This way."

She sets the timer on her phone and puts it away as her assistant precedes her through the lobby. She is due to meet a client at the bistro next door, and it is, quite frankly, the last thing she wants to do. She is suffocating beneath good fortune and success, not that anyone can tell. Nor will she let it show. Only Sterling knows. Discreet, intelligent Sterling. She trusts Sterling to know.

They move through the lobby to a set of adjacent halls. As they walk, he drops back to escort her. His deference is quiet but as real as the ground beneath her feet. She feels his hand at her back—close but not touching. Never touching. He never would. Not until she says.

"Turn left here, Ms. Page."

Sterling rarely comes to the courts, but he moves them through the halls as if there's a map in his head. She smiles, enjoying his competence. Competence is an intensely attractive trait.

"Will this do, Ms. Page?"

They've stopped at an alcove deep within the maze of halls. It's quiet. Private. As private as one can expect.

"Yes. This will do."

"May I, Ms. Page?"

She nods, impassive.

"Yes, Sterling. You may."

She turns and presses the tips of her fingers into the pale blue wall as he comes up behind her, shielding her from view. She checks her watch.

"Now you have eight minutes."

He nods, but does not rush as he draws her skirt up over her hips with his lovely, long-fingered hands. She loves his hands, loves the way they look when he grasps his cock and when he makes her tea. They're the distillation of him—sensitive, competent, and intensely discreet. She knows his hands will do precisely what she needs.

He rests one on the swell of her hip as she leans back, pressing the length of her spine into the wall of his chest. His other hand reaches into the hollow of her thighs. Then he allows the fabric to drape back down over his wrist. She sighs, soothed by the hard-on pressed against her ass, while he strokes her through the panties she knew she shouldn't have worn.

"More."

He knows his role. He knows it well enough to know that this moment isn't precious. She doesn't want emotion and she doesn't need romance. Those are for other times. Right now, his function is to make her come.

He nods and pushes the lace aside.

Her hips rise to meet his fingers as they slip past the damp fabric and into the folds of her cunt. She's plump and ready. Not in the mood for games.

"Sterling, there's no time."

"Yes, Ms. Page."

His hand withdraws but she doesn't notice. She hears his belt and a zipper and then his cock is in her hard. Sterling is often hard. He knows she wants him that way.

She moans, low and soft, as her body opens up, coating his cock with a well of arousal. His breathing hitches but he fills her. He hasn't come in over a week. He struggles but he does it. He sinks himself into her, slow and deep, so she can feel every inch.

"Don't fucking come."

She knows she doesn't have to say it. She knows what he'll say.

Of course, Ms. Page.

"Of course, Ms. Page."

He reaches around again and touches her clit as she

pushes back. Then he holds himself still so she can fuck herself on him.

His touch is light. Just enough. He moves with her, as she rolls her hips. The orgasm swallows her, hard and gritty, as his knuckles turn white against the wall.

"Feel better, Ms. Page?"

His voice is husky in her ear. Her entire body feels clean as she slowly opens her eyes.

"Yes. Much better, thanks."

Mindful of the time, he withdraws though she knows how hard it is for him. Then he gently replaces her panties and straightens out her skirt. After a moment's hesitation, he presses his cheek to hers.

Mallory knows that he wants to kiss her. The hard-on that he sports says he wants much, much more. But she knows he won't ask. He would never ask. He is a very disciplined man. She strokes his cheek. An acknowledgment. Then she straightens and turns around.

"Go home and wait for me, Sterling. I'm going to make this meeting short," she says, allowing her lips to drift past his mouth, just a whisper from his skin. "And Sterling. I'm going to want your cock. Don't come until I return."

"Yes, Ms. Page. Of course."

He smiles. She can practically taste the curve of his mouth as she slips her hand between them and squeezes his rigid shaft. "Excellent," she murmurs. "Then I'll see you very soon."

Dismissed, Sterling nods. Then he straightens his

cuffs and leaves the way they'd come. Mallory follows a moment later, emerging into the lobby just as Sterling passes through the old-fashioned revolving door.

For the first time that day, Mallory smiles, a fully unguarded smile, as she watches him hail a cab. She feels rested and calm and refreshed. Only Sterling can manage that. He is something more than merely her assistant. He is pure, fucking gold.

SWITCHING STRUGGLES

Leandra Vane

Charlotte held Nate's wrists together, his warm pulse thumping against the pads of her thumbs. The hum of conversation and snapping of whips across the dungeon faded away as he kneeled before her. She had topped Nate in the past, but now they were waiting on James, who had been Nate's Dominant over the past year. It was going to be a mindfuck scene—no restraints, just Charlotte holding Nate's wrists, and she was more than willing to fill the role.

Charlotte noticed Nate was trembling, and she sensed it wasn't from anticipation. She was about to ask him what was wrong when Nate forced his hands apart and pushed her back. A second pair of hands clasped around Charlotte's wrists, capturing them above her head.

James's voice sounded above her, his words crisp

and defined. "Nathan, please inform Charlotte what is taking place."

Nate's gaze sharpened in attention and his body shrank into his submissive demeanor.

"So...sticking to the parameters of the struggle scene you negotiated last month, Ian considered the names on the list and has appointed James and me to help him. I'll be acting on behalf of my Master who will be giving me commands in order to complete the scene Sir Ian has requested. Since we're in the dungeon your safewords are red, yellow, and green. Sir Ian informed us that, knowing you, the F word will also suffice as green. Is there anything you need before the scene begins?"

"Fuck off you fucking traitor," Charlotte spat.

Nate nodded. "Good to go, then."

"Thank you, Nathan," James said. "Now get out of the way. I will let you know when I need you."

Nate backed away and kneeled. "Yes, Sir."

Charlotte's nostrils flared as heat, excitement, and arousal seized her all at once. A primal fight-or-flight urged her muscles to tighten and made her fingers tingle.

Warmth flourished on Charlotte's ear as James whispered to her, "You get a five-second head start. I suggest you make the most of it."

James dropped her and Charlotte caught herself with her palms flat on the carpet. Charlotte launched back up but she only managed four or five steps before James crashed behind her, seized her arms, and immobilized her flight.

"Nathan. Shoes."

As her flats were pulled off and tossed aside, Charlotte caught a glimpse of her rose-red-painted toenails.

"Shirt."

Nate carefully began to unfasten Charlotte's shirt. His breath was shaky, along with his fingers. James quickly grew impatient.

"If you can't be faster, my pet, I'm not going to let you help anymore."

Nate grimaced, but clutched the fabric in his hands and tugged, the snaps flying open, and he forced the shirt down around her shoulders.

Nate then reached around and unclasped her bra with an ease that was admirable considering how much Charlotte was writhing and reminding him what things she could do to him in revenge for his treachery.

James had to rearrange his hold on her to get the rest of her clothes off. His warm hands cupped her plumped muscles, holding her firm against her best efforts to get away. Nate unbuttoned her jeans and peeled them off along with her panties. With James's arms wrapped around her and Nate's hands on her bare skin, Charlotte began the blissful descent into subspace.

The two men dragged her naked through the maze of players to a massage table near the back of the dungeon. Her tits bounced ferociously as she made the most of her permission to struggle. Despite her screaming and thrashing, she was lifted onto the table and held in place.

A single glance stopped Charlotte's hopeless protests with a gasp.

Ian strolled over to them, his long hair pulled back, a sharp suit transforming him from the peaceful, laid-back guy that everyone else knew. But as he towered over her, she knew Sir Ian was vexed by her show of being the loudest person in the dungeon that night.

Charlotte prepared herself for a lecture, but he remained resolutely silent.

Ian ran a hand over her jawline and his thumb slipped over her bottom lip. She nipped at it and for a moment he let his guard down. Charlotte sucked his thumb into her mouth. She rolled her hot tongue over his thumb and pushed out her lips, brazenly locking eyes with him, knowing how much it turned him on and how he knew she was still defiantly testing his authority.

When he pulled his hand away, she expected a swift retaliation, but none came. Instead, he placed the tips of two fingers firmly on her sternum and slowly brought them down her abdomen, around her navel, and through the coarse coils of her pubic hair. He nudged her legs apart and directed the other men around her where to hold her. His voice was far away now, and he made it a point to show he wasn't talking to her. About her, yes, but not to her.

Ian wasn't going to use restraints, or blindfolds, or even commands. The three of them were going to hold her down and he was going to do to her what he saw fit.

Charlotte's mind danced in a jagged waltz. Had she

seen any toys stored under the massage table? Did James or Nate have room on them to hide floggers? Was Ian going to take off his own belt to use on her?

The possibilities dissolved in her mind as she gave in to the sensations of hands on her body, the divine pressure on her wrists, her ankles. Her legs were pried apart and a strong hold braced her thighs, opening her for all to see.

Ian's two fingertips returned, plunging deep into her wet cunt. He began to thrust and caress and unravel her with his simple touch.

With every move or spasm of her muscles, the men's strong hands held her in place. As she gasped and whimpered, tears pricked the corners of her eyes. She surrendered and allowed herself to be turned inside out by her love for them, the complete trust she held toward these men to let them do this to her.

With that, she found the molten center of subspace and vulnerability. It wasn't orgasm, but it was a release she'd been needing for a long time. When she resurfaced, her body was limp and the hands were holding her up rather than holding her down, supporting her, helping her sit up.

Charlotte was trembling all over, drunk on subspace and adrenaline. A blanket was wrapped around her shoulders. She saw Nate was sitting on the edge of the bench with her. She blinked, realizing the scene had been for him, too.

As their tops went to fetch some water, Charlotte

drew Nate close to her, nuzzling her face to his.

"I fucking love you; don't forget it," she said, and felt him smile against her cheek. After a moment, she nudged him away. "But don't think I won't give you a punishment for your betrayal."

Nate's smile only widened.

"Yes, Mistress," he said. "I did my best to earn a good one."

FLAGGED FOR REVISION

Elna Holst

It was pelting down. From what she could make out through the dizzying web of droplets that had turned her reading specs into a blindfold of sorts, the overcast sky showed no sign of letting up. Yes, she was wearing her glasses. Nothing but her glasses, in fact.

Edith shifted her weight to her left, in an attempt to give her right leg a rest. Pins and needles were all the thanks she got for this. She sighed and put her foot down in the mud again, rivulets of rain streaming down her sides, down her thighs, as if she were the centerpiece of an overflowing fountain. It was a nice image. Pity it was freaking freezing.

The slick flagpole to which she was strung up, arms hoisted high above her head, creaked in the wind. The cold was eating into the very core of her, her skin mottled

with goose pimples, her short, usually spiky hair saturated, flattened to her skull. And then there was the
other kind of exposure, though Edith doubted anyone
else would be barmy enough to climb the steep path up
the hill in this weather.

And that, right enough, was the reason she was
standing out here in the first place. Turning her head,
she tried to squint over the rim of her frames to where
she had last seen her companion on this miserable quest,
marked in their respective diaries as a "leisure activity."
In other words: their much-anticipated summer vacation, which Edith had energetically lobbied they should
spend not on some tedious, everybody's-doing-it Medi-
terranean cruise (who were these "everybody" anyway?
There wasn't a single soul among their acquaintance
who was going on a cruise this year), but rather on a
walking tour of their native soil, getting in touch with
nature, roughing it, free as larks, lonely as clouds, setting
up camp beneath the stars.

She ticked off her list of inane arguments to the
steadfast rhythm of the driving rain. The rain. Of course
it would bloody rain. This country was fucking famous
for it.

As they locked up and left their car in the long-term
parking lot this morning, some ten miles south of their
current position, her wife's face had been a blank slate of
silent quiescence—a sure harbinger of a storm to come.

The weather gods had taken the hint. They'd been
going for no more than an hour before the first drops

fell, and Edith's chest had tightened with foreboding. Selma had stopped to look up at the sky, her right eyelid twitching. Then she'd shrugged and asked Edith to take their waterproofs out of her rucksack.

Sel always came prepared. Even when Edith knew she'd much rather have brought a pile of light reading, and some even lighter swimwear.

A crack of lightning blotted her already blurry field of vision, followed by the rattling of thunder. She swayed with the surprise, slipped in the mud, but didn't—couldn't—fall. Selma knew how to tie a knot.

Oh, didn't she just.

Heat flashed through her, momentarily, as she remembered how—after she herself had pitched their tent, and Selma had prepared their meal in the relative dryness of the campsite's permanent shelter—Sel had asked her, very quietly, to get undressed after supper.

Edith never disobeyed a direct command. Once she had swallowed down the last of her broth and bread, she stood, rinsed and put their things away, and proceeded to zip off her rainwear and remove her jumper, jeans, socks, tank top, and underpants. The chill of the damp air made her nipples pucker, and it took all of her mental strength not to wrap her arms around herself.

Selma smiled faintly. Edith felt a trickle of moisture responding between her legs. She sat up straighter.

"I'm not happy with you, Ed."

Edith's head fell forward. There was a lump in her throat, tears burning at the corners of her eyes.

"Do you know why I'm not happy with you?"

"You wanted to go on a cruise."

Selma shook her head. "Try again, Ed."

"You said it would rain."

"You're getting closer. I had my suspicions. But more to the point: what did you say?"

"I said it wouldn't rain."

"Almost. What exactly did you say?"

"I promised. I swore to god it wouldn't rain. I…" Edith's voice broke off as she remembered *precisely* what she had said. "I said you could strip me down and put me out for the night if it did."

Selma's smile widened.

There was a glint of yellow on the outskirts of her impaired vision. Edith's head was spinning; her considerable muscular stamina—always a source of pride and pleasure with her life partner—had turned to putty in the downpour. She made an effort to stand tall, but failed ignominiously.

The bright marigold raincoat drew closer. Warm hands touched her numb skin and pulled her slippery body into a tight embrace.

Edith made a sound somewhere between a moan and a sob.

"Hush, baby, there's a good girl. You're on your last leg, aren't you?"

Ed nodded. Her teeth chattered too much for intelligible speech.

"I've decided to revise your plans for the night. It is my prerogative, after all, even if you are the most adorable ornament this old pole ever had the honor of being bedecked with."

Selma slid her hand up Edith's flagging arms and released her bonds. Her arms fell free; her whole body would have fallen, except Selma was there, holding her, half-carrying, half-dragging her toward their tent. There was the unmistakable sound of the zipper opening the canvas door, and Edith tumbled onto soft, dry, slightly rough material. Towels. Terry-cloth towels spread over their joint sleeping bags. She heard the rustling of Selma removing her waterproofs and boots under the flysheet, then the zipping of the door closing up again.

"There we go," Selma said softly. "Now we'd better get you dried off, or I'll have no use for you tonight."

Edith managed to roll over on her back, making a feeble gesture with her bloodless arm. Selma tutted her tongue and set to.

The hard, insistent rubbing of terry cloth against her flesh made sensation flood back into Edith's hands and feet, arms and legs, in turn. She tingled all over, her toes and fingers curling with the sweet, minute ache of it.

As her tormentor worked over her torso, the material grating her swollen tits, a new kind of storm was brewing in Edith.

She wet her lips. The rubbing abruptly stopped. She groaned.

"You know, I think I know what will make us both hot enough."

Selma finally removed Edith's spectacles. Her adored face was prettily flushed as her finger trailed down to Ed's half-open lips.

"You want me?"

"Yes." Edith struggled to shape her mouth around the key phrase. "P...please."

She was amply rewarded.

GROCERY RUN

Rose P. Lethe

With only two items on the list—cumin and dish soap—it should have been a quick trip, especially at this time of day. At just past eight on a Tuesday night, even the crowds at the big-box store Jess frequented would be thinning. She would pop inside, grab the two items that hadn't made it onto her weekly grocery list the first time, and then pop back out. It would be easy—ten minutes at most if she hurried.

And Jess would hurry. Valerie had certainly seen to that.

"You tend to get distracted," she had said, with Jess bare-bottomed and bent over her lap, ponytail swaying as she wiggled. "Let's see if we can't do something about that."

A pair of Ben Wa balls in her cunt and a metal plug

in her ass—"The sooner you get home, the sooner they come out." So yes, Jess would hurry.

The plug in particular was a bully. It was small but heavy, with a curve so sharp that she felt it in her pussy as well as her ass. Even through two walls of skin, the thick bulb at the end could put a pressure against her stupidly sensitive G-spot that was heavenly, usually.

With the added Ben Wa balls, it was hellish. Both holes felt overly full, and every step seemed to rock the toys' weight into her sweet spot, producing a sensation that was almost like a cramp. It made her want to stay in her parked car, just curl up in the driver's seat and not move for hours.

But she had the shopping to finish.

So she got out, trudged across the asphalt, and passed through the automatic doors into the harsh fluorescent lighting of the store. She was waddling a bit, walking like she had a massive pole between her legs. It seemed unreal that something so small—each toy could fit in one palm—made her throb like this, not just in her cunt or ass but throughout her whole abdomen. A pulse of discomfort, dull but insistent, moved through her like ripples in a pond until she was walking with one arm curled protectively around her lower belly, her handbag threatening to slide off her drooping shoulder.

Cumin, she reminded herself, *and dish soap*.

The baking aisle was deserted, so Jess paused in front of the spices for a brief respite.

Valerie had used a veritable flood of lube earlier,

inserting the balls and then the plug. It was beginning to leak out of her now. She could feel her panties clinging to her vulva as she tilted her hips, her labia slipping along her clit as she squeezed her thighs together, a growing wet sensation between her asscheeks even as she stood still.

It was filthy and embarrassing, but the bad sort. Why was she doing this?

Her handbag buzzed once, then twice. She shrugged it off her shoulder and fished her phone from its depths. Sure enough, there was an incoming call. *Valerie mobile*, said the screen.

Jess answered with a tense "Hello?"

"Hey." There was a melodic quality to Valerie's soft, chipper voice, the way she drew out the vowel like a musical note. Just hearing it drained some of the tension in Jess's body. "How's it going?"

"It's…" Jess considered. It would be so easy to say, *I don't like this.* So easy to say, *Red*, and be allowed to make the discomfort stop. "Intense," she decided.

There was a pause. Jess pictured Valerie on the couch, twirling her glossy brown hair around one finger as she analyzed Jess's tone. "Are you alone?"

Jess glanced around. The aisle was still empty, but she could hear the shuffle of footsteps nearby and the distant squeak of cart wheels. "Yes."

"Yes, what? What do you call me?"

And just like that, Jess remembered herself. The discomfort didn't matter, nor did the filthiness and embarrassment of standing in the middle of a store with both her cunt and asshole slick and full. She wasn't here because she needed to finish the shopping; she was here because Valerie had told her to come. Valerie had *wanted* her to do this.

Jess swallowed, ducked her head, and answered in a barely audible whisper: "Daddy."

She burned from her cheeks to her ears and all the way to her nape. Another glance reassured her that no one was around, no one could hear her, but even the possibility that someone could walk by, see her standing here calling her girlfriend *Daddy* over the phone...

"Is it uncomfortable?" Valerie asked. There was a smile in her voice that made Jess want to hide her face in shame—the good sort—knowing she was about to be toyed with.

"Yes, Daddy." Jess shifted her weight, jostling the toys and making them press into her G-spot anew. Her breath caught, and there was a quaver in her voice. "It's too much. I'm too full."

"I know." Valerie's voice dripped with mocking sympathy. "You're so sensitive, aren't you? Hmm. How about this? Give me a little squeeze of those thighs."

Jess did hide her face this time, covering it with her free hand while humiliation and—god help her—the stirrings of arousal poured over her like hot wax. Squeezing her thighs was how she liked to come. She breathed into the receiver, "Daddy, I'm in public."

"Alone in public. Or did you lie to Daddy?"

Lowering her hand, Jess scanned the aisle. Still

deserted but for her, no one even passing by on the ends.

"Of course you didn't," Valerie said warmly. "Because you're a good girl. So be good and squeeze for me."

For you.

Jess crossed one foot over the other and squeezed her thighs together. The balls slipped a little deeper into her cunt, and the plug gave a little wobbling thrust into her ass. It felt like she was being jabbed in her G-spot, but fuck if her clit didn't throb at the motion.

"That's it," Valerie crooned into her ear. "Another."

Jess obeyed, squeezing again and again while her gaze darted from one end of the aisle to the other, watching for passersby. When she came, it was a pitiful thing, nothing more than a weak ripple through her clit, accompanied by a huff into the receiver, but it didn't matter. It wasn't her orgasm. It was Daddy's.

"That's it. Perfect," said Valerie, sounding so pleased, so proud, that something in Jess pitched upward and soared. "You did so well."

Feeling light and giddy, she snatched the cumin from the shelf. It wasn't quite the floaty nothingness of subspace, but it was as near as she wanted to come to it in public. Her cunt was looser and wetter now, the pressure and the fullness less uncomfortable than before.

Heading for the dish soap, she whispered into the phone, "Thank you, Daddy."

"Don't forget to get yourself a candy bar," Valerie said. "You've earned it."

CONFERENCE CALL

Elizabeth Coldwell

It's close to six, and I'm still waiting for the call. Lifting a slat of the blind with my finger, I gaze wistfully into the parking lot. Patti and Linda are heading for Linda's car, laughing at something as they teeter on their heels. They'll be going for drinks at Muldoon's, our usual Friday evening haunt, and I wish I could join them. But I can't. Once, bored and frustrated, I skipped out on a conference call. I haven't made that mistake since.

"Juliana." At the sound of that oh-so-familiar voice, I swivel in my chair, back to face the monitor. He's watching me from his seat in the office down the hall, his brow raised.

"Sir." The response is automatic.

"Max, are you with us?" he enquires. Another,

smaller window opens on the screen, as our colleague in the London office joins us.

"As always. Good to see you, Iain." Based on the time difference, it must be almost midnight where Max is, but he looks bright-eyed and alert, handsome in his sober black business suit. "Miss Winston." He acknowledges me with a nod.

"If we're all here, then we can begin. Juliana, remove your jacket."

"Yes, Sir." There are no niceties, but I didn't expect them. We've been sharing these calls long enough for me to know that, with him, it's always straight down to business. It's why he makes such a good Master; he knows how to read the mood in a room, and give me what I need, sometimes even before I know I need it myself.

Aware of Max watching from his vantage point across the Atlantic, I shrug off my jacket, and hang it over the back of my chair. The white blouse I wear is sheer enough to reveal the pink-and-black underwired bra beneath. A bra too tarty for office wear, but my Master likes it. As does Max.

"Undo your blouse." Another curt order, and one that sets a pulse beating heavily between my legs.

I fumble with the buttons, unfastening four before I'm told to stop.

"What do you think, Max?" My Master's voice holds a note of disinterest. He's aware, of course, how much the idea that he's not in the least bothered by my display turns me on.

"Very nice."

"She has gorgeous breasts, doesn't she?" Master comments.

Max seems to be fidgeting in his seat, as though he needs to readjust himself. "Mmm. Two perfect hand-fuls, I'd say. But I don't feel as though I'm getting the best view of them here."

"Well, I'm sure we can do something about that."

I'm expecting to be told to take my bra off, and my hands are almost halfway to the catch at the back when Master says, "Lift your tits out of the cups, Juliana."

Hurriedly, I obey, thrown a bit off guard by the request. In moments, my breasts rest on the silk fabric, pushed up a little way by the wiring. It's a sight that's somehow much ruder than if I'd been asked to take it off entirely.

Max lets out a small groan. He has so much less composure than my Master, and I know it won't be long before he's freed his cock from his suit trousers so he can jerk himself off to the sight of my willing humiliation.

"Pinch your nipples, Juliana," comes the command.

I do as I'm told, wishing it were Master squeezing the tight nubs between his fingers. Or Max. I've never felt his touch. I wonder if he'd be rough, or whether he'd prefer to use his teeth to bite them. Juice trickles from my pussy as I imagine Max taking my breast in his mouth and sucking greedily on it.

"She has a surprise for you, Max." Master's voice cuts into my reverie. "Stand up and show him, Juliana."

It's obvious what he's really asking me to do. Without hesitation, I get to my feet. Aware of Max's gaze on me through the video link, I slowly ease my tight skirt up my legs. I know he's a stocking man, so he'll adore the sight of the black hold-ups I'm wearing, and the soft flesh above them, revealed as I lift the hem all the way up, to show that I have no panties on. Max bites back a moan, and I swear I hear the sound of his zipper coming down.

"Fuck—she's shaved," he murmurs. "Oh, that is exquisite."

"I got her to do it especially for you. Don't you wish you could reach out and touch that pussy? Feel how soft those juicy lips are?"

"Yes, I do." Max fights to spit out the words, and I'm sure he's uttering them between strokes up and down his dick. "You're a fucking lucky bastard, you know that, Iain?"

Master chuckles. "Well, right now, neither of us is able to have the pleasure of feeling that wet cunt of hers, so I guess she'll have to do it for us. Touch yourself, Juliana."

I shouldn't be so eager to do this, but I put my hand to my pussy without hesitation. When I skim a finger over my clit, tremors shudder through me, so strong that I know it'll take all my willpower not to orgasm without permission.

"She's such an eager little slut," Master comments, "but it's a beautiful sight, isn't it?"

"Absolutely gorgeous." A stranger's voice. A *woman's* voice. I don't look at the monitor to see who's joined the conference call. I can't. Just the thought that a third party is watching me play with myself has me coming all over my fingers, sobbing and gasping as my legs threaten to give way from under me.

I'll be in so much trouble when Master gets me home, but I don't care. As my breathing slows and I gather my scattered wits, I risk a glance at the screen, but the woman has gone. So has Max. Only Master smiles at me, love and fond indulgence mixing in his expression. There are so many things I want to say, chief among them, "Who was she?" and "Please tell me that wasn't a one-off," but Master doesn't give me the chance to ask.

"See you in the parking lot in five, boss," he says. "We've got a table at Muldoon's and the drinks are on you."

And with that, our roles revert to normal and Iain, the best PA I've ever employed, shuts down the call.

LISTENING TO HER

Eve Pendle

I listen to her every night. Whatever time she gets back, whoever she's with, I'm there, eager cock in my hand, desperate to hear her doing unspeakable things to someone who I wish were me.

I hear them laughing in the corridor, my housemate and the man she's brought back. He's got a deep voice that complements her husky drawl. I've been lying on my back in bed, waiting for her. As I always do.

She goes out every Friday and Saturday night. She must go to clubs, though she doesn't frequent the usual student places. Every time she goes out, wearing tight leather trousers or a short red dress, she comes back with someone. Usually a man, but sometimes a woman.

She put up two eyelets above her door when she moved in. I asked her about them after she'd been giving me study advice in the corridor, and she said they'd been there when she moved in. I didn't say anything, but I looked at all the rooms when I arrived, and I don't remember seeing them.

"Take your clothes off." Gemma's voice is warm and authoritative, even through the wall.

I hasten to comply, stripping off my boxer shorts under the duvet.

"Demanding, aren't you?" There is the sound of clothes crumpling onto the floor.

I do this sometimes, playing along with whatever she's doing, imagining it's me she picked. But I'm quiet. These walls are ridiculously thin. I can hear everything. When Gemma masturbates, on the days she doesn't go out, I hear her every moan and sigh.

"Yes." Her voice is teasing. "I demand that you hold up your arms."

He laughs.

I slide my hands up the sheets. The cotton sheets rub along my skin, the smallest friction but it feels like a burn and it sensitizes me. I imagine I can hear Gemma pacing around him. I fantasize I'm there and she's moving around me, securing ropes around my wrists and slipping the other ends through those eyelets.

"Spread your legs."

I do as she says and my feet are now at the corners of the bed. With me spread-eagled under the duvet, if someone saw me they'd just think I slept like a bed hog. Except my cock is making a bulge. Just the sound of her commands makes me hot and hard, especially since I've been anticipating this since she smiled at me in the corridor earlier on her way out. She was wearing a short dress made elegant by its high neckline and pattern of flowers and birds. It was so tight you could easily see the outline of her every curve. I tried not to drink in the sight of her when I wished her a good evening. But she's a drug.

He gasps.

My mind blazes with what might be happening through the wall. She's grasped his naked dick and is roughly jerking it. She has a sly smile on her face, satisfied at her power. He's at her mercy, knuckles white as he holds his bonds and she plays with him.

My left hand has snuck down between my legs, and my fingers are stroking along my dick. In the dark, I imagine myself her toy. I can almost deceive myself that it's her hand on me and her bonds that hold me down.

"Mmmm. You taste delicious."

There's a wet noise and a deep groan from the man.

She's sucking him. He'd be able to see her dress riding up since she was leaning, or even kneeling to take his length in her mouth. He would see the soft shape of her breasts from above and her blonde hair falling all around his dick. I have to stop touching myself for a second because the vision is almost too much.

It's perverted, but I spit on my hand and the lubrication for an instant is a facsimile of what is going on next door. Sliding my finger and thumb firmly, I allow my foreskin to slip back and the super-sensitive flesh underneath, the head of my cock, to emerge. I do it again, and again, focusing on the top inch as I listen to Gemma and her latest pickup toy make noises of pleasure.

A thud of hard hitting soft bangs through the air and he grunts. Gemma giggles.

"Fuck," he says in an undertone, "that—"

Another strike and he cries out again.

"Take it like a man. Or do I have to go easy on you?" I can hear a little bit of scathing, a bit of teasing in Gemma's tone.

The next smack is loud. My hand has sped up. I can't help it.

She's hurting him. My fingers dig into my cock and I stifle a gasp as the sharp pressure shoots into me. It's so good and so wrong to like this vicarious pleasure-pain. I don't know whether I'm a sadist or a masochist, enjoying the sound of this man's discomfort as well as wanting it myself.

"Give in. Come," she urges him and delivers another blow.

I won't listen to her again. I swear. She's too much. But even as I think this, it's a lie. How many times have I said I won't? Still, I'm here, cock in my hand, keeping myself on the edge, forcibly resisting orgasm.

Just this once more.

The man's breath is coming quicker now and so is mine.

"I like to see you so desperate. I'm soaked, and I'm going to make you lick up all that cream," Gemma croons, even as there's smack after smack of blows, only slightly muffled by the wall.

That's too much. I explode, my climax wracking through me, blocking out everything.

I hear a door close, followed by heavy footsteps in the corridor. I open my eyes, but it's dark. The sheet above me is sticky with come. I feel the familiar embarrassment creep across my skin, even as my dick is still semi-hard under my fingers.

"Did you enjoy that?"

I look around without thinking, but of course Gemma's voice is coming through the wall. *Yes, I did,* I want to say. *I want you to do everything to me that you did to him. I want to be yours.* But I stay silent.

"Arjun, answer me."

The sound of my name rips through me. She said my name, through the wall. I heard it and now I am completely still. I am paralyzed with mortification that she knew I was listening, arousal that she knows I liked it, and fear that perhaps I imagined her saying my name.

I lick my lips. I want to say something. I want her to come in here and force me.

There's the sound of water running. Footsteps from the corridor.

"Arjun." Her tone is stern and seems a bit louder, as though she's walked over to the wall that divides her room from mine. I didn't imagine that. Surely I didn't?

"Next time, you'll have to join in."

THE BACK ROOM AT THE SALOON

Donna George Storey

S he pulled her wrapper over her nightgown and tied the sash snugly. It felt odd to be in her nightclothes with her hair still properly dressed, but John had asked her to leave it up tonight.

A good wife gladly submits to her husband's desire.

Her pulse quickened at the thought. She felt like a bride, unsure what lay ahead. On their real wedding night, John was gentle and full of sweet words. Afterward, he promised their relations would become more mutual as they adjusted to married life. Men of experience assured him it would be so.

As time passed, she did indeed respond to his caresses with increasing ardor, but had yet to share his final pleasure.

Until one night, when they were tipsy on champagne after a dinner with friends, she dared ask him shyly about his education in matters of the flesh. Even in the darkness of their bedroom, her face burned with the brazenness of it. She was surprised at how readily he confessed: he first knew a woman at eighteen when his uncle took him to a parlor house. The woman was pretty, plump, and kind. That encounter lasted all of five minutes, John told her with a rueful chuckle. He'd indulged a few times more in college—always careful to take precautions for his health—but had since renounced that vice.

"Nothing compares to what we have, my love—a true union of hearts and minds."

She was reassured of his devotion, but his story left her unsettled in a different way. The images that filled her head—the woman baring her large, pink-tipped breasts to his virgin eyes, her soft arms pulling him close, John's grunts as he found oblivion in a stranger's body—inflamed her so keenly that she knew the fullest joy of the marriage bed at last.

Her response delighted him, and he coaxed a shameful confession from her in return—that while he'd embraced her, she'd imagined she was his harlot.

The next time they lay together, he whispered forbidden words in her ear, painting pictures of sensual license no decent woman should see.

Once more she reached satisfaction.

She wondered aloud if there was something wrong with her that she craved such depravity.

"It's nobody's business what a man and his wife do in private. Trust me, dear, and all will be well."

And so, at his confident knock, she opened the door.

She found him in his shirtsleeves and suspenders, his collar open about his sturdy neck. Gone were the coat and vest, and along with them, his proper demeanor.

"Come to the back room with me, my girl. Don't be afraid. I'll treat a fine miss like you just right." His tone, too, assumed the impudence of the lower orders.

She gave him her hand and followed him down the hallway. The walls around her shimmered, melting like candlewax. Suddenly they were walking through a saloon, redolent with the earthy scent of whiskey, the hum of male conversation. The men at the bar stared, undressing her with glittering eyes. This was a place a decent woman could only dream of, half with fear, half with longing. With John as her guide, she could finally enter into the heart of this mysterious realm.

The back room—his dressing room—served their needs well: a standing closet, a washstand, a camp bed. He'd prepared the side table with a napkin and a glass of water. She caught her breath. So that's how it would go tonight.

John closed the door and turned the key in the lock, although the hired girl had gone home hours before.

"Let's see you in your shift." He pulled her wrapper open and gave her an insolent once-over. "You look too proud a lady to come to a place like this, but we all know looks can be deceiving. You'll give me what I want, won't you?"

She nodded, her eyes trained on the carpet.

"Well, no use lingering with idle chatter. Lie down on the bed."

Thrilled at his audacity, she obeyed.

He stretched out beside her and began to make love to her. Pushing her nightgown up to her neck, he caressed her breasts and stroked her between her legs, patiently and knowingly, until she relinquished all dignity in a chorus of soft, lewd moans.

Then came that velvet voice in her ear: "You *are* a frisky one. What d'you say we take a trip to Paris tonight?"

Only a few weeks before, John had taught her about "French love," how sporting men would pay extra to get their pleasure from a woman's mouth. Curious, she found the courage to try it, for just a moment.

A good wife gladly submits to her husband's desire.

John lowered his trousers and sat at the edge of the bed. She knelt between his legs.

Submit to him. A good wife submits gladly.

His manhood was so long and thick, she wondered how she'd managed before. Timidly, she kissed the length, then took the tip in her mouth. He'd been thoughtful enough to wash and smelled faintly of soap. Soon she found her courage and was moving up and down like the dasher of a butter churn.

"Your French is well nigh native tonight," he said in a thick voice.

Apparently satisfied with her progress, he lifted her to the bed and mounted her quickly. But then he was patient again, letting her move against him as he suckled her breasts and stroked her neck and shoulders. "That's right, my pretty whore," he whispered, "fuck me good, you sweet, wet trollop."

How was it that such wicked words could uplift her, free her, make her soul soar?

You like it all, don't you, you little cocksucker?

With that final endearment, she came undone in his arms.

He held her for a moment, his own pleasure still unquenched. Usually he spent on her belly as they wanted to wait to start a family, but she found herself overcome by a perverse desire: "Darling, would you... please...finish up in Paris tonight?"

She knew John was never one to deny a lady's wish.

He felt harder this time, and she took him so deep he knocked against the back of her throat. She could taste herself on him, but that excited her even more. In but a few minutes John stiffened and groaned. His flesh pulsed against her tongue, flooding her mouth with thick, salty wetness. Thus he revealed a new masculine secret to her—the taste of the essence of his lust.

Afterward, he gallantly offered her the napkin for her lips, the water to refresh her mouth.

"Was that truly all right for you, dear?" he asked with concern.

"Oh, yes. I felt so bold. Did you like it?"

He laughed. "So very much. That was a first for me, you know. I'm the luckiest man alive."

On her wedding day, her mother confided that a good wife must find it in her heart to submit gladly to her husband's desire.

She never said how easy that would be.

WINTER GAMES

Allyson Shannon

No one's out here. Are you going to do it?"

I glance around and it's true, we're alone. This public park is empty, as one would expect in the midst of winter in Michigan. There's no snow on the ground but it's cold and ugly out; everything is varying shades of gray. We're in a parking lot far from the water, where there's nothing to see but bare trees and asphalt, the kind of place where people go to do the kinds of things he's proposing I do. I turn the heat up a notch and look at him sideways. "I will but only if you tell me to instead of asking."

"I'm working on it," he says, his gloved hands curled around the steering wheel. I get wet imagining those hands on me, pressing me down to my knees once he really gets the hang of this.

"It's okay. If I don't want to do something, I'll say

my word. All you have to do is tell me and I'll do it. So tell me."

His hands tighten on the wheel, he clenches his jaw, and I can see the quick rise and fall of his chest under his puffy coat. He licks his lips and his eyes make another sweep of the area before coming to rest on me. "Sorry. Newbie nerves." He smiles, his teeth flashing movie-star white against his deep-brown skin. "Take off your mittens and pull your tights down. No panties, right?"

Even with the heat on, the seat is still cool against my bare ass where my skirt has bunched up. "Right." I flip it up so he can see that I complied and then tilt my hips forward and spread my thighs so he can see how ready I am.

"Fuck," he groans, his gaze riveted to my hard clit, nestled in my trimmed bush like a fat pink pearl. I watch, fascinated, as he gives in to his desire and lets his cool, commanding side take over. He sits taller in his seat, the smile fading as his eyes rake over me like he owns me. "Touch yourself. Make yourself come for me."

Yes, Sir. I don't call him that out loud; I don't call him anything but his name when we play. It's not a necessity, at least not yet, while he's a baby Dom. I simply say yes and do it.

The sound of me fucking myself is obscenely loud in his small, eco-friendly car. This won't take long. Being told what to do has me halfway there, but I hope he stops me a few times just to make me suffer. I want him to make me beg for it. I'm silent, focused, my teeth sunk into my bottom lip. He's watching me, his eyes flicking back and forth between my face and my fingers in my slippery cunt, and occasionally out at the parking lot around us. One minute he's over there on his side of the car, practically vibrating with lust; the next, he's looming over me, yanking my coat open and shoving my sweater up around my neck. I left the bra at home with the panties so there is nothing to get in the way of his squeezing hands or his lapping tongue.

"Don't stop," he grumbles around a mouthful of tit and I feel it in my pussy, my fingers moving faster as the need to come intensifies. I try to touch him, to hold on to him with my free hand, but he catches my wrist and holds my arm down the way he knows I like it. I'm close and I feel compelled to let him know, hoping he's feeling cruel enough to make me wait.

He cuts off my warning with a hand over my mouth. The gloves are still on because he knows how much I love the smell of leather warmed by his skin. He tells me to stop, but I'm not sure that I can. I'm in the place where a well-chosen word can set me off.

"Hey." He's in my face, one hand still covering my mouth, the other tightening around my wrist in a way that I'm sure he thinks will ground me but is instead pushing me closer to the edge. "Hey," he repeats. "Look at me…breathe. That's it. Good girl."

Once I've got myself mostly under control, he takes his hands off of me and slumps back in his seat, huffing and puffing like he's the one who's about to blow while it's me who's sprawled out half-naked in a car in a public park in broad daylight, desperate to come but struggling not to.

"Don't move." He pops his door, letting in a blast of cold air that makes it difficult to keep still. By the time he gets around to my side, he's already got his belt undone, his jeans unzipped, and his cock out. He opens my door just wide enough to wedge his body between it and the car.

"I'm literally going to freeze my tits off."

"Then turn the heat up and get busy." He leans down and gives me a smug look. "Unless you've got something else you want to tell me."

In the month or so that we've been doing this, there hasn't been one instance where I've had to safeword out and I'm not about to now because of a little frigid air. I crank the heat up to high and place my hand over his on his cock, scanning the area once more.

He cups my cheek, stroking my lips with a leather-sheathed thumb. "I won't let anything bad happen. I'll take care of you."

I know both of these things are true. We wouldn't be playing these games if we didn't completely trust each other.

"You're taking too long." He winds my braids around one hand and holds my chin with the other so that he can thrust into my mouth, a power move that he knows my body will respond to. "Maybe we should just go home." His threat of delayed gratification might as well be an order to come, and my clit obeys. For a moment, I forget where I am. I don't care about getting caught out here or about the cold or even about him. The only thing that matters is how good he makes me feel—until he pounds a fist on the roof of the car, his cock pulses, and I hurry to swallow his come down.

"Are you okay?" Once he's dressed and in the driver's seat again, he helps me get back into my clothes and passes me a thermos of hot cocoa. He zips my coat, pulls the furry hood up, and tucks my braids away inside of it, pausing to take my face tenderly in his hands for a kiss.

"I'm fine. A little chilly but nothing you can't fix with more cocoa and a nice, long cuddle session." I get warmer just thinking about the way he pampers me after we play. "You're getting so good at this. How do you feel about me calling you Sir?"

PRIVATE MESSAGE

Erzabet Bishop

Her bare pussy had touched his chair. It was the only coherent thought running through Dale's mind as the meeting ran into the two-hour nightmare that as CEO he had to endure every Tuesday. He always hated Mondays but after yesterday he was going to have to rethink that one. He'd known the new senior engineer was a firecracker when he interviewed her, but never in his wildest imaginings had he quite envisioned this scenario.

And he'd bet money the reason why lay somewhere in yesterday's decision to put the new project in the vicinity of his old standby principal engineer instead of rewarding her with the account she'd brought to the table.

But she was too new. Untested.

She had a right to be angry. But this… The fucking shock of it had almost rendered him speechless. Picking up the phone thinking it was another one of the security team's test drills, all he could do was stare.

Steve's monotonous financial rhetoric had left his brain in a fog, but the instant the alert went off on his phone, Dale's eyes snapped to the screen. Georgette stood in his office doorway, her expression mutinous, a single piece of paper crumpled in her hand as she took in the empty office. He took in the tight black skirt riding up the sculpted planes of her ass, the sweater molded to her perfectly lush breasts.

She must have waited until his secretary had gone off to lunch to try and corner him in his den. Checking his watch, he grimaced. It was well after noon and the team was starting to get restless. But they wouldn't leave until he did.

And clearly she'd expected him to be at his desk—unlike yesterday, when she'd entered his office thinking no one was looking. Today, displaying an awe-inspiring measure of boldness, she'd proceeded to raise the hem of her skirt, draw down her panties, and sit in his favorite chair.

Sliding her fingers inside of her slick sex, she'd writhed and moaned her way through a vigorous bout of self-pleasure, her legs splayed out, hips thrusting as she'd stuffed her hungry pussy with first two fingers, then three.

Not to be outdone, she'd fondled herself to a boisterous completion, using his personal handkerchief that he kept in his desk drawer to tidy herself up.

She hadn't known he was watching. She also didn't know that he'd barely made it to his private bathroom to tame the lust boiling in his veins at the thought of her finger-fucking herself. He watched it, over and over again, stroking his length until he was spent, hot jets of come spurting against the shower wall as he nearly collapsed.

No doubt she thought she still had the upper hand. The woman was a human resources field day, only he had the evidence he needed to keep the situation contained. And the ball was very much in his court.

Well, he wasn't about to disappoint her in her quest to teach him a lesson.

"Excuse me, gentlemen." He rose from his place at the head of the table, handing the reins of the meeting over to his more than capable second in command.

Gaze sharp, his eyes narrowed at the footage streaming live from his office.

Fuck. She was in his chair. Again.

Are you ready to submit?

He'd typed the one-line email before the meeting, his mouse hovering over the SEND button. Just sitting in the chair where he knew she had been only hours before had hardened his cock until his suit felt like it was suddenly a couple of sizes too small.

Installing the cameras hadn't been his idea, but with the constant threat of industrial espionage and hackers, his security team had insisted on one located in his office, that only he had access to.

He rounded the corner of the hallway, passing his secretary, Meredith, on the way into the outer office.

"Give me two hours. I have a private meeting."

"Yes, Sir." Meredith gave him a brisk nod and continued on her way.

He entered his office and shut the door, locking it.

Georgette lounged in his chair, legs crossed and heels up on the desk. Her elegant eyebrow shot up in question, the rich scarlet waves of her hair falling in soft waves down her shoulders.

"The answer is no." She rose, her heels sliding off the desk and to the floor.

Instead of saying anything, he laid his phone on the desk, the picture of her from yesterday, fingers buried inside her gleaming pussy, emblazoned on the screen.

"You bastard."

"You may want to rethink that." He stepped forward and yanked her toward him, her breasts mashed against his chest.

"I want that account."

"No." His cock hard, he walked her back toward the desk, pushing her onto the spacious wooden surface.

"I could sue you," she whispered against his lips before biting down until he groaned and tasted blood.

He met her gaze, his own then trailing over to the phone. "You started this, kitten."

Something clicked behind her eyes, and he felt her tremble against him.

"What do you want?"

"I sent you a private message earlier. That should have made everything quite clear."

He flipped her over so her body was draped over the desk, the rounded curve of her ass taunting him through the fabric of her black skirt. He thrust his cock against her and a soft, strangled sound erupted from her lips.

"You're insane."

"Am I?"

He ran his hand down her back, finding the flesh beneath the elegant sweater. Curves. She was all woman and as his hand pressed firmly against her, she struggled, turning over so she faced him.

"Why are you doing this?" Her eyes were wide, reality setting in.

"Because I can."

"It was a prank." She wiggled against him, but he held her fast.

"Never tempt a wolf who's hungry for dinner, Red. You might end up on the menu."

"You're just trying to scare me." The sheen of tears glistened in her eyes. "You could have any woman here."

"But I want you." His fingers slid along her inner thigh, brushing against the sopping, thin barrier of her panties.

"Why?"

"Submit," he whispered. She had started this game. And he would finish it.

"No." Her response was strangled, but her lips opened in invitation.

He wound his fist into her hair and edged his right hand beneath the elastic, his finger sliding inside of her heat at the same time he tugged her head back, dragging a gasp from her lush mouth. She bucked, his knuckle teasing the erect nub of her clit.

And then he stopped.

Heavy lidded, her eyes met his and she licked her lips as he peeled off his tie and reached for her hands.

"Last chance."

"Yes." All the breath left her as his fingers worked the silk tie over her wrists, his cock twitching with every movement.

But not yet. His hands cupped her generous breasts, pinching her nipples as she arched against him, the soft skin of her thighs opening to him at last.

METAMORPHOSES

Emmanuelle de Maupassant

There's a dark cloud coming over. Hurry, Miss Jenkins, or you'll miss the quarter-to-six bus."

"You're a good girl, Evie."

Miss Jenkins's feet are aching and she's more than ready to head home. "Cheerio then. See you in the morning."

Miss Jenkins puts on her headscarf and gloves, and readies her umbrella. She made a good choice in appointing Evie as assistant librarian. Such a helpful young woman; it's the third night in a row she's offered to close up.

Miss Jenkins encourages the last few stragglers as she goes. "You'll be late for supper, boys. They'll be ringing the gong. Put that one back carefully, Philip—it's heavy. No running now. The prefects are on the prowl."

She's out the door, the boys ushered ahead, and Evie is alone. The first drops of rain are hitting the window. The lights flare, then dim. The electricity was only put in the year before. Better than gas, more reliable, unless there's a storm.

Evie's tidying the card index when she hears the door open, the swish of a gown, and the familiar footstep.

"Good evening, Headmaster," she says.

"Ovid's *Metamorphoses*. Third stack down I believe, top shelf."

Evie comes out from behind the desk, heading to the Classical Literature section. Yesterday, it was *Alice in Wonderland*, the day before that, Byron's verse.

She slides the rolling ladder along from its resting place at the end of the row.

The upper shelves are dusty. She makes a mental note to clean them; Miss Jenkins can hardly be expected to climb ladders at her age.

Evie's on the fourth rung, stretching up, when she feels his hand on her ankle.

"The green volume, not the blue," he tells her.

Her fingers fumble on the spine. It's now, before-hand, that she feels most unnerved. She's still herself: apple of her father's eye, church on Sundays, doesn't stay out late. She's a good girl, isn't she?

Since she began working here, she's not so sure.

Beneath her dirndl wool skirt, his palm traces her calf. She shivers as he skims the crook of her knee. On and up, until his fingers are hooking the top of her nylons.

She knows his wife wears silks. Not as practical; they catch so easily.

He unclips the suspenders, just on one side, and rolls down Evie's stocking, until it's bunched at her ankle.

With one side up and one side down, she feels faintly ridiculous. She supposes that's the point.

Evie rests the lower edge of the slim leather-bound edition on the shelf in front of her.

Cool against her warmth, his hand waits on the bare flesh of her inner thigh.

"Begin, Miss Evesham. It's a translation. You'll have no trouble."

She lets it fall open. Evie knows what's coming. She aches for it, has been waiting. Yet her fear and excitement are like the first time.

He'd asked for Milton's *Paradise Lost*. Out of sight of others' eyes, his fingers had snaked about her wrist, his lips placing a careful kiss there, claiming her pulse. Like Lucifer, he'd tempted her: with knowledge, with experience, with the unthinkable.

He'd read *her*.

She forms the words, her tongue dry and thick.
The lamps flared up, and all the rooms were bright
With flashing crimson fires...

He seeks out the soft fringe of her fur.
...and phantom forms
Of savage beasts of prey howled all around.

Evie's voice flounders on the final word, as his thumb pushes to enter her. His fingers are never explicitly invited. Nevertheless, her legs part and she swells at his touch. Her slipperiness comes quickly. The hungry mouth of her sex draws him upward.

There is no going back. She pauses to swallow, gripping the shelf in front of her as she reads.

Among the smoke-filled rooms, one here, one there,
The sisters cowered in hiding to escape
The flames and glare...

He withdraws his fingers to remove her knickers, guides her feet as she steps out. He drapes them, peach with a lace frill, over Cicero's *Collected Speeches*. His cap, the mortarboard denoting his status, he places on top.

The lights flicker again. It's dark outside, rain heavy on the windowpane opposite the fourth stack. If someone pressed their nose to the glass, they'd see them, surely—if they wanted to, if they came close enough.

Five buttons on the back of her skirt, and it drops. He folds the garment carefully, beside her underwear.

Her buttocks are exposed to the chill of the room. She shivers, but it's only partly from the cold. She's glad for her cashmere sweater. Darned at the elbow, but who notices such things? She continues, a slight tremor in her voice.

... and, as they sought the dark,
A skinny membrane spread down their dwarfed limbs,
And wrapped thin wings about their tiny arms,

"What beautiful diction you have, Miss Evesham.

We should have you join us in assembly. You might read to the boys, just as you are doing now."

His hand on the small of her back indicates his desire that she bend at the waist. She squeezes her shoulders through the open rungs of the ladder, only just keeping hold of the book. It's undignified, the metal pressing cold against her lower belly.

He taps at both her ankles, reminding Evie to part her legs. She feels his breath, from his mouth, his nose. She's never looked as he's looking, at her sex laid bare, exhibited.

In some ways, he knows her better than she knows herself. In their Eden, he doesn't see her as a single floral note. Her scent is complex: lily, jasmine, and hellebore, bitter orange and tuberose.

The electric lights dwindle, flare brighter, then settle, but dimmer than before. She has to concentrate to see the print.

And in what fashion they had lost their shape
The dark hid from them.

The flat of his tongue runs through her wetness, stroking, probing, drinking her, and she's helpless in her shame, choking out the words through a sob of humiliation and desire.

Not with feathered plumes
They ride the air, but keep themselves aloft
On parchment wings...

Tires crunch the gravel outside: Evie's father, driving from the bank, collecting her on his way home. Twin beams arc through the window, illuminating shelves of European history and politics.

Taking her toward the edge of where she wants to be, the tongue inside her flicks. He never smiles, but she imagines him doing so now.

Barely a whisper, her voice is ragged, catching.

And when they try to speak
They send a tiny sound that suits their size,
And pour their plaints in thin high squeaking cries.

Ribboning, her wail lifts and rises, winging bat-like over the stacks, leaving her mute and breathless, transformed behind the red veil of her ferocious blood-beat.

He has no need of the book, as he takes over.

They loathe the light; from dusk they take their name, and flit by night.

The car horn summons her.

Rolling up her rumpled stocking, Evie clips it into place, reassembles herself, until her appearance is as it was.

It's inside that she shimmers: knowing and known, transformed.

WAY OF LIFE

Selena Kitt

Y ou've been a bad girl."

My heart sank when he shut the bedroom door and locked it behind him.

I couldn't remember anything I'd done but he always said I was too impulsive. And it was true—I couldn't seem to help myself.

"I'm sorry," I said immediately, even if I couldn't remember what I'd done. It was always the best way to start. "I won't do it again."

"Down."

That was all he had to say. I sank to my knees, hands resting on my bare thighs, shoulders back, gaze fixed on the carpet.

He had taught me this.

He had taught me everything.

The leash snapped onto my collar—my only adorn-
ment—with a resounding click. My body reacted
instantly. My nipples formed tan, ridged peaks while
anticipation forced a leak, like a hairline crack in a dam.
The trickle between my legs would eventually threaten
to flood. It was only a matter of time.

I was going to be punished, and although I knew I
wasn't supposed to like it—I did.

"You enjoy my new toy, don't you?"

A surge of shame seared my cheeks.

Now I remembered.

He'd purchased a large sex toy, one with a saddle.
It had attachments. They buzzed like a thousand bees
making sweet honey deep inside me. We'd used it once,
and it had felt so good, I couldn't help trying it out
myself when he was gone.

I thought I'd been careful.

How did he know?

"I can smell your cunt." He yanked the leash, lifting
my face. "Even when you wash it off, pet, I can smell
you."

He pulled me along and I crawled after him. The
machine was on the floor. I noticed he'd put a different
attachment on it—for double penetration. I winced, but
didn't object when he lubed up the dildos and ordered
me to climb on.

They were cold and it was hard to maneuver to get
them both to slide in, but I managed. He used a foot
pedal controller, starting the motor purring, and I began

to purr right along with it. The dildo in my pussy whirred softly, vibrating and turning at the same time. The one in my ass just hummed deeply, making me moan.

"Suck."

I knew what to do. I released his cock from his trousers and worked him into my mouth. The machine shuddered between my legs as I whimpered, rocking, rubbing my clit along the ribbed, silicone surface.

"Dirty whore." He thrust deeper into my mouth, making me choke on it. "You love having all those holes filled, don't you?"

I flushed scarlet, nodding, admitting my humiliation. The heat of my shame only fueled the flames that licked fiercely between my legs.

"Let's try these on for size."

I didn't stop sucking as he reached into his shirt pocket but I did cry out when he attached a clamp to my throbbing nipples, first one, then the other. They bit into my flesh, a sharp sting that built to a slow, steady burn. He watched me writhe on the machine.

"Keep sucking."

The new sensation had distracted me and I went back to work, using just my mouth, the way he'd taught me, following his lead when he wanted to fuck my throat more deeply. His foot worked the pedal, kicking the machine up a notch, making me twist and thrash, caught somewhere in a torturous quagmire of both pleasure and pain.

I avoided his gaze, trying to keep my feelings hidden,

not quite understanding them yet myself. But they tasted delicious. Sweet, with just a hint of smugness.

Did he really believe this was *punishment?*

"You're not allowed to come, pet. Not until I say." He slipped one hand under my long, dark hair, making a fist. I nodded, gulping down his length. I knew that. *"No matter what I do."*

I groaned as he tilted my head back, shoving his cock in to the root. Forcing me to take it, to taste the bitterness of this punishment deep in my throat. There was a diabolical method to his madness after all. I had defied him on this machine and now he was going to torture me with it.

My pussy dripped wildfire as he pressed the foot pedal, taking me higher still. My nipples had gone blessedly numb, but my breasts felt heavy, too full, ripe and ready to burst with feeling. I didn't know how long I could stand it.

He was the epitome of control, even though my saliva coated his length and I guzzled his cock as fast as I could. Watching my face, he somehow caught every minute change in my expression and adjusted the settings accordingly, pushing me—forward, back, forward, back—until I thought I'd go mad with desire.

"Master!" I gave up, pressing my cheek to his belly.

I only called him that when we were here, like this, after he'd ordered me down.

"Please…" I begged, needing the release he kept just out of my reach.

"Not yet." He toyed with the chain between the

nipple clamps, tugging gently, making my hips buck. I gave in, submitting to his will, continuing to fight the rising tide. My limbs trembled with the effort.

"Stroke it."

My hand moved, the tip of him wet with precome, making it an easier slide. He grunted and moved closer, aiming at my breasts.

"Are you ready, pet?"

"Oh yes, please!" I arched, pleading with my eyes.

He tugged on the chain, a slow, steady tension, pulling. I gasped, feeling it in my clit somehow as the nipple clamps slid off with a hot, stinging pop, my breasts coming alive, a sudden inferno of sensation.

"Now," he commanded.

I surrendered, my body wracked with my climax, convulsing uncontrollably with one final, blissful release. He thrust into my hand with a deep, determined roar, splashing my tender breasts with liquid fire, burning my throbbing nipples with his heat. I cried out in pleasure and pain, completely his.

He turned off the machine. I whimpered, leaning forward on it, still shivering.

Then he unhooked the leash from my collar. "Up."

I went to him, whispering his name—not "Master" now, but always Master, even if I wasn't saying it—as he cuddled me in the crook of his arm. He led me to the bed and cleaned me up. We rested, quiet, the room filled with the musky scent of our sex. I loved the smell of us together.

"You like my new toy?"

I smiled. "I'll say."

"Perhaps you'd like permission to use it when I'm gone?"

Eagerly, I nodded. "Yes! Please. May I?"

He kissed the top of my head, breathing me in. "All you had to do was ask."

I bent my repentant head, resting it against his heart, a silent apology.

In that moment, I knew this was what I needed. What I was born for.

I loved it—and I loved him. Beyond sex. Or words. Or even life.

He was my life.

This was our way of life.

And neither of us would have it any other way.

SYMPHONY
OF
SUBMISSION

Jordan Monroe

Y ou're too quiet. We must break that."

You don't look up at Sir. Your back is sore, yet you dare not relax. Years of kneeling in pretend prayer have you disciplined to remain composed and rigid. Your eyes are downcast in supplication. The air is cool, raising goose bumps down each limb, hardening your nipples. You fidget with your fingers behind your back.

"Nothing to say to that, pet?"

When Sir asks a question of you, Sir expects an answer.

Your voice trembles. "I am yours to command, Sir."

Cloth rustles. Sir's footsteps, even and deliberate, are sharp against the hardwood floor. His fine Oxford shoes stop at your knees, black and shiny, recently polished. You desperately want to look up, but you suppress your desire.

"Look at me."

Sir's sonorous voice reverberates. You could listen for hours. Blinking, you raise your mascaraed eyes and meet Sir's piercing blue gaze.

"Without auditory confirmation, I don't know whether I give you any joy. I don't merely take pleasure; I expect to give it as well."

You listen to Sir, inhaling his rich cologne mixed with the light layer of sweat that has accumulated throughout the day. Your face is at Sir's crotch, the zipper of his suit trousers peeking tantalizingly from the fly; you could lean forward and grasp it between your teeth with ease. You hold your ground and continue listening.

"No more of that, pet. No more silence. No more wondering if I am wasting your time, for your continued silence wastes mine. If I don't know you are enraptured, then there is no purpose. Do you understand?"

Of course you understand. Sir's ego requires diligent stroking. You know Sir is an excellent lover and feeds off of your energy. You also know your own stubbornness and are defiantly silent. Above all things, you challenge Sir to break your composure; toying with him this way is your idea of a game night.

Sir asked a question. You answer, "Yes. I understand, Sir."

Sir reaches down to caress your cheek with a large, gloved hand. The black leather is soft. You lean into it, taking the thumb into your mouth and sucking, letting the bitter flavor of leather and saliva trickle down your throat. You hear Sir sigh, and you cast your eyes back up to stare at his bearded face. It's a face that is striking: composed, but with crystalline eyes that betray a latent wildness. It's a face that demands undivided attention.

Sir's grip tightens slightly on your cheek. "Good. Lie on the bed facedown. Keep your pretty ass in the air."

Without using your hands for balance, you stand and walk toward the elegant black four-poster bed. Sir swats your ass sharply, but you don't cry aloud; you release a soft gasp. You swing your legs over the footboard. The covers and pillows have been removed, leaving only the cream-colored Egyptian-cotton sheet. As Sir instructed, you lower onto the bed, your breasts and belly pressed flat against the cool fabric, your wide buttocks on display, your thick thighs spread so that your entrances are available.

You wait patiently.

You hear the whistle before you feel the sting. The leather tip of the flogger against your skin is so sudden, you are more surprised than pained. Digging your fingers into the expensive sheets, you remain silent. You feel the sliver of flesh on your ass redden, yet you do not shy away.

"I want to hear your resolve break. I want to hear your ecstasy. I want you to vocalize your surrender not to me, but to your pleasure. Do not hold back your personal symphony. Cry out!"

With that last syllable, there is another strike of leather against your flesh. You grip the fabric, tighter this time, but still remain quiet. You hear Sir grunt in frustration, then his heavy steps against the hardwood floor. Your hands are pulled to the corners of the bed, palms forced open and flat. You turn your head to the side to watch Sir snake a leather cuff around your wrist. Before you can inquire, Sir has gone to the other side of the bed to imprison your other hand. When you have been shackled, Sir leaves your field of vision again.

"You rely on your hands too much. You are not to grab the fabric. As I have stated before, I require you to make noise!"

Once again, Sir has raised his voice. While you want to please Sir, you also want to push him. There is a part of you that gets off on goading him like this. You're not a brat in the typical sense: you don't whine, tease, or openly defy Sir. You are more interested in being a challenge, because you so desperately want Sir to rise to the occasion. With another sharp smack, you release a loud gasp as your composure wavers.

The sound has pleased Sir: you feel the warmth of leather caress your sore flesh. Sir is stroking you pleasantly, and you exhale languidly.

"That's a good start, but it's not enough. I shall do this until I hear you scream. Generally I use gags and bits, but not so with you. The opposite, it seems."

You yearn for more of the brutal strikes. Something deep within you wants Sir to use those wide hands across your ass, turning the expanse of flesh red and sore. The riding crop Sir has been using is not enough.

You feel the leather tip of the crop trail down your spine. You arch your back into it, letting your attempt at feline grace indicate your desire. When the cool leather reaches your private places, you inhale through your teeth. In an instant, the leather is withdrawn, but it does not strike you. As though Sir has read your mind, something larger and warmer sends a shock against your skin.

Sir's leathered hand comes down with such force that you rock forward on the bed. You quickly resume your position, wanting more. Sir strikes your ass again. You are now panting, anticipating more of this. In rapid succession, Sir rains hot, leathered slaps across your quivering flesh. You gasp with each, until Sir lands a blow between your legs, slapping your cunt. That elicits a sound you have never uttered before: something foreign and far too base for your liking.

There is a pause in the play. Sir gently rubs your softness. "That, my dear, was a lovely sound. Let me hear it again."

As Sir rewards you with a similar swat against your inner seam, you reward Sir with an ecstatic cry. You find the sounds increasing in volume and intimacy. With a final blow, you realize that Sir is the only person who is able to unlock this release.

TWELVE

R.A. Buckley

One!" I squeal as the paddle lands on my ass, the burn already beginning even before He's warmed up. I can't believe that He's punishing me for this; it's so unfair! The last time I sassed Him in public He gave me ten paddles, not twelve. It was eleven at first, but when I mentioned this to Him He added another. Like I said, it's so unfair. I wasn't even sassing Him, but rather the stupid Dom who thought he was making me feel good on that Saint Andrew's cross. I was bored, and I barely felt anything; that's why I called him a pussy.

"Two!" The paddle lands across my ass again and I know that my cheeks are going to hurt tomorrow. When He's really mad at me He doesn't say anything during my punishments. That's really the worst thing of all; silence is not my friend. And He knows that; I guess that's why He does it. It makes me think about what I've done wrong, and also how to make it up to Him. Was that Dom as stupid as I thought? He was using a cane but it didn't even hurt. But Master has said that I'm a pain slut who can take a lot more than most dish out, so maybe it wasn't the stupid-head's fault. I could have asked him for more.

"Three!" I yelp as I announce my count this time. This is as hard as He ever hits me. But looking back on the evening, I know I deserve it. I was bratty the whole night. I complained about the outfit He had me wear, and how cold it was in the dungeon as well. He shot me that look, the one that says "You're skating on thin ice, little one," and I should have realized what He meant. But no, I had to go mouthing off to the owner of the dungeon (although if he owns a dungeon he should know how to hit harder) and I embarrassed Master. When He was quiet on the drive home I knew I was in trouble.

"Four!" The tears start welling up in my eyes as I announce my count this time. The pain is pretty intense, but I'm more upset that I disappointed Master. How could I have disappointed Him like that? He loves me and he usually is so proud to show me off. I love to be the perfect little sub for Him, but tonight I was that brat everyone talks about when she leaves. Oh, shit, I can feel the tears really flowing now.

"Five!" The tears continue and I sob as I call out my punishment. Tonight was supposed to be a fun night, and all I did was ruin it by acting like a petulant child. Why do I do this? We can be in such a good place and then it seems like I will purposefully screw up, like I'm scared that this perfect thing will end, so I sabotage it. Master would probably use some psychoanalytic term to describe what I did since that's His job, but I just feel like I can't handle it when things go too well.

"Six!" I'm sobbing hard now. I fucked up and I know it. I know this is penance for not only what I did to the gentleman at the dungeon, but because I was acting like a brat all night. I should have had a great time. I love showing off my body, and wearing nothing but a body stocking in the club should have been the perfect thing for me. But I had to whine and complain and it wasn't for any real reason other than that sometimes I just have to rebel.

"Seven!" The sting in my buttocks intensifies as I begin to hiccup from taking in too much air at one time from the sobs. Oh, I have that ugly crying face now on top of everything else. Master knows that I'm going to rebel; I'll never be that perfect service-oriented sub that you read about in those books. I have to act out; it's just part of who I am, and honestly part of my submission. I need to push Master's limits so that I can feel safe knowing he'll never let me fall or go to far.

"Eight!" My sobs are slowing down, the sting in my ass is lessening; oh yes, I'm starting to get there. When I need a good beating Master always delivers and sometimes I get to heaven. People call it all sorts of things—

the most common term is subspace, I guess—but for me it's heaven. All I can feel is the paddle reddening my bottom, and Master's gaze upon my body as I react for Him. He loves me so much and He knows that I need this from time to time. If it were a normal thing it wouldn't be so special, would it?

"Nine!" The pain is almost gone entirely now. I feel like I'm floating, even though I'm on my hands and knees on the living room rug. I can feel my pussy reacting to Master's attentions, even though He hasn't come anywhere near it. I'm a pain slut and I love to feel my body being used for His pleasure, for correction, for punishment, for whatever He desires. He makes my body sing and react in ways that I never thought would be possible. I've orgasmed from His bare-handed spankings many times in the past, and other ways as well. It's part of our dynamic and why I love Him so.

"Ten!" It's now like an out-of-body experience. I can almost see my body, taut and tense as it awaits the next lash from the paddle, craving the feeling of Master's paddle, reminding me that I am His girl and I am expected to obey Him and make Him proud at all times. It feels like I could come at this moment, but I don't want to; I want this moment to last and for my Master to tell me when I can release. I am His and want to make Him proud.

"Eleven!" I barely recognize my own voice as it echoes throughout the living room. I look over at the windows overlooking the backyard and see Master, the paddle in His hand as He prepares for His next strike, in the reflection. I see the smile on His face; He knows that I am repentant now.

"Come."

"Twelve!" My body explodes as Master says one word and the paddle lands across my ass for the final time. I heave and convulse as my body and pussy spasm. I never grow tired of this—serving Him, pleasing Him by accepting punishment and pleasure at the same time. He is my Master, my Love, and my body sings for Him in exactly the key He wants.

It's over. I collapse onto the floor and feel His strong arms envelop me. There is nowhere else I need to be. No more punishments tonight. Just love.

AROUND THE BLOCK

M. Marie

Since having their baby two years ago, Jason and Alexandra had implemented a secret routine.

Every couple of days, when they needed a release, they would ask Jason's mother to babysit while they went for a "drive around the block." They made the excuse of needing some quiet time together, and the doting grandmother was only too happy to fuss over her grandchild for an hour or two, so no further explanation was needed.

No questions were ever asked about the small bag Jason brought along, either.

They lived in a small farmhouse just outside the city limits, so they simply had to drive around a bend to find privacy. They would park on the shoulder of the road a few miles away from the house, turn off the ignition, and allow themselves a brief escape to indulge their sexual kinks.

It wasn't ideal, of course. A hotel room—or a dungeon—would have served their needs better, but with their daughter so young, and money a bit tight, it was hard to justify that kind of expense. All they truly needed was each other and a safe space to play in, after all, so with their house out of the question now that Jason's mother was in residence, their car had become their secret playroom.

Tonight, after parking and killing the engine, the pair stepped out of the car to quickly check that the area was indeed vacant, before sliding into the backseat. Alex settled in beside her husband, before getting right to business: "Safeword?"

Jason's eager grin filled the backseat. "Venice," he responded.

She smiled softly at him—that was where they had been married. Alex loved Jason's romantic side…it paired so nicely with his submissive nature.

Gracefully, she straddled his lap. As her warm weight dropped down onto his thighs, Jason's body reacted instinctively to the feel of her body pressed so closely against his. His pulse quickened, his skin flushed, and, as he felt his cock begin to harden, Jason shifted so she could feel it pressing against her.

"Not yet," she admonished.

Alexandra's short black dress had shimmied up her thighs as she settled into his lap, baring smooth, porcelain skin. Slowly, she slid her hands up her legs, from knees to waist, pulling her skirt up completely as she did so. Jason's hungry eyes followed every movement, and settled quickly on her pussy as it was bared. She never wore panties when they went for their drives.

His hands twitched at his sides, desperate to touch, but he resisted. Pleased, Alex leaned in to press her lips against his. Her kiss was demanding and desirous, but brief.

Pulling back, she wrapped her arms around his neck and whispered, "Did you bring my bag?"

Instantly, Jason's cock swelled with excitement. "Yes! It's on the floor."

"Close your eyes," she instructed.

He obeyed. There was a rustling of fabric as she shifted on top of him, then the metallic purr of the bag being unzipped. Next, *silence*. He tilted his head, listening; her fingertips tapped his chin, making him start slightly. Her fingers traced his jawline, down to his throat, then disappeared, only to be replaced a heart-beat later by a familiar, heavy sensation.

Jason practically purred as Alex slipped his well-worn collar around his neck and carefully buckled it, being mindful not to fasten it too tight. With it placed to her satisfaction, she slid even closer and let her firm body press flush against his. His breath caught in his throat as she pulled his wrists behind his back. There was another familiar noise—metal clinking together—and then the cold sensation of bands encircling his wrists.

The handcuffs snapped shut with a sharp *click*, restraining him.

"Good?" she checked, in a throaty whisper. He nodded consent.

Satisfied, she reached between their bodies and stroked his stiff erection through his pants. Her lips were against his neck now, and her fingertips had found his zipper. Her teeth nipped just below his jaw as she lowered his fly and reached inside. He cursed in a low voice as, after squeezing the base teasingly, she slid her grip up to encircle the head of his shaft and pull it out of his pants.

Jason's groans deepened. "Can I open my eyes?" he begged.

"No."

Grinning, Alexandra didn't loosen her grip as she slid off his lap and dropped to her knees on the floor of the car. Above her, Jason spread his legs and blindly thrust his pelvis upward as she lowered her face to his crotch. Alexandra's tongue lapped a lazy circle around the head of his cock, before she opened her mouth wide and took the whole organ.

She wasted no time on a slow buildup. Immediately she began to suck hard; her left hand was gripping the base of his cock and squeezing rhythmically, while her right hand cupped his heavy balls. As she slid her mouth up and down his swollen cock, her tongue swirled around the hard shaft and, occasionally, she pulled her lips back from her teeth and let them graze tauntingly over the sensitive skin of his erection.

It was maddening. Jason wanted to bury both of his hands in her long hair and rein her in to a steadier pace, but the cuffs kept him from doing so. She increased the pressure of her teeth for a moment, enjoying the way he squirmed and shuddered, but once his breathing grew labored, she relented and climbed back into his lap.

"Watch me," was her brusque order.

Jason's eyes snapped open. Under his heated gaze, Alexandra reached between her legs to spread her pussy open, then slowly lowered herself onto his stiff, throbbing cock. Helpless to touch or interact, he merely groaned and panted, offering breathless cries of pleasure as she rode him roughly.

She came first. Her cry of climax made him keen in frustration. She could feel him trembling beneath her and took pity on her pet. Affectionately, she slid two fingers under his collar and tugged lightly as she commanded, "Come for me."

Jason climaxed with a hoarse, breathless bellow. His wrists strained against the handcuffs hard enough to leave bruises. As his tremors subsided and he sagged back into the smooth leather seat, Alex gently stroked his damp forehead and whispered praises against his temple.

When he had recovered somewhat from the exertion, Jason rolled his head to the side and looked out the car window. The sky had darkened considerably since they'd left the house. Alexandra confirmed the late hour beside him.

After adjusting her clothes and freeing his wrists from the handcuffs, she decided, "I don't think we have time for any other toys tonight. We need to get back."

There was a time when Jason would have protested; he would have insisted they stay and that his Domme focus her attention solely on him, but they were no longer simply submissive and dominant. As partners—and parents—other responsibilities often had to take priority.

Without complaint, he bent his neck so she could unfasten his collar. After all, their next indulgence was always just around the block.

THE OLD-FASHIONED WAY

Angela R. Sargenti

My wife thinks I'm working late. She'd be shocked to know where I really am, lying facedown, shackled to a table at my Dominatrix's place.

Unfortunately, my Domme knows I'm here betraying my wife's trust in me. The flogger snaps against my buttocks, causing me to gasp, then moan.

"You little shit. You don't deserve a woman like her."

It's true. I probably don't, because she'd be crushed to find out about Mistress Lorena and the kind of activities I involve myself in.

She hits me again, and I strangle a cry.

"You should be home, or working late like you told her you'd be, you lying dog."

"Yes, Mistress."

"You probably couldn't wait to get here, you scum."

I feel tears well up in my eyes, because she's right, she's right about all of it. I could be home making sweet love to my wife, but the problem is, she's not very adventurous when it comes to sex, and her sex drive is low. She rarely lets me get inside her, and even when she does, she's flat on her back with the lights either off, or down so low I can barely see her. As for her doing the work of Mistress Lorena, that wouldn't happen in a million years.

My wife doesn't have a kinky bone in her body, whereas my Domme is a deceptively petite lady, with flaming red hair and a temper to match. All of her commands must be promptly obeyed or she works me over extra-hard.

She wields the flogger again.

"Did you hear me?"

"No, Mistress. I'm sorry, Mistress."

"I told you to pay attention. What are you thinking about in that stupid little head of yours?"

"My wife."

"Oh ho, so you do think about her. You're not just a thoughtless little fool?"

"No. It hurts me to treat her this way."

She starts flogging me—once, twice, three lashes— and then she stops.

"It's going to hurt you even more, because I'm giving you an assignment," she tells me. "I want you to confess by our next session."

"Confess?"

"Yes. I want you to tell your poor, long-suffering wife the truth about your late nights at the office."

"You can't be serious."

This enrages her and she moves down the table and starts whipping me again. I start crying, but I don't know why.

"But how?" I ask her.

"Just open your piehole and speak. Show her your welts. I don't care how. Just do it. And I want proof that you've done it. A note, a phone call, a personal visit. I don't care which. Just tell her, or else."

"You ask too much."

She beats me again.

"I'll teach you not to disobey me," she says through gritted teeth. "Talking back to your Mistress like that. And stop your sniveling, before I really give you a reason to cry."

And I know what she means, but I can't help it. I deserve to be tortured, so I make no effort to squelch my tears. She stands there patiently, and when I don't stop, she sets the flogger down and unclips my shackles.

"Turn over, and make it snappy."

I obey her, and flip over onto my back. She clips my shackles back into the rings in the table and picks up the riding crop lying beside the flogger. I'm already hard, and the sight of that crop makes my insides ache with need. When she realizes this, Mistress Lorena strolls over to my head and looms over me.

"Time for the blindfold."

I open my mouth to beg her not to blindfold me, but she silences me with a smack to the knee. I shut my mouth and she retrieves the blindfold from the tray and goes to slip it over my head. I raise up for her, for it will be far, far worse if I disobey her now.

My cock throbs. It's so hard now it hurts.

"What a naughty boy you are, Phillip."

"Yes, Ma'am."

"Such a bad, bad boy."

She runs the crop up and down my cock. It twitches, and I fight back a moan. She grabs hold of it and smacks me on the balls quickly, before I can start pumping into her hand.

This does nothing to diminish my hard-on. I want her to touch me again. I might be able to come if she touches me again, but the devil made this woman to torment me. She slaps the crop against my cock. Not too hard, but still.

A groan escapes my lips and she whacks my cock a few more times. It hurts like hell, but the snap-back is incredible. I squirm on the table and she caresses me with the crop again.

"I don't know why you're being so stubborn tonight."

"Oh, please don't make me tell her."

"You'll do it, or else."

But Mistress Lorena knows how to torture and tease. She continues punishing my cock, but none of her cajoling will make me break.

And then she does the unthinkable. She yanks off the blindfold and slaps my face.

Hard.

"I've had it with you tonight," she tells me. "Just lie there and watch me pleasure myself."

She's never done this before. She grabs the vibe off the tray, and she's so fucking sexy I think I'll burst. She gets herself off pretty quickly, and I'm half out of my mind with lust. I pull at the restraints, but of course, it does no good. She slaps my nipples and tickles my dick, but not enough to be useful.

"Please, Mistress, please make me come," I beg. "I'll do anything you want, just please make me come."

"You'll tell her, then?"

"God, yes."

"Swear."

"I swear I'll tell her. I swear on my mother's grave, I'll tell her."

"Then, here," she says, unhooking the shackles again. "Go pleasure yourself, then get dressed and go home."

The talk with my wife is painful and tear filled. At first she doesn't understand that Mistress and I haven't slept together, have never slept together, but when I finally make her believe it, she stops me.

"Then what do you go for?"

"To be punished, absolved of all my transgressions. It's kind of like confession for the Catholics."

"This is your biggest transgression of all, if you ask me, sneaking around and lying."

"I know. Lately I've been feeling worse and worse about it."

"Feel better now? Because give me your belt. You want to be punished, let me do it."

And the miracle is, she does. She punishes me atop all those welts on my ass. It takes her a few minutes to get into the swing of it, but she really comes through, and when it's over, she calls Mistress Lorena herself and tells her she doesn't think I'll be needing her services any longer.

"We're going to do it the old-fashioned way," she tells her. "At home."

THE GIFT

Victoria Blisse

He'd known to expect a present, known it would be something good, but he hadn't known what it would be until he opens the hotel room door and sees his present on the bed.

Naked.

He locks the door behind him and approaches the offering. From this angle he can only really see her ass and spread legs, stretched apart with the aid of a sleek, steel bar, her ankles encircled by black leather connected to the restraint with a few chain links. Her hands are bound with cuffs at the middle of her back, the same black leather, steel attachments, and chain.

Her hair is spread haphazardly over her shoulders, her cheek pressed to the sheets, facing away from him. He walks to the other side of the bed, wanting to see her face.

He smiles, noting his implements lovingly arrayed beside her. Crops, paddle, flogger, and something new. Black, long, threatening, with a beautifully turned wooden handle. Picking it up, he lovingly caresses it, looking intently as it shines, the Delrin plastic hard and unyielding. Joe notices her straining to watch him. So, with a smirk, he flexes the cane in the air. The unmistakable sound makes her nostrils flair. He repeats the action.

She hates canes but she loves them. They've been a talked-about thing, threats and promises, but he's never used one on her before. Unwilling to force her forward—that benefits neither of them—he's waited for her to make the first move.

And now it's resting in his hands.

Bending low, he places his face in her line of sight.

"Well, Elizabeth, I can see you've been busy."

He uses her full name when they play. It puts her immediately into his control.

"I knew you would treat me—you always do—but this is just the perfect gift for me."

He watches the corner of her mouth curl in satisfaction.

"Now, what do I do with you? It would be particularly evil of me to just leave you there, wouldn't it?" Joe turns and sits at the head of the bead. "To deny a pain slut what she desires would really rather satisfy my sadistic streak. The ultimate punishment."

Sitting silently, he watches her. She moves her fingers

and intakes breath. He lets the silence roll on, uncomfortable and heavy. Taunting her with its emptiness.

"But you have been such a good girl, going above and beyond to provide me with the perfect birthday present. Although you did deny me the pleasure of watching you getting all trussed up like that. I bet that was wonderfully entertaining."

More silence. She hates to wait, but it is an essential part of any scene for them.

"And you have left out all these beautiful implements for me, including something shiny and new. It would really be a shame not to break in my new toy."

Joe picks it up, taps his left hand with the tip.

"Maybe it'll be *all* I use."

Standing, he grabs all the implements and moves them out of her line of sight.

He takes his time undressing, slowly unfastening his belt, making sure it clinks loudly so she knows what's going on.

When he touches her, she startles. Trailing just one finger over her buttocks, he contemplates his next move as she moans, a little release of pressure.

"What's this?" he asks, taking the finger between her buttocks, lower, through her wet lips and running up and down between them. "You are soaked already. What a slut. Bound up and waiting and so fucking wet for me. Damn."

A sharp slap to the left buttock shakes her whole body. He follows quickly with a strike to the right.

"I think I want to physically hurt you, Elizabeth. I want to let you give me the exact gift you planned. Tell me. Tell me what you want to happen."

"Well, Sir. I wanted to surprise you. Give myself to you to do with as you will."

A hard, flat-palmed slap shakes her.

"Not the clever answer you think I want to hear, Elizabeth. What do *you* want?"

"But Sir, if I tell you, you won't give it to me," she whines.

"If you don't, I won't give you anything," he growls.

"Well, in that case—" Another crack makes her squeal and dance her feet within the give of the straps.

"I was hoping you'd come in and hit me with all the things, Sir. To give me amazing marks, to leave cane stripes, Sir. Then I want you to fuck me, like this, use me. That's what I want."

Gripping the cane, he presses it against her flesh.

"You want to be hit with all the toys but I just want to play with my new one." Tapping it gently against her, he continues. "I'll give you those stripes. Red, burning stripes across your delicate, white skin."

Lifting the cane higher, Joe brings it down with confident ease, hitting but not at full strength, not yet.

"Ah!" she yelps.

"Hush now. Don't want the whole corridor to know what a pain slut you are."

Another impact, a little harder, and she whimpers.

Joe switches back to light taps, gently stinging, then

pulls his arm back into the air. Elizabeth clenches, antic-ipating the hit. He cuts the air with the cane but stops the strike before it lands.

She lets go of her breath, relaxes, and then he hits, without warning.

"Fucking ouch!" she yells.

"What did I say?"

"Fucking ouch, Sir," Elizabeth repeats at a normal level. "And sorry but it hurt a lot, Sir. It just exploded out."

"Damn, impulsive woman."

A hit to the back of her thighs elicits a whine, quietly blown through clenched teeth.

"Better."

The next blow has her calling for leniency. If she meant it, she would call amber. It is just part of the game. So he leaves her another rapidly developing stripe of red across the backs of her thighs.

"How does it feel?"

"Hot and tight, and rolling and stinging and it really fucking hurts, Sir. It won't go."

"No? What about if I do this?"

He hits again, once, twice, three times in quick succession.

"That," she squeaks, "that makes it all the worse, Sir. Thank you, Sir."

"My pleasure." He smirks.

And the strikes continue and she strains harder and harder not to make noise and he delights more and more in his control and her submission. When she is striped, sore, and snuffling back tears, he fucks her.

"Jesus Christ, you're wet and tight, you pain-loving, submissive sub."

He doesn't hear her response; her face is buried in the sheets and she is not forming words. It's just pure pleasure spilling from her lips.

Joe pulls on her cuffs, arching her back and using that extra stability to fuck her all the harder. Her cunt clutches; she is rolling in pleasure, in the zone, completely and utterly used, hurting and in ecstasy. He feeds off that, coming hard when he just can't take any more.

"Happy birthday, Sir," she mumbles, as he begins the process of releasing her.

"Thank you, Elizabeth. You're the best."

BOTTEGA LOUIE

Zoey Trope

"Hi. I'm Gavin."

That was the first and last time He referenced himself by name. Later it would be Sir, then Daddy; perhaps eventually Master. It makes me blush every time I hear His actual name in public now, knowing that to me, He represents so much more.

But it started with "Gavin." I knew I was in trouble because I wanted Him immediately. It's surreal how all my previous "looking for" criteria seem to have described exactly Him, a Dominant male with a cast-iron soul, seasoned with salt-and-pepper hair; aged, mellow, and neat...just like His favorite whisky. We barely touched but I could feel His eyes on me the entire night, lassoing my body as I walked through the door.

The intensity escalated as we were seated across from

each other. It formed such a tight grip on me that it was difficult to breathe. I'd barely caught my breath when He presented a small pink box of chocolates from Bottega Louie. I was already smiling; now I was smitten. Needless to say, the attraction was immediate and He pulled me in with every detail he revealed about himself. When it came time to order, I was prepared for my palate to be one of the first things he would claim and refine until it was as He wished. Everything He ordered, I craved. It fed my hunger to be across the table from a man who knew He could have His way with me, but chose instead to slowly mold my attention to fulfilling His desires and denying me mine.

Before dinner ended, He casually mentioned that he had another gift for me, and handed me a folded Ziploc bag. Confused, I unfolded the empty bag and asked what it was. What he said next sent my mind racing. His soft words silenced the entire restaurant. "I want you to go into the bathroom, take off your panties, and bring them to me in this bag." His voice was calm and stern, and my body was paralyzed by His words. I desperately wanted to invite Him to take them off at the table, but that would lack the discretion and class that I needed to present in order to impress Him. I raced to the bathroom, eager to present Him with my submission. I returned and proudly handed Him my panties, carefully watched as He tucked them into His coat pocket. He helped me into my coat and said, "Let's go for a walk."

As we walked toward the pier, the cold breeze tickled

up my thighs. His words tugged on me like a leash and I followed obediently until He stopped to reward me with one kiss. His warmth made me weak and I wanted more. But no matter how much I threw myself at Him, He continued to withhold His touch.

Foolishly, I reached out to pull myself closer into Him to satisfy my hunger for Him. He reacted with a single glance that signaled the utmost disapproval and disappointment. With His rough hands, He grabbed a fistful of my hair, peeling my desperation away until I was hovering within a breath of His lips. I was shaking, not from the cold ocean air, but from the unbearable distance and silence from Him. Suddenly, He struck my left cheek with His forceful hands.

"I don't like being grabbed."

"I'm sorry, Sir."

He leaned in and softly whispered into my ear, "Good girl." The waves crashed into the pier and my world was silenced. My gaze was fixed on Him even as He looked away, making sure no one saw Him. The heat and sting from His palm on my cheek finally dissipated. The slap awakened my desire for submission. In one gesture, He reminded me of my place and made me want more. But I knew I had to wait.

It would be another week before He planned to see me again. He sent me home with my first assignment. I was allowed to indulge in one chocolate a day from the pretty Bottega Louie box. And as a thank-you, a sexy photo dedicated to Him. "Remember, just one chocolate a day," He reminded me before he said good-bye for the night. I was thrilled to comply and committed to pleasing Him.

During the cab ride home, I carefully plotted out my daily photo shoots. I had seven photos with which to seduce this man into giving me more of His irresistible self. I decided I couldn't wait until morning for a taste. I opened the pretty box as soon as I got home. I stripped naked, posed with one piece of chocolate melting in my mouth, and confessed to Him that His kisses taste much sweeter.

My ritual continued daily with careful attention to the mise-en-scène. Wine, chocolate, and a bubble bath seemed like a no-brainer. I could tell He approved. He taunted and tortured me with the reminder that He was carrying my Ziplocked panties with Him everywhere He went. "You're in my back pocket, underneath me, where you belong," He teased. By the end of the long week, He'd sent a photo of His big brown leather bag, torturing me with the details of where my panties were stored along with His toys and, most importantly, my collar.

When we finally reunited, He sent me straight to His hotel room. I felt completely naked as I walked through the door. He had seen every part of me. I recognized His leather bag and my eyes widened as I scanned through His collection of restraints, spreader bars, paddles, and floggers. He ordered me to strip and drop to my knees. He pulled out a black leather collar with multiple rings.

"I need you to recite this to me every time you put

your collar on. This is how you serve me from now on. Repeat after me..."

"Desire..."

"Devotion..."

"Obedience..."

"Gratitude..."

After I recited my mantra, He pulled me up to my feet. I was struggling to stand up, but He kissed me in a way that made me yearn for Him even more. He held my face in His hands and quizzed me. "How do you serve me?"

"With desire, devotion, obedience, and gratitude, Sir." He gently pulled my hair away from my nape as He wrapped the collar around my neck and locked it into place. "Good girl."

Twelve months later, I can barely make it through my entire mantra or taste a piece of salted caramel from Bottega Louie without being reminded of how I felt that first week. He gifted these rituals to me, allowing me to feel closer to Him despite the distance between us. When I wake up without Him, I slap myself five times, repeating my mantra. When I go to bed without Him, I taste a piece of His chocolate and bring back the memory of our first night together. All of these rituals please Him. I know that I have to earn His adoration, His attention, His authority, and most importantly, His love, with my desire, devotion, obedience, and gratitude.

LASHED

Dr. J.

The waves lulled us in the middle of the ocean. On the side of this historic replica of an eighteenth-century sailing ship, I sat with Nelson. Sailing this vessel had been Nelson's dream. As he toyed with his new rope, we watched the palette of the early morning sky flash a sailor's warning of red.

Nelson was a seadog from way back. His skill set made him reliable at our craft.

"Do you trust me?" His hesitant words hit me as he stood and faced the sea.

His question seemed out of place. His stance was edgy and agitated. I knew this behavior well.

Nelson had always taken care of me, my well-being, my safety. But today, he expressed a need. It was evident he wrestled with it; I could feel it. I became privy to a personal process of his, with me.

For him to grapple with an idea meant that I would too. For when he pushed himself, he pushed me. When he surrendered to his true nature, I yielded entirely to mine.

I joined Nelson, looking out. I picked up the end of the rope and offered it to him. "Show me."

With both our hands on the line, he caressed my thumb. When our fingers touched, I slipped mine to intertwine with his, and the dominant place in him expanded. Warm, firm, calloused fingertips pressed into my hand. He let out a deep breath.

"Undress. I have something unique in mind."

I created a pile. My bra and panties followed my shorts and a tank top.

Nelson opened a bench seat and pulled out a gauzy piece of fabric. He draped it over my shoulder, and it floated past my hips on both sides of my nude body. I felt more naked wearing the flimsy material than only sporting my bare skin.

Nelson pointed. "Stand in front of this pole." I faced the bow of the boat as a wave rose, and salt spray misted my face.

Nelson looped my hands to the pole. The intensity with which he worked the loops suggested an artist weaving on a loom or a fisherman making nets. The sentiment was gratification.

"How's the tightness?"

"It's good."

"You know I like a particular tension."

"I do."

I was mesmerized by the sensation of the pattern he created on me. As the gulls overhead squawked, I owned a secret part of myself. I had yearned for another level. *Did he know?* His calm almost made me combust. I was dropping into that other place inside myself when I realized he was talking to me.

"Sorry, what?"

"I want to create you as my 'Neptune's Wooden Angel.'"

The intensity and control of his words shattered something deep inside me, primal, urgent.

"May I ask what that is?"

He nodded. "At one time in history, carved maiden figures graced the prow of wooden sailing ships." Nelson paused to test the rope's tension across my flesh. "Lookouts, if you will. There to ensure safe passage for sailors."

The morning light caused a sparkle in his eyes. "Am I that to you, Sir?"

He secured a knot then kissed my cheek. "You are and more."

"Tell me. I will go there."

"I intend to photograph you, bound to this pole. You are my personal maidenhead, recreating history and demonstrating, as in the days of old, my might and wealth as an owner. Your beauty will grace this ship and me."

He grabbed my face and kissed me fiercely, nipping my lip, drawing blood.

Marked.

He was mine; I was his.

The sting of the salt settled into my cut lip, as he lashed me to the pole. I inhaled the ocean scent. The strength of her nature grew in me.

I imagined how I would look as his Neptune's Angel, my red hair unfurled like the banner of a beautiful sailing vessel. I was his treasure. Now he was making me his jewel of the sea.

Nelson tapped my foot, and I lifted it. He bent my leg, placed the sole of my foot on the pole, and knotted it in place.

He had never used these particular rope designs before. They highlighted the femininity of my breasts and the lips of my vulva.

After he had finished the design, he rubbed sunscreen on my fair, uncovered skin. He executed a future visual plan of enjoyment. No burn, just rope marks. His sure and steady fingers worked me with the motion of the waves, causing my arousal to build. I shook.

He shifted me and the pole to an angle, replicating the maidenhead's direction pointed out to sea.

He retrieved his camera, snapping pictures of me as I hovered in this wanting, needy phase. I hung forward into the world of the sea. My breathing shifted. The shudder clicks grew distant, and I felt consumed by the churning ocean.

Nelson stimulated me by alternating strokes to my erect nipples and then my clit. The ocean whispered to me. "You are his. Submit."

He read me so well and knew exactly when to stop the touches before I moved into an orgasm. Sweet torture. Today, it was amplified. But I would do this for him, for us.

He revved me up, and then backed off, over and over.

I ached, I craved release, and I wanted him.

The wind whipped me, the sun cooked me, and the rope held me in my angled position as a roar belted out of me and spewed into the air. Its potency would have done the job of keeping another safe, Nelson safe, from everything. That was the last thing I remembered until I felt his wet, warm mouth in the heart of my sex.

As Nelson's hand held my bent, roped leg, his lips and tongue devoured me. He pulled on my lips with his mouth. I was lost in pleasure. His teeth grazed my clit, and he drew it into his mouth with pulsating sucks. My urgency and his determination might be the death of me. The ropes allowed the orgasm to rumble through me. It broke me apart. At that moment, I was the maiden on the front of the boat, and the waves broke over me, again and again.

Nelson righted the pole and removed the ropes. His tender touches and kisses nudged me to wakefulness as I lay in his arms.

"There you are."

"Nelson."

"My beautiful sea angel."

"We went there, into the deep."

"We did, love. I have the pictures."

"I expanded myself to take it all in."

"I know." His thumb stroked my thigh and then he traced the rope marks on my skin. "It's imprinted on you."

"Yes, and the ocean has pounded it into me, forever."

WHAT SHE WANTED

Olivia Foxe

Dev wasn't a pussy, he just wanted to fuck one.

He repeated the thought to himself while his knees shook with the urge to buckle for Camille. His cop's uniform felt rough on his skin as the breeze from the hot afternoon brushed his face.

Standing on the balcony of his apartment, he crossed his arms, aware of the bulge of his biceps and the way Camille's eyes latched on to them, then moved down his body in appreciation. His cock twitched in his pants. Beads of sweat rolled down his spine.

Dev wanted to claim Camille like he'd done to the other women he took to his bed, but that wasn't what *she* wanted.

"Well, Dev?"

Her voice dragged over his senses, rough like a cat's tongue.

They'd been playing this game for weeks, her asking, him *not* saying no. At least *he'd* been playing, hoping she'd change her mind. But she hadn't. Her gaze licked over him again and she leaned back against the railing, then turned to look over her shoulder to the street below. The afternoon light and shadow played perfectly over the lines of her face, the mahogany skin, her long and delicate neck.

When he first saw her, he imagined her riding him, her pussy clenched around his cock while his hand tightened around that seductive neck of hers, her gasps toward orgasm dragging his up from the base of his spine. But it never happened that way.

"It's getting late," she murmured.

He'd invited her over after work with the promise that she'd get what she wanted. But now his pride rebelled.

"You don't have to go," he said.

Camille straightened. She was tall, taller than any woman he'd ever dated—or fucked—but still only managed to match his height in the high heels she always wore.

"Why should I stay?"

His lust was a hot brand in his belly, firming his cock even though it should have made him limp to think of the things she wanted. But he only grew harder when her gaze dropped to his crotch. *Not now.* But his dick wasn't listening.

"You're very…impressive." Her voice hummed with

approval. "Nothing you say will change how much of a man you are." She paused. "How capable and strong."

Her words soothed something in him. Something he hadn't known needed gentling. He'd had a long day at work. Some asshole tried to blow himself up and used a fake connection to terrorists in the Middle East as an excuse. Everyone on his team had been on edge, and after that shit show, the word came about a cop brutalizing a Black kid in a nearby suburb. His fellow cops weren't perfect, but he wished the bad ones would just disappear so the rest could do their jobs in peace. He wanted to release all of that.

"Tell me," Camille said.

A sigh leaked out of him, and he thought she didn't hear it. But her eyes latched on to his.

"Hm. Maybe you're right. I shouldn't leave yet."

After another pointed look, she walked past him, brushing the sleeve of his uniform with her bare shoulder. Her stilettos rang against the tile floor.

She headed for his bedroom, her leather purse in hand.

Camille had never been in his room before, but she easily made herself comfortable. Flung the windows open, refilled the glass of water Dev kept on the table. She even turned down the bed, leaving the dark expanse of sheets an ocean of invitation for her body, and his.

Camille slipped off her high heels. And although she was abruptly shorter than him for the first time since they'd met, she suddenly seemed more powerful.

"You're tense," she said. Her hands landed on his biceps and his muscles trembled. "Come."

Camille tipped her head toward the bed, an order, and Dev couldn't find it in himself to resist.

He stripped and climbed into the bed.

"May I?" Camille asked.

The "Yes" spilled out of him. He knelt in the bed.

"Good."

She reached for her purse, pulled out something red. Rope. It spilled from her hands, slithering onto the sheets. Camille stroked his cheek.

"Tell me about your day," she said.

Then, as he talked, the words apparently waiting to fall from his tongue, she tied him up.

The rope felt like silk and her touch both soothed and aroused him, stroking the already-there desire until his cock was *aching*. Any resistance drained from him with each knot, each stroke of her fingers. The rope bound his wrists behind his back and to his ankles, the silk brilliantly red over his muscled thighs. At the end of it, he felt...secure.

"Dev." He lifted his head but it was an effort. "How do you feel?"

He licked his lips. "Good. Fine." He actually felt better than fine, the tension from work gone, leaving only the heat of his arousal, his dick thick and dripping.

Camille brushed her thumb against his mouth at the same time as he licked his lips again. She caught her breath when his tongue wet her finger. Her nipples hardened under the thin blouse and the smell of her wet pussy changed the scent of the room. Dev's mouth watered.

"What would you like?"

Dev confessed what he wanted most in that moment. "I want to taste you."

The corner of her mouth curved up. Then she stood on the bed and pulled her skirt up, revealing plump pussy lips and slick arousal dripping down her thighs. Surprise and desire slammed into Dev.

"Ask and you shall receive."

With one foot balanced on the headboard, she put her pussy to his mouth. Gratitude rushed through him, and he opened his mouth wide to devour her like a starving man uncertain of when his next meal would come again.

Camille's clit was firm under his tongue, her sounds of pleasure falling into his ears, washing over his body, pooling low in his belly. Her hand tightened in his hair, a familiar pain he welcomed. The lust gripped him harder. Her pussy moved against his mouth in a desperate rhythm.

"You're so good for me." She groaned and bucked against him, her nails pressing the back of his neck, holding him firm as she chased her pleasure. His name fell from her lips, then she shuddered, whispering how good he was. How strong. How perfect. How—!

The orgasm burst over him, a sudden and overwhelming tide.

Dimly, he felt the splash of warmth on his belly, his chest, heard his own groans while he came, untouched except for the rake of her nails down his neck, her pussy dragging over his mouth, the silken ropes on his flesh.

"Gorgeous," Camille murmured.

Then she untied him. A pillow appeared under his head and her sighing breath gusted over his lips, a kiss hovering a touch away. Leaning over him, she was like his own guiding star.

"Good?" Her breath brushed his lips.

He closed his eyes and his body surrendered into the sheets, relaxed and thankful. "Very."

Her mouth touched his, and the sensation of it, light and firm at the same time, followed him down into sleep.

LIGHTNING STRIKE

Sommer Marsden

There are no hidden places inside me. Not from him. From the rest of the world, yes. From Jackson, never.

He knows what I crave, what gets me off, and takes great pleasure in keeping me off balance. My pleasure is his pleasure but it comes on his timetable, not mine. It comes in his rhythm, and I have to keep up.

The room is drenched in the odd underwater light that only comes at true dawn. His fingers skate over my hip bones, circle my mons, travel up my belly until the muscles shake. My brain is overthinking and he damn well knows it. Will he go down on me? Use his fingers? Will he flip me and fuck me the way I crave? There is always that moment when I'm airborne for a split second and I cry out. Then I crash back down, gravity doing its work, and he's sliding into me. What will it be, what will it be...

My mind races but Jackson knows the secret ways to silence it.

He puts a fingertip on my forehead and puts his lips to my earlobe. "Shh..." The heat of his breath and the utterance cause a tremble, a line of goose bumps marches up my neck and disappears beneath my hair. My scalp prickles. "Stop trying to see it in advance."

Then his fingers are back, stroking down the tops of my thighs, drawing patterns and loops on my belly.

His hand drifts up until he covers one small breast and groans against my neck. Because according to him, my breasts are perfect. Perfect size, perfect feel, perfect smooth skin and pink nipples. I smile...until his fingers close over my nipple and pinch. Hard. I hiss between my teeth and my hips shoot up like they're on a string and he's just yanked it.

"I know you like that hard." His teeth are raking across my shoulder as he talks. Now there are teeth on my skin and the pain of his pinches. The rat part of my brain, the part that is trying to see three steps ahead, begins to weaken. Soon it will shut down.

I relish the shutting down the way some people relish a good meal or an expensive garment. The silence in my head is golden. A gift. Treasured.

He pinches again, and I feel my body ripple.

"Don't move," he says. "If you move, Nick, I'll stop."

Nick...Nick... No one calls me Nick. To the rest of

the world, I'm Nickole. In this bed, with him, when I am to obey or be denied, I am Nick.

My brain flares with anxiety. So that's the game. To stay still despite the urge—the need—to move. No cuffs or butt plugs or ropes today. Just my own strength and willpower. My ability to control my body when he touches me, which is like holding back a tide during a storm.

His fingers have moved from my hips to my pussy. He delves into the folds of my sex and brushes a fingertip over my clit. His fingers already slick with my wetness. I'm soaked and he's barely touched me yet. Not the way I need.

I bite my tongue to keep my body from arching up to meet him. It's second nature, like breathing, and I nearly fail. That fast I almost lose my chance to go to that place he always takes me.

He dips his head to kiss my neck, drags his tongue down along my shoulder, then follows with a nip of his teeth where he's kissed. I moan, both from the pleasure of the things he does and how well he knows me, and the strength it takes to keep my restless body utterly still.

His fingers drive into me, two fingers surging into my wetness. He curls them, finding my desperate places. His thumb finds my clit and presses. I clench my fists, my body caught between pleasure and focus. I need to keep myself under control when all my body wants to do is scatter like ashes on the wind.

"Good girl…"

I recognize my urge to curl toward him at the last second and stay the way I am. On my back, his body pressed against mine, my legs splayed in a sluttish way that says, *Please do all the things you do to me. Please make me feel all the things you make me feel...*

He kisses down my body and his mouth finds my mound. He licks me softly. I'm nearly crying as he parts me and traces my labia with his tongue, getting close but not close enough. My body wants to slam up to meet his wet mouth and yet I have to hold on. My fingers clutch his dark-gray sheets, my eyes prick with tears that I pretend are from the brightening of the room, but are due to sheer frustration.

When he finally closes his mouth over my clit, I sob. My body shakes slightly just from the force of it and Jackson pauses. "Careful, Nick."

I go as still as I can. His tongue circles and flicks my clit. His fingers drive in and out, and I am trying so hard not to move that sweat dots my chest. "You may come at will," he whispers.

And just like that, I do. A gunshot. A lightning strike. I come even as I struggle to keep my soaring body tethered to earth.

He's helping me now whether he knows it or not. Big hands pressed to my thighs, keeping me flat.

Just as I adjust, I'm moving. Being flipped. I lose contact with the bed for a heartbeat and then crash down again as he hikes me to hands and knees. His hand comes down on my right asscheek. A flurry of blows that make my pussy flood and my brain shut down. I always try to count, whether I need to or not, but I can't. It's too fast and the pain and heat is too much to keep my mind on a leash.

I love it.

I buck when the blows land but grit my teeth to focus on no motion beyond the ones I can't control. The assault moves to the other cheek. The resounding crack of his palm on my ass is deafening. I bow my head and breathe, tears leaking from my eyes.

They end as suddenly as they begin, the silence in the room a tangible presence.

"You've done very well, Nick." His chuckle is dark. Cold black water rolling over rocks in the winter. "Now you may move if you need to because I'm here for mine. And mine won't be gentle."

A shiver slips up my spine, and I arch my back as he drives into me. One hard smooth thrust, and his fingers bite into the meaty part of my hips. Every time he thrusts his cock drags across the sweet spot. He chuckles again, hand in my hair, tugging.

"Come with me," he commands.

Another lightning strike. They say it never strikes twice. They lie.

IMAGO

Anna Sky

The hypnotic buzz of the gun before it touches me is enough to send flickers of need shooting through me. It's a Pavlovian response; my nipples harden, my cunt pulses and flutters, and dammit if I don't nearly salivate.

You might think I'm a slave to the tattoo gun, but you'd be wrong. The loops and swirls, whorls and shading, the colors and monochromes are reminders of who I am but they do not define me.

It's the process that does: a multifaceted reflection of everything I am and want to be. The injection of ink into my dermis is cathartic. The pain as the needle pierces my outer shell hundreds if not thousands of times a minute takes all thought away, leaving just me and my breath. And I do breathe; I breathe to physically still my body and to explore the echoing emptiness of my mind. Later on, I'll masturbate hard, allowing the heaviness in my cunt the release it so desperately craves.

I'm careful now, choosing a new tattooist if I feel my desires have become too obvious. In my head, they're always Master or Mistress of my flesh as I submit but I want to keep it pure, not marred by their discomfort as my lips slightly part and my cheeks take on a pink flush.

My body has become a canvas, a riotous carnival of ink. It's an homage to the pain I endure and showcases my ultimate, unquestionable submission. Every time I go under the needle, it refreshes my fervor and what started as a small, butterfly-shaped challenge between friends is now the story of my life.

I'm the quiet girl, the introvert. Cocooned and cosseted, I was brought up to think tattoos would damage my job chances and were an ominous thing that "other" people did. Somehow though, before we went our separate ways to university, my best friend persuaded me to get something small, easy to hide. It would be our secret connection, a reminder of having known each other since before either of us could remember.

I still remember that first time, walking into the shop with Kel. She was suave and confident next to my awkward jumpiness. We scanned the boards trying to find "our" design, sure that we could bond over a stock image. In my naïveté, I didn't know a whole world of custom design work existed. I know better now; I understand the pride of a tattoo artist, the culmination of honed artistry and the application of pigment to create a permanent piece of art. Unique images combining on my flesh in a living, breathing canvas.

The shop smelled odd to me that day. Now it's comforting, like coming home. Disinfectant and other, unidentifiable, unpleasant scents assaulted my nasal passages. I winced as I first heard the gun, its mosquito-like buzz emanating from behind a curtain. My signature on the consent form was shaky and distorted, a clear indication of my nerves.

Kel went first; I nearly turned and ran when I saw how much it hurt. Her previously cool demeanor drained from her face to leave her with a gray, sickly pallor. A grim curiosity kept me there; perhaps it was the guy doing the work. I guess he'd be described as a hipster now: beard, full sleeve of ink, checked shirt. Yeah, the whole damn clichéd package that Kel and I would giggle over afterward and take turns in making ever more lewd suggestions. The look of concentration on his face captured my imagination and for those few minutes that I really watched him, Kel was his entire world and everything else fell away. He had slender, precise hands that inked and wiped and inked and wiped and that's why I stayed, fascinated.

I wanted to be the center of his universe. I wanted him to treat me so tenderly yet have the power to alter me at my very core. My rising primal urge shocked me. And thankfully, he didn't disappoint. From the way he applied the stencil, his eyes boring into me as I nodded my assent, to the warmth from his fingers seeping through to my skin as he stretched it outward, I was hooked. "Ready?" he asked.

I took a deep breath, then said, "Yes."

It hurt. It hurt like fuck but all I could think of was how he cherished me in those moments and so I endured, instinctively breathing hard and deep to counteract the deep gouging scratch of the needle. Inside, I was in turmoil. Pulse quickening, the pain taking me to somewhere I'd never been before. Everything seemed slower and quieter until it was just me, the needle, and the deep concentration of the tattooist.

It pierced deeper than sex; in spiritual overtones it whispered to my very soul and I knew I was forever changed, purged of the old and blessed with clarity and purity of thought. My lungs moved in and out to keep the oxygen flowing but I was unaware, riding a divine wave of ecstasy.

Later that night, I peeled off the film to rub balm into my injured flesh. It was hot to the touch, bruised and sensitive, but I didn't care, I lovingly caressed it anyway. And deep into the night, I furiously rubbed at my clit, imagining each stroke of my fingers the push of the needle. When I came it was hard and relentless, my cunt clenching like it had never done before. But it wasn't enough and, soaking wet, I came again and again until I fell asleep, sated.

The healing process was metamorphic. Dead layers of skin sloughing off to reveal shiny, new, permanent ink. With multiple daily applications of moisturizer the sheen disappeared until the tattoo was just another part of me. It was an outward reflection of my transition, a chrysalis evolved.

My body is filling up and I know the day will come when I can no longer have the satisfaction I still crave so very badly. There are only so many cover-ups and gaps. Now they're fewer and fewer. Every single piece of ink tells a story, my story, and I cannot distort or destroy my body's narrative. My bright façade will remain, but on the inside I'm sure I'll shrivel and fade away.

HER TURN

Martha Davis

Olivia works in a bookstore and enjoys reading her latest shelf find before bed every night. A few months ago, she said, "I want to try something new."

"What do you want to try?" I asked with a sleepy grin as I drew a line down the length of her spine with my index finger.

Olivia purred in response to my touch. I traced the small of her back just before the swell of her perfect ass. I loved the way Olivia's silky cheeks were both firm and giving.

She said, "You can fuck me there if you want to."

Did I want to? I'd never had anal sex before, but I did indeed want to. Soon I was enjoying some of the best sex of my life. My hands squeezed Olivia's asscheeks as I watched my cock thrust in and out of her back hole.

We emptied the bottle of lube that night and both Olivia and I found so much love for butt-fucking that we made it a regular addition to our sex life.

I should have known there'd be a catch. A few weeks later it came. "I want to fuck you in the ass, Liam."

"What?" I let out a cross between a gasp and a choke. "No!"

"Why not? You fucked me in the ass."

"I have a cock. Last time I checked, you don't."

"I can get one." Olivia grinned. "As big as you think your tight little butt can handle."

I shook my head. "I don't know."

With every other aspect of our relationship, Olivia was carefree and let things go if they didn't fit. But she refused to surrender on the whole pegging thing. "What are you afraid of?" she whispered into my ear. "I promise to be gentle."

Without hesitation, the words fell from my mouth. "I'm a man. My ass is exit only."

"My female ass is the same as yours, but when a creative, open-minded couple sets their minds to explore..."

My mind didn't budge easily. But Olivia moved slowly, taking her time. The occasional sex article magically appeared in my email. "An Attraction to Anal Sex Isn't a Gateway for Homosexuality." She came home with books and gave her opinions on the subject. "It would be hotter for you because I don't have a prostate. When you massage it, your prostate transmits all these sensations from a batch of nerves straight into the base of your cock. Bam! I bet you'd come buckets."

Whenever we fucked missionary, Olivia "accidentally" slipped the tip of her finger in my ass. "It feels so good, doesn't it? Admit it makes you harder."

I couldn't lie. It did feel good. Eventually I said, "I'm willing to let you fuck me in the ass, Olivia."

I'd never been sexually submissive before, and went through a pendulum of responses. At the store, Olivia chose the harness, but I wanted to choose the dildo. Olivia grinned and put what I held back on the shelf.

"Yeah, you're totally macho, Liam, but let's start a little smaller." She chose another and escorted me to the counter.

I couldn't look the cashier in the eyes. He was a guy I'd discuss football with, not reveal I'm getting ass-fucked by the five-foot-three blonde purchasing a strap-on and, damn it, asking for a giant bottle of expensive lube located behind the register. Olivia flashed me the sexy grin that made me ask for her phone number the day we met. That's probably the only thing that kept me in the store.

At home, the acts that aroused me, Olivia did twice, but with the parts that made me buck, she slowed down and petted me into submission. My breath caught when she wiggled the strap-on and dildo free of their containers as she gave me the instructions. I liked assembling everything myself to make sure it was done right, and sliding the "cock" up the length of Olivia's plump legs was exciting. We finally stood facing each other, comparing my cock to hers until one look of glee mirrored the other.

Olivia dropped to her knees and started sucking my cock. I grew hard in her mouth, watching the purple cock bob between her legs. When I got excited enough to start fucking her face, she pulled away and had me help her back onto her feet. Standing once again, Olivia put a hand on my shoulder and pushed me down onto my knees. "Give me a blow job."

"What?" I stared at the cock she thrust into my face.

"I always wondered what it would feel like to have a cock and get a blow job." Olivia bit her lower lip. "I want a sloppy one like in a dirty movie."

"I want one of those too," I snorted.

"You do me, and I'll do you. Lady cocks first."

She had an expression of complete delight. I couldn't refuse her, so I put on a show, licking and sucking her silicone cock, slobbering all over it until some of my saliva landed on my bare thighs. I even swallowed enough of her dick to make me gag. Surprisingly, the act pleased me, but when finished, my cock had softened again.

Olivia showed no worry. She commanded me to get on my knees in the bed. "I want to fuck you doggie-style!"

She'd made sure the lube was warm, but the newness of it made me jump. Her thumb made gentle but firm strokes around the bit of flesh between my cock and ass and, sure enough, my cock started to grow again.

Olivia described all the dirty things she wanted to do to my tight ass between swats on my buttcheeks with lube-sticky hands. When she slowly slipped a finger in, I gasped. I felt like I had to pee. "Don't worry," she said. "It's supposed to feel that way." I'd grown so hard, precome dripped from the head of my dick, more than I had ever produced before.

She caressed the length of my back and placed the head of her cock at the opening of my ass, just deep enough to get the tip in. "You're fucking hot on your knees, Liam. I'm going to have so much fun fucking this ass."

Olivia started to slowly thrust her way in. The way she grunted and trembled, the base of the dildo probably hit her in the right spots too. When she found a rhythm, she clutched one asscheek in her palm and slid the other hand underneath to jerk off my cock.

Olivia rode me until I flooded the sheets with come and I think she got off too. She fucked me after I came, until she trembled, but there's no way she could have come as hard as I did.

We cleaned up and crawled in bed together. I buried my head in her breasts and let her tell me how she wanted to spend a lifetime fucking me. I wanted Olivia to fuck me again too. I'd beg her to do it if I had to. Hell, beg even if I didn't have to.

MAKING HIM MINE

Evoë Thorne

I snuggle up to Jaxson, my breasts pressed against his back. The thin layer of sweat between us makes my hips slide a bit against his ass. Our breathing begins to slow, but the heady aroma of sex and warm skin permeates the air. Even though I just came three or four times, there is still tension in my body. Unlike many couples who have been together for years, Jax and I have a great sex life. Maybe that's why I sometimes feel like we should keep exploring. Tonight, I'm thinking about trying something new. I'm excited, and a bit nervous.

My love for Jaxson is so intense that I want to know everything about him. We've shared all of the normal things: childhood experiences, family history, job stressors, and past lovers. I know that his favorite breakfast is Lucky Charms with banana slices and he secretly wants to give up his job as a lawyer to write travel guides. He's catty as hell behind people's backs. He recently confessed to having sex with his college roommate. I want all of him.

I run my fingers through his chest hair and across his nipples. I grind into his beautiful butt, and lick the sweat from the hollow between his shoulder blades. Jax takes my thumb into his mouth and sucks, causing mild spasms in my cunt. Something in my brain explodes and I decide I'm going to do it.

I growl and push him over onto his stomach. Pinning his arms over his head, I lean down to his ear, my breasts barely brushing his back, and ask, "Jaxson, are you mine?"

"Of course." He laughs, his body shaking. "The same way you are mine."

"No Jax, for serious. I mean that I want to take you. Will you let me do what I want to your body? Will you trust me with your secret places?" I'm afraid I sound crazy, but I know what I want. I'm almost in tears out of need and fear of rejection. I am all ferocity and desire. "Surrender to me, Jaxson."

His muscles relax under me, but I can feel his heart rate speed up. He doesn't say anything for a moment. I wait, still holding him down, wishing that I could see his face, but unsure of how to move. When he finally responds, his voice is different than I've ever heard it before. "Yes, I am yours."

I wait for more, but he doesn't add anything, so I

clarify, "Do you agree to let me do what I want with you?"

He kind of groans and rocks his hips. "Oh my god, yes."

Intrigued, I ponder what to do next. I order him to stay still and run off to the closet, coming back with four neckties and an Amazon box. His fancy silk ties don't work very well, but I manage to secure his arms and legs to the bed. Jax seems sort of happy but faraway. Once he is spread out and tied up, facedown on the bed, I smack him on the backside a couple of times experimentally. He shudders all over. I pull his head up. "Sweetheart, do you like this?"

He nods. I spank him more, totally getting off on the look on his face. I kiss him. "You're making me so hot, Jax! I want to take you in the ass. Do you want that?"

His reactions are so complex that I realize I'm getting what I want: more of Jaxson. Briefly, I am staggered by the thought that even as close as we are, there are things we haven't shared with each other. I hope what we are doing now will make us closer, but I fear it might tear us apart. Either way, this is the most intensely sexy thing I've ever done. I want more. Jax nods his consent, and his whole body says yes.

I dump the contents of the box on the bed and grab the bottle of lube off the nightstand. While Jaxson watches, I put on a leather harness and a purple dildo-like plug. I'm amazed at how his body is so tight with wanting. He orgasmed pretty recently, but I bet he's ready to go again.

I untie his wrists and order him onto his knees. Yep, he has a huge, gorgeous hard-on. Interesting. I want to put him in my mouth, suck him off, but that would mess up my plans. Instead I laugh and tell him to go down on me. Jax does so unflinchingly, no hesitation, like he was already thinking about it. His mouth engulfs the whole probe, then he stops and looks up at me. I swear I can feel him blowing me. He holds eye contact while he slowly sucks at each rounded segment of my shaft. I almost come right there. I tangle my fingers in his hair and rock my hips toward him, pushing him to take me deeper.

In a haze of lust, I can only think about fucking him. I realize I'm still holding the lube. I break free of his mouth and move behind Jax. He is totally open to me, head down, ass up. How is it possible that he is submitting so completely to me? Unsure of this next part, I pour a lot of lubricant into my hand and rub it all over the purple butt plug. Hesitantly, I rub some on his asshole. I've never seen one up close before. I spread the lube around, exploring. Jaxson clearly wants more of this because he is shaking and whispering, "Please," over and over.

I slide a finger inside him, edging in a little at a time. He feels warm and slick and tight. I bend my finger and he moans. I slide in and out. He gasps. He begs.

I give him just the first section of the purple probe. He wriggles, trying to impale himself all at once. A quick slap on the ass gets his attention. "Jaxson, hey, you're mine!"

He stills slightly under my hands. "Please, please fuck me?"

As gently as I can manage, I slide into him. My entire body is throbbing by the time I'm buried deep. I lean over his back, aching with love and longing. Holding on to his hips, I fuck him, slowly at first, then hard and fast. We go wild. My nails rake down his back. He makes primal noises like an animal rutting. I stop thinking.

When I feel myself on the verge of orgasm, I reach for his cock. I beat him off to the same rhythm I'm using to pound his ass. We come together, but I lose my sense of whose body is whose.

After that moment of blinding ecstasy, I worry that getting what I want might be more of a curse than a blessing. I never set out to be a Dominatrix or anything; I only wanted us to be closer. Then he looks back at me. In his eyes, I suddenly see that I have surrendered as much as he has. I fall into Jaxson's arms and we are laughing, crying, and coming.

ROPED IN

Adrea Kore

I thought I knew what rope felt like. Hard, salt-roughed rope that rigged a sail. The chafe of hessian rope against thigh on a makeshift swing. And knots? Practical things. Functional elements that kept your shoes on.

But this—this seductive slither of an embrace, trailing around my neck, snaking over and around both arms, encircling my waist like a possessive lover—this, I am not prepared for.

He hasn't even tied a knot yet.

You wanted me here. Wanted to experience more (how did you put it?) *elaborate* possibilities than tying my wrists to the headboard.

Over dinner, you pushed the flier across the table: *The Japanese Art of Shibari—Erotic Rope Bondage.* I sighed, knowing there was no escape. You're indefatigable when it comes to your kinky predilections. The sigh was partially an act; I'm more reserved than you, and relish coasting in the slipstream of your adventurous nature.

"I love it when you rope me into new experiences." I raised my wineglass to yours to emphasize my pun.

"You know it's my pleasure. Next Thursday night— I'll pick you up." You smiled, a conspirator's smile.

On our first date, three drinks in, I revealed my tendency to orgasmic excesses. Six months later, our connection remains intense; you enjoy discovering just *how* multiorgasmic I am. You see sexuality as a skill to be practiced and developed, like cooking or tango dancing.

We arrive at the workshop and exchange hellos within the group. At the first opportunity, you nudge me forward as a volunteer.

"When you're tying, you may have preconceived ideas about what knots you'll tie, what shape you'll create… but the rope, once it makes contact with that body, may have other ideas." The facilitator, Nick, introduces himself as a rope *dojo*, a master practitioner of Shibari.

"This is a beginner's class—no human origami creations for you guys yet."

People laugh, relaxing visibly. I feel you watching me.

"There's lots to explore, without even tying a knot. I'll teach you two basic knots later, but first we'll explore weight. Gravity. Connection." His eyes, ice blue, project a clarity of purpose.

I glance down at the rope. Red, not dull brown.

Gleaming with a silken texture, not rough. It slides sinuously against my skin, reminding me of last night; the teasing sensation of your thick tresses along my torso. Your fingers deep inside me, your breasts against mine, I'd writhed with each orgasmic surge you coaxed from my cunt.

Focus.

"Rope has its own intuitive intelligence. It responds to different bodies in different ways."

His movements are deliberate, yet fluid, like a jiu-jitsu master. As he speaks, he knots my wrists together in front, then bends my elbows up into prayer position. He loops the rope around my neck, exerting gentle pressure, until my head tilts forward, as if in supplication.

I hear sounds of appreciation. He's captured an archetypal pose. For a moment, I feel like a penitent saint. *Sans* halo.

I flush—he's somehow intuited my submissive tendencies. As the knots were tied around my wrists, a tumult of emotions moved through me. Vulnerability. Desire. *Need.* I feel the rope around my neck like a snaking current of energy, whispering erotic possibilities.

"I'm getting ahead of myself, but I wanted to show you the beautiful potential of Shibari."

His expert hands retrace the path of the knots, releasing me from my silent prayer, leaving the rope looped around my arms. My body shivers involuntarily from the release of tension.

"Think of the rope as a tangible manifestation of

connection with the person you're tying."

Tangible. Connection. Each place the rope has touched, heightened awareness flares across my skin. Surveying me, his eyes glint with the intent of a craftsman creating a masterpiece.

"See—no knots yet. But even with something simple like this, you can begin to experiment with the connection, to play with weight and gravity."

He moves closer behind me. I'm aware of the scent of pine, his warm breath across my shoulders. He hauls gently, destabilizing my balance. I fall backward onto his chest and his hand moves to the small of my back, supporting me. He rocks me, back and forth, rights me, and topples me again onto the broad expanse of his chest. Being rocked in this way transports me into a pre-lingual state. I feel the thud of his heartbeat through my back, sending pulsations of heat into my belly, shooting down into my sex. My lumbar spine bucks against his hand. Several times. I look up at him.

"You could just play here for a while, slowly building trust. Or…" He pauses, and in my ear, whispers, "Ready?" I nod.

In one lithe move, he takes all my weight, lowers me to the floor, and turns me onto my stomach. I sense more rope being coiled around my upper arms.

Dizzy. The circle of people feels out of focus.

"To be a good tier, you need to be able to read the body and flexibility of your subject. To be an exemplary tier, you must learn to listen to the rope."

I feel him tying an intricate knot in the center of my back; hear the subtle swish of ropes through the air as they're deftly manipulated. The knot seems to radiate heat, as if a hot stone has been placed on my skin.

He runs a hand down to my foot, bending first one knee, then the other, securing both ankles. This constant play of tension and release, this deft manipulation of my body in ways beyond my control, tugs at a primal place deep inside my womb. The traction caused as my stretched arms strain back to reach my lifted ankles releases pent-up sexual energy, coiled in my abdomen. My whole body begins to writhe as waves of orgasms course through me.

Nick crouches beside me, turning me on my side, his hand remaining in the small of my back, grounding me. "Are you okay?"

"Yes," I nod, smiling. "*Very* okay. I'm just, umm… sensitive to stimuli."

"Wow," he says. "Beautiful." He addresses the group as he begins to untie me. "You'll sometimes see this response in particularly receptive people. In any group, you'll see a diverse range of responses. Let's take a quick break, then we'll start exploring in partners."

People disperse, some smiling at me, as Nick helps me to sit up. I'm panting and disoriented. You move toward us.

"I think I need some water," I venture.

"I'll take care of my Yasmin." You help me up, and lead me toward our bags. "That looked intense," you whisper, as you hand over my water bottle. I nod, gulping thirstily.

"It was. Beyond words."

Afterward, people chat and mingle. You've disappeared. Five minutes later, you're back, smiling your conspirator smile, and when we're alone again, you announce:

"I've arranged a one-on-one Shibari session for you. My treat."

I hug you, appreciating your generosity. Then I motion to the merchandise table.

"Marla? Can we get some of that rope? In fact, can we get a lot of it?"

You take my hand, and kiss me.

"You're not going anywhere tonight."

ONE WORD
LEADS TO
ANOTHER

Pearl Monroe

B rian gently laid down the letters R-E-S-S and slid them snugly aside Julie's last word, MIST. "Mistress for twenty-seven points, and victory," said Brian rather glibly.

Julie eyed the board and took in all of Brian's words for a moment. "Wait right here," she said. She got up and walked down the hall to her bedroom and returned with a long black scarf. She stepped behind Brian and quickly wrapped the scarf around his eyes.

"Why are you blindfolding me?" he asked.

"You're right, Brian. Victory is yours and tonight you shall have your reward," she said as she started to unbutton his shirt.

"But why blindfold me? What are you doing?"

"I want you to let your imagination run wild. I do

not want you to see your good friend Julie. I want you to imagine the Mistress of your darkest desires."

Brian's heart started to race. Maybe he had pushed things a little too far this time. Since his breakup with Claire, he had expressed his sexual frustration more than a few times to Julie.

"That's a creative set of words you managed tonight, Brian. Let's see, there's PRICK, TWINK, HARD, LIPS, OOZE, MISTRESS, and, oh yes, CUMSLUT. Well, my dear, you're going to get a little hard prick and come oozing off those lips of yours tonight."

He heard Julie unzip her pants. Then she took his hand and gently ran it across soft denim and cold metal zipper. She then placed his hand on her flat stomach. He could feel the rise and fall of her midriff with each breath that she took, and the shallow cavity of her belly button. Slowly, she directed his hand to the waistband of her panties and then slipped his fingers beneath.

Brian felt the soft silky hairs of her closely cropped bush and the firmness of her pelvic mound. His fingers were exploring her labia and he had just begun to rub her clitoris when she pulled away. Julie took him by the hand and led him to the living room floor, where she laid him down with a cushion beneath his head.

He heard her peel off her jeans and the gentle chiming of her belt buckle as she tossed her pants to the floor beside his head. Next thing he knew, she had straddled his face and pinned his wrists to the floor with her hands. He could smell her sweetness and he was quivering with desire.

Julie brought her pussy up to Brian's face and parted her labia with his nose. "Do you like this?" she asked.

"Yes," whispered Brian.

Julie caressed his chest and then pinched his right nipple hard. "What?" she asked firmly.

"Yes, Mistress," said Brian.

"Eat me," she said as she started to rock her pussy on his face. "Stick your tongue in deep."

Julie was riding his face, moving from his nose down to his chin and back. She was getting into a groove and breathing heavily. Brian was beyond aroused and one hundred percent focused on the task at hand. Her pussy and his mouth had become one as he swirled his tongue around her clitoris. Suddenly, she quivered and pushed down firmly. He could feel her juices flood his mouth and cover his face. "Do you like the taste of my come?"

"Yes, Mistress, very much."

"Would you like to come now?"

"Yes, please, Mistress. I'm about to explode."

Julie stepped back and unzipped Brian's pants. She pulled hard, and they slid right off. She toyed with his underpants, teasing him by slipping her fingers under the elastic and grazing his hard cock trapped beneath the fabric.

She hoisted his legs in the air and pulled his underwear to his ankles. "This is a pathetic sight," she said.

"Here you lie, your face covered in come, your cock ready to explode, and your ass in the air just asking to be fucked."

"Oh, Julie, please, I'm dying…" Brian started to say when he felt a stinging slap on his right buttock.

"What did you say, Cumslut?"

"I'm sorry, Mistress. Mistress, please let me come."

"Don't worry, you'll be coming soon enough, slut," she said. "You really are a horny little bastard, aren't you?"

"Yes, Mistress."

Julie pushed his legs down so that his knees came to rest on the floor on either side of his head. Brian's stiff cock stood at attention right in front of his face. Julie dribbled a little massage oil on Brian's cock and asshole. She began to massage his asshole in a circular motion and pushed her finger in every few rotations. Brian began to moan with pleasure. At the same time, she was softly stroking his balls and shaft.

"Take a deep breath and exhale," Julie commanded. "Again," she ordered. "You're going to keep breathing until you've relaxed enough that you can reach your cock with your mouth."

Brian was awash with desire. He had never sucked a cock before in his life, and nothing could have prepared him for the excitement that flooded his body as his lips felt the tip of his cock. He licked off a drop of precome.

"That's it, my little cumslut. Lick the head; wrap

your lips around your warm, soft cock," Julie taunted as she continued to stroke the length of his cock and run her finger in and out of his well-lubed ass.

"You like being fucked and sucking cock, don't you?"

Letting his cock slip away from his lips, he said, "Yes, Mistress." Then Brian wrapped his lips tightly around the head of his cock and began to suck with determination. He swirled his tongue underneath and around the head of his penis. His ex-girlfriend Claire had given him blow jobs before, but they were nothing like this. To be on both the giving and receiving end of a blow job was incredible!

"Then say it. Say it out loud that you like to be fucked and suck cock!" commanded Julie.

Brian barely got out the words, "Mistress, yes, I love to be fucked and suck cock," when he started to come. The first spurt of come landed thickly on his lips and tongue. Julie applied a little more pressure to his lower back, easing about two inches of Brian's dick into his mouth. She could see and feel his cock and balls spasming, sending streams of come into Brian's mouth.

"Swallow. Swallow all of it, you cumslut." After a minute or two of milking his cock, she stopped stroking him and pulled her finger out of his ass.

Julie lowered Brian's legs and his cock popped out of his mouth. He was spent and felt a euphoria like never before in his life.

Julie stood up, and he heard her zip up her pants.

"Next time, maybe I'll invite my friend Ray to join us for Scrabble. Would you like that?" she asked.

A smile came across Brian's face, and he said, "Yes, Mistress, I think I'd like that a lot."

THE
BROKEN DAM

Rob Rosen

I run my own marketing department with seventy people reporting to me, millions of dollars riding on my every decision. Because of all that responsibility, my blood pressure was higher than the penthouse floor I lived on. I ached for a vacation—not from my job but from my life. I wanted to give up, give in, even for just a day, an hour. I didn't want to think, didn't want to act, just wanted to submit.

I thought about going to the gym, but decided on Craigslist instead. Seemed more expedient.

He arrived in no time flat.

"Nice place," he said, entering my loft with a swagger and a gym bag that rattled at his side. He was tall, lanky, handsome in a rough way. I had people working for me who looked like him, people dozens of floors below me.

I never talked to them; I didn't feel much of a need now. I didn't want to talk, after all, didn't want to even think.

"Do what you will," I said, feeling my cock harden as the muscles in my neck relaxed.

I locked eyes with him, his a startling blue, haloed as they were beneath a mop of unruly auburn hair and a thick beard below. He simply nodded and tossed his bag to the carpet. It landed with a dull thud, as did I as he flung me to the couch and pinned my hands behind my back.

He rammed his tongue down my throat, and then pulled an inch away, taking me in, perhaps deciding what he was going to do with me. I sighed and waited. He spat on my mouth. "Lick it up." I did as he said. I would do so for as long as he remained there, gladly. Or perhaps *resignedly* was a better word for it.

He stood up, got undressed, and told me to do the same. "Quickly," he added.

I stripped, panting a bit now as his lean body came into view. He stared at me in return as if I was a toy to be played with—which is just what I was.

"On your knees," he said.

I fell from the couch and landed in front of him, his cock already aimed my way. He slapped it across my face. I felt the sting. He grabbed my nipples, and I yelped. He quieted me down by shoving his prick between my lips. I gagged, a tear streaming down my cheek. His cock was like a crowbar; mine was suddenly even thicker than that, harder.

He smacked my cheek and yanked my hair, all while I sucked him with abandon, my hands submissively behind my back as I did so. He tossed me to the ground when he'd had enough of my attentions.

I watched him unzip his bag; saw the ropes, the gag. I was trussed in mere moments, unable to move or cry out. I went limp. It was a delightful feeling, terror mixed with acceptance. My fate was in his hands, not mine. My brain at last flatlined.

He spanked me, slapped me, tugged at anything that protruded. I breathed through my nose. My prick throbbed, leaked. I would've sighed had it not been for the gag. I squirmed instead as he abused my body and slapped my prick, sending it reeling.

He spat into his hand, stroked his cock, spanked my hole. I longed to be penetrated, to be nothing but a puppet for him. I didn't have to wait beyond a minute as his spit-slickened fingers found their way inside me, one becoming two, two shifting to three. He pumped my chute with ferocity. My cock felt like it could explode.

"Don't come," he said. "You come, I leave."

I nodded. Acquiescence was met with a yank on my nuts. I howled into the gag. He pumped farther into my ass, teasing my cock with his free hand, bringing me to the verge before letting up. Sweat cascaded down my face, come welling up from my aching balls.

I didn't think of work. I didn't think of money. I fought not to come. That was all I needed to do, all I was commanded to do.

His fingers were replaced by a black dildo, then a plug, though he had enough mercy on me to use lube this time. He ravaged my ass as he freed my soul. He jacked me and released, jacked and released. I was in pain. I was in ecstasy. I didn't even know his name and I'd nearly forgotten my own.

He eventually stood over me and stared down, clearly enjoying the sight of me. He pounded his prick and spat onto my chest. I watched his balls slowly rise. His eyes rolled back into his head a moment later. He moaned loudly as he came, thick gobs of aromatic come splattering my belly before gliding down my sides.

He removed the gag and untied me, then kissed me, hard. He jacked my cock as he strummed on the plug still embedded up my ass. He played my body like a musical instrument until I was finally in tune.

I came with a gushing release, as if a dam had broken.

In all, it lasted forty minutes, tops. It felt like an eternity.

He left without another word.

I lay there, naked and battered. I'd gone into this broken; I came out the other side whole.

I went to my computer. I did my work. My blood pressure felt normalized. I typed even as the butt plug remained, a gift from a stranger, a gift that would keep on giving long after the bruises healed.

CHASED BY
THE WOLF

Mischa Eliot

Who is it?" The person I saw through the peephole wasn't someone I recognized. I didn't live in the safest area, so I wasn't about to take a chance and open the door to a complete stranger.

"Ms. Hartley? I'm Samuel. I drive for Mr. Clark. He has sent me to fetch you and I have a package, as well."

Samuel held up the dark magenta box wrapped with a black bow. My eyes widened, as those were the signature colors of a very specific boutique I enjoyed window-shopping as I walked to work. I had no idea how Mr. Clark had found me, but I was going to give him a piece of my mind. This was crossing a boundary. We weren't supposed to meet outside the club.

"Madam? Are you still there? Should I give your regrets to Mr. Clark?"

Samuel. I had forgotten he was standing there as the blood rushed through my veins. Even though he couldn't see me, my face flushed beneath the beauty mask I'd just applied. I opened the door and let him come inside.

"My apologies. Please come in." My flush deepened as he entered my tiny apartment. It was small, but I didn't need a roommate and I relished that.

Samuel set the beautiful box down on my little side table near the door. With barely a glance around, he stepped back out into the hall. "Once you are ready, Ms. Hartley, I'll take you to the location specified by Mr. Clark."

Confusion reigned as he closed the door behind him, content to wait in the hall as I readied myself. He hadn't given me a time limit. I hadn't planned on going out tonight, so I was wearing fuzzy pajama pants and a tank top. A gasp of horror escaped me when I realized I still had on the clay facial mask.

"Crap." Focusing on being gentle, I untied the ribbon from the box and opened it. On top of the softest silk were a mask, a collar, and shoes. I plucked the envelope out and opened it. The paper was expensive.

Dearest Ms. Hartley,

I meant to discuss this event with you at our last meeting, but we were interrupted. Please forgive me for any offense at finding you. I have not delved any further than to acquire your address. It would be an honor to escort you to the

*Predators and Prey Ball tonight. You are not to
put the collar on as I wish to have that honor.*

Warmest Regards,
Mr. Clark

I forgot how to breathe. The Ball was the biggest event of
the year. It was held at a local zoo. Dominants dressed as
predator animals and chased the submissives, dressed as
prey. Only the uncollared, unleashed submissives would
be chased. I'd seen the collar. Desire built up inside as I
pulled out the costume he'd picked for me.

A beautiful faux-fur bunny outfit greeted me. I pulled
out the floppy ears and couldn't hold in the laughter that
bubbled up and out. I knew I couldn't say no. Laying the
costume back down, I opened the door. Samuel stood in
the hallway.

"Please let Mr. Clark know that I'll be joining him
this evening. I'll need a short time to get ready."

"Yes, Madam." I closed the door as he pulled out a
cell phone, most likely to text or call Mr. Clark.

I flew to the bathroom and started the shower.
While the water heated up, I stripped and set out the
favorite scented lotion Mr. Clark had gifted me with a
few months back for the holiday season. Before long, I
was lightly scented and wearing a beautiful floppy-eared
bunny costume complete with fuzzy tail. I tucked the
collar into a small pouch-purse that I could easily carry
without hindering anything my Sir planned.

Upon arrival, I saw many Dominants dressed as predators; lions, tigers, and bears. Oh yes! Mr. Clark was dressed as a wolf. His grin suited the costume perfectly. I lowered my eyes and offered the pouch. Other submissives were uncollared all around me. The prospect of being chased by Mr. Clark sent shivers down my spine, and I couldn't wait.

"My dear." Mr. Clark held his arm out for me and I placed my hand in the crook of his elbow. We went into the zoo and found the center gathering place. "Would you allow me to be your only Master, Ms. Hartley?"

"It would be my pleasure, Mr. Clark. *Sir*." Heat filled me. I had never thought he would be so bold, but it filled me with joy.

"Then I shall hope to catch you, my pet." I lowered myself to my knees in front of him and before I could lower my eyes as well, he lifted my chin. The heat of a thousand suns fell upon me, and I felt love blossom inside.

An emcee started speaking and we all listened as he welcomed us to the zoo and gave us information about it, the animals, and how our contributions would be used. The rules for the game were stated. My wolf had to catch me, or I'd belong to another this evening. Then the bell rang and the submissives were off like greyhounds.

Moments later the second bell rang and the predators gave chase. I had found a place to hide in some thick shrubbery after outrunning someone dressed, oddly enough, as a cheetah. Listening to her call, "Here bun bun," did not coax me one bit. I held my breath as she stalked around looking for me. My shades-of-gray pelt blended with the shadows. Animals made noises in the pens nearby, rustling and snuffling, sounding anxious like me.

After she left, I took off the way I'd come only to have a falcon block my way. The feathers on their mask were amazing but before I was forced to take a closer look, I was scooped up and carried off. Struggling, I attempted to slip out of the hold, until I heard Mr. Clark's soothing voice.

"Calm, my pet. I have you now." He held me tightly in his arms as if he were afraid I might be taken away at any moment. Mr. Clark headed to the stage and set me down there. It wasn't long before others joined us and the game ended.

Mr. Clark took the collar from his pocket and I settled on my knees, my eyes lowered, chin pointing up. The collar settled around my neck. It was a simple black strip of leather with a charm in the shape of a floppy-eared bunny just like the one we'd originally bonded over in the pet shop.

That night I went home with Sir. He bathed me and petted me until I begged for more. And, like the teasing Dominant he is, he made me wait as we curled up together for a good night's sleep, whispering naughty ideas of his plans for me tomorrow and the next day, and the day after that.

THE AMAZING LUCINDA

Heather Day

It's not the kiss of the rope on my skin that does it, nor the well-placed strokes of her fingers on my helpless body. It's the look in her eyes that drives me wild and gets my pussy throbbing with want. The look of pride at her work as she reclines, arms crossed, on our sofa. The look that says: *Go on then, get out of this one.*

My arms are tied securely behind my back. I start to flex them, testing out the bonds. She raises an eyebrow and turns over the hourglass. The subtle whisper of the sand threatens to set my nerves on edge, but I can't afford to panic. I have three minutes to escape and need my wits about me.

There is a professional reason for our games; onstage she is the Amazing Lucinda, Mistress of Magic, and I am her glamorous escapologist. We make quite the handsome double act, her with her top hat, tails, and long black hair, me with my blonde bob and tiny, sequined outfits. We've garnered a bit of a cult following over the years—mostly queer women, I can't help but notice.

But once the curtain falls, she is again my Domme, my love, and my wife. The one who captured my heart as soon as we started performing together five years ago. That doesn't mean she goes lightly on me though, far from it.

She knows locks present no challenge to me at all, buckles even less so. She knows that my joints are particularly supple and that I can reach around rope to untie knots with my long fingers. But she also knows by now exactly how to strip away these advantages.

That is why, after securing my arms behind my back with a complicated series of knots, she wound another length down the front of my body, between my breasts and up and under my pussy so that it sits there snugly, rubbing my vulva and teasing my clit in the most maddening way with every movement I make to try and free myself. It is why she added, in one final touch of cruelty, the silver nipple clamps that bite into my sensitive buds in such a way that I can never decide whether I love or hate them.

She is very pleased with herself. I can hear it in her voice when she says, "Two minutes left, my dear."

I force myself to breathe steadily, to ignore as best I can the sensations of pleasure and pain flooding through my body and instead analyze how to break the bonds she has woven around me. I stretch my wrists up toward the knots and wriggle my arms methodically, trying to loosen the rope's hold on me. She's wrapped me up tight, and although I adore the feeling of being held in the embrace of her ropework, my professional pride forces me to try and find a way to escape.

"One minute," she says, standing over me, hooking a finger under my chin and looking straight down into my eyes. "I can't wait to carry out your punishment."

Oh, she is cocky. I close my eyes, trying not to think about how wet her words make me, but the slick juices flowing between my legs, coating the rope, make this almost impossible.

Nevertheless, my fingers finally reach the first knot and work quickly to untangle it. Eventually it unravels and I feel a small surge of triumph, but this is tempered by the knowledge that there are several more knots between me and victory. I flex my arms again, seeing if I can shrug any of them loose, but they hold tight. I realize I am in danger of failing at this task and a fresh wave of adrenaline—part determination, part anticipation—pulses through me.

I stretch my wrists farther and move my nimble fingers with a new focus, methodically tugging at the knots. I don't want to fail. I know I can do this. Sure enough, the rope begins to loosen and the next knot unravels. The rest will be easier.

I am almost there, nearly free, when my Mistress decides to make things more interesting. In one swift movement she releases the clamps from my nipples, causing them to throb and stiffen with a sudden rush of blood, forcing a gasp of pure, agonized pleasure from my lips. My hands go limp and useless, their task forgotten.

"Thirty seconds."

I would say that was unfair. I would say she plays dirty. But neither statement would cut any ice, and complaining would only make my punishment ten times worse. After all, she would say, she is my Mistress, and she can do as she pleases. And she would be right.

As she begins a countdown of the final ten seconds, I smile. I hear the last of the sand whispering its way through the hourglass. I know I am going to fail. If my pussy wasn't aching with want, if my nipples weren't still sending tiny shocks of pleasure through me, I would be able to focus enough to untie that final knot. But instead, I give in. I give in to the pleasure and the pain and to whatever delights and horrors she has in store for me.

Because sometimes, with a Mistress as devious and beautiful as Lucy, losing can be the sweetest reward of all.

HIS

Jade Melisande

Ava stood trembling in the deep shadows of the alcove, her heart hammering in her chest. She stared, an unseen observer, as Noah leaned over the woman's body, blade in hand. As one, the woman and Ava both caught their breath as the tip of the blade slid across the flesh of the woman's back.

"Easy," she heard him say. She felt the air go out of her lungs softly, sweetly, like the kiss of his blade across her lips. She heard the woman's expulsion of air at the same moment. A trickle of blood, shockingly bright against the woman's pale skin, trailed down her rib cage and dripped onto the floor. Noah reached up and wiped the blood away gently; the woman moaned beneath his hand.

Ava felt an answering tightness in her belly. She

imagined his hand on her like that. It had been so long since she had felt any man's hands on her. Two years, to be exact. Her eyes closed; she bit back the familiar pain. Oh, to let the pain go, to have it cut away... Why couldn't sorrow work like that? She longed to give herself over to his touch, as this woman had done. To lie there beneath his hand, allowing him—trusting him—to carve upon her body with his blade.

To lay herself open to him.

Desire, hot and sweet and fierce, swept over her, and she gasped with the intensity of it. For so long she and Noah had danced on the edge of this desire, each playing the role of hunter and hunted, as desire and fear and longing had flared and banked only to flare once more between them. She wasn't sure she still had what he wanted her to give. Noah insisted she did, insisted that it hadn't died in her the day that Rubin, her partner, her lover, had died. That it was merely hidden away inside of her, waiting for her to surrender herself to it again. To him.

She opened her eyes and found him watching her, the tip of his blade raised in one hand, the woman's body an intricate swirl of lines and liquid beneath the other. His eyes were dark, almost as dark as the blood on his hands. The woman moaned again, shifting on the table, every movement a plea for more. Still Noah watched Ava; watched her watching him.

Heat curled its way up from her belly, spreading across her chest, into her face. It curled downward, too, swirling and pooling between her legs. Her skin burned, her breathing quickened. Her body throbbed in time to the music coming from the speakers.

She wanted him. Wanted to be his, wanted to feel his mark on her.

The woman sighed, a breathy exhalation of pleasure. Noah held Ava's gaze for a moment longer, and then turned his attention back to the woman. With gentle strokes he began to wash the blood away, leaving behind the tracings of the cutting.

Ava turned abruptly, backing deeper into the shadows and then out of the alcove altogether, feeling guilty for her intrusion upon their scene. Still, she felt Noah's eyes on her, the question in them, long after she had left them.

She lay curled into the corner of a couch in a small side room, enjoying a moment of solitude after the noise and excitement of the party. Kurt's parties were always well attended, and a quiet spot was hard to come by. In days past, she and Rubin had been a fixture here, along with half a dozen others. Noah was part of that inner crowd as well. After Rubin had died, Ava had sequestered herself and locked all her needs and desires away. But little by little, Noah had chipped away at her reserve, drawing her farther and farther out. Ava was a submissive at heart, but that heart was not easily won, and in the end it wasn't Noah's dominance that had called to her. It was his quiet strength, his boundless patience with her as she struggled to come to terms with losing not only the love of her life, but the man she had considered her Owner.

Still, she held back from him. How could she give herself completely to another, when losing Rubin had been so devastating?

Ava looked up as Noah entered the room. "Ava," he said, stopping in front of her, "it's time."

Ava's heart began a slow, steady hammering. He touched her cheek.

"Say yes," he said. "Be mine." He held out his hand.

With a shaky breath she rose and placed her hand in his. He led her through the warren of rooms, her mind and heart racing. Finally, he stopped just inside a small, intimate space in which a table stood before a fireplace.

"After this," he said, his lips close to her ear, "this will only be for you and me. Your body is the only one I want to mark. Your body, your mind, your heart."

Moments later, she lay facedown on the table, naked before him. She felt his eyes, then his hands, tracing the curves of her body. Her skin glowed with heat that had nothing to do with the flames flickering in the fireplace.

"Ava," he said, "sweet Ava. You're all I've wanted for so long. Will you be mine?"

Ava turned her face to his, gazed up into his dark eyes. "Yes," she said at last, and surrendered to his touch. To her own need. Her mind slowed. It felt as if the world held its breath as she waited for the first touch of steel against her skin.

She shivered as the flat of the blade touched her, but

it wasn't cold. It was warm, heated by the desire that flowed between them. Her body thrummed, painfully attuned to his every touch, to the roughness of the pads of his fingers, to the blade against her skin as he teased and caressed her with it. She shuddered as she felt his warm breath on her shoulder, on the nape of her neck.

Then he had turned the blade edge-side down, and she felt him beginning to trace a pattern in her skin. He drew the blade carefully down her back, and it stung, but as it penetrated her body it was as if he penetrated *her*, opening her, peeling away the layers of doubt and fear and loneliness. She felt the darkness being cut away, leaving only her desire for him, her desire to be his. The sting of his knife was an exquisite accompaniment to the ache between her legs, to the ache that he was releasing from the center of her. She felt herself floating free of everything that had held her down, that had kept her from him.

"Look," he said, after. He had washed her blood away tenderly, and raised her to a sitting position. She looked over her shoulder at the mirror on the wall, saw his strong hands cradling her. Then, a single word etched in her skin: *mine*.

CARI'S RECITAL

Rod Harden

The pretty young woman stepped onto the stage to polite applause. The dress she wore was flowing, full length, pale yellow in color. It covered her from ankles to chin, with sleeves so long that only her fingers were visible from the ends. Walking to the piano with tiny, dainty steps, she bowed briefly to the audience before turning and taking her seat on the piano bench.

Her posture was impeccable—shoulders squared, back straight, head high. Her jet-black hair fell to the middle of her back, shimmering as it caught the stage lights. Her expression seemed rigid, almost unnaturally so. She sat for a long moment in silence, broken only by a brief, faint, "Hm," as if she were moaning as she stared at the keys. She shifted her weight several times, each time extending her hands to the keyboard and her right foot to the sustain pedal, before pulling them back, only to shift again. The audience grew impatient, clearing their throats, coughing. At last, she seemed to find the right spot, and began to play.

As the opening measures of the Chopin Nocturne reached their ears, the audience could tell at once that this performance was going to be very special. The emotion the performer was pouring into the music was palpable. Was that another moan they heard? Were those tears welling up in the young woman's eyes?

Only Cari knew the secret behind her performance. Cari and her Master, that is, as he had helped her prepare as only he could.

Her face showed little expression because there was a foam ball in her mouth. Easily compressed to fit between her lips, it expanded once inside. Cari was sure it made her cheeks puff out, but Master assured her she looked fine, and no one would know it was there, as long as she kept her mouth shut. "Like a good girl," he'd said.

The long dress hid numerous secrets as well. Beneath its high collar was another collar of thin, supple leather, secured in place with a tiny padlock. It helped ensure she would hold her head high. And hidden under the long sleeves, each of her wrists was locked in leather as well. The cuffs served no purpose while she played, of course, but she knew that later at home they would certainly be used to secure her for Master's pleasure. Perhaps high overhead to one of the ceiling hooks, or, she hoped, simply to the headboard.

Lower down, the dress hid another pair of cuffs. These were fitted around her thighs, just above the knees. A short, delicate chain connected them, forming a hobble that forced her to take dainty steps, yet leaving her feet free to work the pedals.

But these things barely registered on Cari's awareness now. For there were other secrets as well. The first was inside her bra cups, which were lined with fine sandpaper. She had been made to wear nipple clamps earlier in the day as she had practiced in the nude. Her breasts always swayed more than she imagined when she played this way, and her nipples were already quite sensitive when she put on the rigged bra. And now the pressure of the gritty paper on them was a constant stimulant that hovered just on the edge of painful, an edge she delighted in skirting, especially in public.

The final secret was the band of steel that circled her waist along with its attachment that extended down between her legs. The chastity belt held in place both a butt plug, which she felt with every movement she made, as well as a small but powerful radio-controlled vibrator locked inside her pussy. Control of the vibrator rested, as always, with Master.

Maddeningly, Cari knew exactly when he planned to turn the vibrator on. He'd told her, even marking the spots so she would memorize them along with the music itself. There would be no surprise involved, only anticipation, intense anticipation. The first time had been before she even started, when she had taken her seat, causing the long delay as she got "comfortable" on the bench. And now she was approaching the section of the music where it would begin buzzing inside her again.

She couldn't help thinking about it, praying it wouldn't cause her to lose control. Master loved doing this to her—tormenting her, teasing her, keeping her on edge. In public, though, it was even worse. Or better. She couldn't decide which. She hated it and loved it at the same time. Exhilarating, frightening.

At last, the moment came and went. Her fingers continued playing, remembering the music for her as her mind disengaged. Had the audience seen her shudder? Had they heard her whimper?

Before the piece was over Master buzzed her three more times. By the time she finally lifted her hands from the keyboard at the end she felt exhausted. Her body continued quivering, her inner thighs damp with her arousal. She looked up and saw him standing in the wings. He smiled and nodded. She'd done well. His approval washed over her like a warm embrace.

Cari stood, tentatively, turned and accepted the applause from the audience, reminding herself not to smile too broadly lest the foam ball in her mouth become visible. As pleased as she was that she got through it successfully, the next challenge now filled her mind: How was she ever going to get through the Liszt?

BEAUTIFUL

Kendel Davi

They say that black don't crack but hands don't lie. I've spent a fortune on moisturizer, lotions, and skin-firming cream but my hands still scream my experience on this earth. Years of typing have given them a long sinewy look. Right now, my veins percolate under the surface of my skin from the red nylon rope securing my hands to the arms of this chair. I try not to stare but the restriction of blood flow has created a sculpted appearance, as if my hands were carved by an expert confectionery artist. If they had been on display at an exhibit, the realism would be astonishing, but what I need most right now is an escape.

Derek clears his throat. I pop my head up to see his reflection of disapproval in the full-length mirror in front of me. I force a smile, but he seems unmoved.

The only thing on my body besides this nylon rope is a pair of black stilettos, so there is no escape for either of us. That's exactly what he wants. He grits his teeth and whispers, "I wish you appreciated your body the way I do."

It's that calm but eerie tone of his voice that grabs me. It's devoid of emotion except for frustration. I glance at him, watching the muscles in his jaw flex. He holds his tongue from lashing out at my focus on what I perceive as my physical imperfections.

"Tonight I'll teach you how to embrace how exquisite you are."

This evening started off as a nice romantic dinner at a five-star hotel. He'd rented a suite on the top floor that overlooked the city. Every few months we'd plan an evening away from the doldrums of our lives to reconnect with each other. Tonight, Derek had gone out of his way to make this evening as perfect as possible. Somehow, between the second glass of Riesling and the dessert, I found myself staring at my hands. Here in the hotel room, the flickering candlelight strobes against my skin. I whisper, "This is what Nefertiti's mummified hands must have looked like."

I never intended him to hear that but the familiar clench of his jaw let me know that he had. Then an unexpected laugh broke from his lips. There was nothing sinister about it, but the way he dismissed my comment should've been a warning. On the elevator ride to the top floor, he gave my hands soft, delicate kisses. He unzipped the back of my dress as we walked down the hallway. By the time we reached the door, it was falling off of me. In a flight of fancy, I let my cocktail dress fall as he opened the door, and stood there naked except for my heels. His eyes devoured every inch of me as his body blocked my path.

"I should make you stay out here." The right side of his lips curled with excitement. "You know they have security cameras in these hallways?" Panic gripped me and I pushed Derek out of the way as I bolted past him into the suite.

"I have something better in store for you anyhow."

I'm not sure if better was the right word. He's tied me up before but not like this. Every element of my nakedness is now on full display. The same strand of nylon rope secures my arms and legs. It also weaves the rope around my breasts and across my thighs, leaving my pussy open, willing, and exposed. The more I struggle, the tighter the rope grips against my flesh. The stress of not being able to move forces me to sweat, wiping away the concealer that covers my crow's feet. The muscles in my neck rage into view under the tension. That one large vein that runs down the center of my forehead throbs as if it's about to burst. The experience of my years is on full display as I turn my focus toward Derek.

His dark gray suit brings out the hazelnut of his skin. His hair, now more salt than pepper, glistens from the overhead light. His appearance has a rugged cuteness. If he had continued to dye his hair he could look fifteen years younger with ease. Then again, as a man, he has that choice and right now I hate him for that.

"Look at yourself, Jamila."

I feel his erection against my naked back as he steps behind me. I lean back, hoping my stimulation against his cock will spark his need to untie this rope and ravish me. But why would it? Derek has me exactly where he wants me. The mirrored closet in front of the bed leaves me no choice but to accept what I see. This is who I am, wrinkles, veins, and all, and for a brief moment, I embrace that this is what fifty-five looks like on me.

The tension in the ropes appears to relax. My eyes scan every naked inch of my body until my stressed breathing reaches a calming norm. That's when I hear Derek sucking on his fingers. I glance up right before he removes his index finger from his lips and places it on my clit. He pulls back on the hood. Tension shoots through my body. Now every muscle and vein in my body appears ready to rip through my skin.

"Watch your body as I make you come." I fight looking at myself, but a pinch of my already erect and aching nipples allows me to give in to him.

"It's okay. Let go for me."

He slips his finger inside my glistening cunt. I squirm in an attempt to get him deeper inside me. My body contorts in desperation as Derek keeps me on the precipice of coming.

I beg, "Please," but his control is relentless.

"Just watch."

He gives my nipples a flick and slides another finger inside me. My face is no longer recognizable. The wooden legs of the chair creak as I try to get his fingers where I need them to be. I gasp with all my focus on my reflection, understanding the purpose of this journey. In this moment of physical anguish, I unearth the beauty of seeing myself as he sees me. He senses my acceptance and bends his fingers, forcing me to come. My head falls limp, and I'm panting from fatigue as Derek glides his fingers from the depths of my pussy. I hear him sucking my juices off his fingers before he lifts my head. He gives me a kiss and turns my head so I can see the results of tonight's escapade.

"How do you feel?"

Through glassy eyes, I gaze at my ravished form. As my body returns to its normal state I mumble, "Beautiful."

He steps in front of me and pulls his hard cock from his pants. He tosses his jacket aside before stepping between my legs. My body trembles from my recent orgasm but my need to have him is paramount. Derek places the head of his cock at the opening of my cunt and fills me up as he purrs, "Yes, Jamila. You are so fucking beautiful."

MY GIRL, MY BOY, MY ENBY

Annabeth Leong

Today I want you to be my girl, the text message said.

I scowled at my phone in a way I never would have done to Rory's face. I had already slicked back my hair. Waiting for me on my bed were dress pants, a pressed white shirt, and my favorite tie. I'd been planning to go *boy* today.

Do I haaave to? I typed back.

Extra vowels are whining, not a safeword. So yes.

Damn it.

Rory didn't mind back talk, as long as it was accompanied by obedience. I went over to my closet to figure out how to handle the change.

The hair could stay, I decided. The tie, too, because I liked it. I put on the white shirt but left my binder off. I swapped out the dress pants for a pair of orange shorts and accessorized with dangly earrings and some sparkly rings. *Voila.* Girl enough.

I snapped a picture for Rory, and I had to admit I felt pretty and coy. *What do you want your girl to do?*

Girls just wanna have fun.

I pouted. Fun? That was the worst command of all, the very hardest, something I would never choose on my own. *All day?*

Yes. The park. The ice-cream store. A treat for yourself to keep. And an orgasm at the end.

What are you even getting out of this?

Haha. Bratty girl.

I did as I was told, as best I could. I walked around the park uncertainly. I managed to order a small ice cream, and I almost enjoyed eating it. After visiting four stores, I found a weird little magnet made by a local artist, painted with colors that matched my girl-mood well.

Then I went home, undid my shirt and shorts, and lay on the bed for the orgasm.

I nestled my audio recorder on the pillow next to my head, then began to touch myself.

I coaxed the pleasure out of my body, slowly, sweetly, gently.

After I finished, I played the recording for myself before sending it to Rory. My breaths sounded a little surprised. My moans were soft, the pitch of my voice high. I came with a full-body exhale. It was the sound of sinking deep into welcoming mattresses.

I attached the audio file to a text. *Being a girl wasn't so bad.*

Today I want you to be my boy.

The instruction couldn't have come at a better time. This was a day when I wouldn't have known what I was otherwise, when I needed Rory to help me out by defining me, to give me enough of a push so I could put clothes on and get out the door.

I pulled on boxers, made my binder nice and tight, picked out low-slung jeans that hung off my hips, and added a boxy short-sleeve button-up. I didn't want Rory's boy to look careless, so I drew on a little eyeliner and put a unicorn-shaped stud in my left earlobe. *How do you like that?*

Very much.

And?

And I want my boy sweaty.

Do I get to come today?

Like a cherry on top.

Oh, that last instruction made me feel mischievous. It begged to be taken literally.

I texted Paula. *You free tonight and horny?*

LOL. Why?

I called her and explained, and that led to me with my pants and boxers pushed down to my ankles in her kitchen after work, crack lubed, Paula slowly feeding a thick plug into my ass—with a handle shaped like a cherry, which I'd remembered from a previous playdate.

Next thing was to get on top and get sweaty, and I made very sure Paula enjoyed that process. I didn't even think about coming until she was begging for mercy, cursing me out, and swearing her clit was too sensitive to take any more.

Then I tried to shock my own pleasure out of myself, hard and fast, and Paula was nice enough to reach around at just the right moment, smartphone in hand, and capture a short video of my asscheeks pulsing rhythmically around that bright-red cherry handle.

Today I want you to be my enby.

My heart leapt in my chest. This command came from Rory so rarely, but these were the days when sex was about neither holes nor sticking things in holes. It became creative and other, and something Rory liked to do in person.

I put on a ruffled skirt over unshaven legs. I rolled a lacy camisole on over my binder. I used glittery eye makeup but left my lips natural. From the back of my closet, I pulled out my heaviest, most ass-kicking boots.

I rushed to Rory's place like genders were ice-cream flavors. I'd picked up one of each, and I needed to get them all into Rory's mouth before they melted.

Rory opened the door. They didn't get into costuming the way I did, so they wore simple black. Jeans, T-shirt, eyeliner. Long black hair tied at the back of their neck.

I spilled into the door, kissing everywhere I could

reach. Rory let me for a few minutes, then reasserted their control.

"Down," Rory said. I dropped to the floor like a dog, not bothering to look around the space. I'd been over to Rory's apartment a couple dozen times in a couple of years, and I always left with only the vaguest impressions of walls, floors, and furniture. Rory was all I ever looked at.

"Put me in your lap and brush my hair for a while," Rory said.

We did it right there in the narrow foyer. Their hair was so soft. I lifted the brush to my nose after every few strokes to smell their shampoo and their scalp. Rory moaned and writhed and smiled blissfully. They rubbed my crotch with the back of their head. They slid their hands underneath my skirt and gripped my thighs with sharp fingernails, making me gasp and tense.

Then their eyes turned catlike, cold and green, and they said, "I'm going to tickle you now, until you can't breathe."

They pushed me onto my back, dug into my ribs and my armpits and the vulnerable places behind my knees and the points of my hips. They let me feel their weight. They shoved their thigh between my legs to hold me in place. When I cried out, they winked, and did everything harder.

I know people who wouldn't call that sex, who would say this wasn't like what I'd done with myself as a girl or what I'd done with Paula as a boy, but those things had only been sex for me because they were for Rory, and now I was Rory's enby and my head floated and my heart filled and my body surrendered and nothing could have felt more intimate.

I lost my breath. My toes pointed. My muscles went stiff. I spasmed everywhere, not just in the traditionally sexy parts. Then Rory and I gave each other goofy grins, and as soon as we recovered enough to move, we went into the bedroom and did it all again.

A JAMAICAN AFFAIR

D. Fostalove

Nelson sat on a chaise longue in the middle of the third-floor studio apartment as Jamaica wheeled two metal clothing racks from behind a curtained partition. He'd been a client of hers since she first appeared in a local alternative weekly five years prior. Although he knew their sessions were business to her, Nelson felt a special connection to the internationally known Dominatrix.

"Do you see anything you like?" Jamaica asked, as she lit another joint.

"I hate when you smoke."

"I know, sweetheart." Jamaica put the cigarette out in a nearby ashtray while Nelson sorted through a few outfits on the first rack before turning his attention to the second.

"This." Nelson grabbed a black-and-beige striped satin dress. "With those tan stilettos I like."

Jamaica glanced at the dress. "It's a little matronly for our plans. Are you sure?"

"It'll accentuate your curves."

Jamaica then wheeled over a metal makeup case and opened one of the drawers, retrieving various shades of lipstick. Nelson surveyed the colored tubes in Jamaica's outstretched hand before pointing out a vibrant cherry color. She asked if he'd like to see her with or without makeup.

"Without, but wear your dreadlocks up in a bun. You know how I like that."

"Whatever you want." Jamaica disappeared behind the curtain to change, reappearing moments later to model Nelson's selections.

He loved what he'd chosen for Jamaica and held up two thumbs. "You look striking."

"Thank you." Jamaica glanced at the gold watch on her wrist. "We're running a little behind. Are you ready?"

He nodded. She walked before him and spun around slowly, briefly modeling for him again.

"You're so good to me."

Jamaica winked and grabbed her keys from an accent table. "Let's go."

"No kiss for hubby before you head off?" Nelson asked as they exited.

"I'm sorry, sweetie." Jamaica leaned down and gave him a kiss. "See you in two hours, okay?"

"Yep." Nelson checked his watch. "Have fun, my dear."

"Thanks. I will." She smiled.

Nelson sat in his car thirty minutes prior to his date with Jamaica. He opened the email app on his phone and pulled up the classified ad they'd written together days earlier: *Sheepish older business exec, younger jet-setting wife looking for aggressive buck to satisfy an unquenchable thirst.* Scrolling down, Nelson's heart pounded at the seductive body shots of Jamaica that she'd allowed him to take.

Closing the ad, Nelson found the email reply from "Brick." When he saw the photos and response from the six-foot-three personal trainer who looked like he'd stepped right out of a prison yard instead of a gym full of suburban soccer moms, Nelson knew he'd found the man to satisfy Jamaica in a way he never could. They quickly called him, explained the details of their exchange, and made arrangements for Jamaica to meet him at a hotel downtown.

As Nelson's mind wandered to Jamaica and Brick, he thought about masturbating but a knock on the window broke him away from his fantasies. He glanced up to see Jamaica waiting with a smile. Hand-in-hand, they entered the Moroccan restaurant and stopped at the host's podium. As Nelson opened his mouth to speak, Jamaica squeezed his hand firmly. He flinched, remembering; he was to be seen but not heard.

"Reservation for two, last name: Cuckold."

The hostess scanned a folder. "Yes. Mr. and Mrs. Cuckold, please follow me."

Nelson almost laughed at Jamaica's absurd humor, but maintained his composure as they followed behind the hostess who led them to a plush booth.

"I hope this is to your liking." The hostess placed two menus on the table as they sat.

"Yes…"

Jamaica shot Nelson an icy glare. "The table is fine. Thank you."

"Your server will be with you shortly."

When the hostess was out of earshot, Jamaica scolded him. "Don't speak unless granted permission. Understand?"

"Yes," Nelson mumbled, loving how domineering Jamaica was.

"Good."

The pair scanned their menus briefly before the server, a tall, bronze man, stopped at their table. He greeted them before serving traditional Berber whiskey poured from a silver kettle into two small glasses. "I'll be back to take your orders."

After a few minutes of silence, Nelson couldn't contain himself. He needed to hear each sordid detail of her evening. "Please, Jamaica, don't keep me in suspense like this. It's killing me."

Her eyes shot up from the menu. "I warned you. Speak again and I will tell you nothing."

He suppressed the urge to smile at being completely controlled and lowered his eyes with a slight head nod.

The waiter returned then and asked if they were ready to order. "He'll have lamb, prune, and almond tagine. I'll have vegetarian couscous. Thank you."

After the server disappeared, Nelson raised his hand.

"You may speak."

"Please...tell me something...anything..."

She smiled, acknowledging that she'd stalled long enough. "As soon as I entered, he took me. Lifted my dress up, ripped my panties off with an angry fist, and jabbed his massive meat in my pussy."

"At the door?"

"Yes. He pinned me against the door and fucked me with a hand over my mouth."

Elbows on the table, Nelson leaned forward. "Did he at least speak first? Offer you a drink?"

"No. He literally pounced and knocked the wind out of me." Jamaica pulled back the shoulder of her dress to reveal several marks. "He was so rough, biting my neck and my breasts. He even choked me from behind after he threw me over the luggage rack."

Nelson felt himself stiffen below the table. He could vividly picture the brute fucking Jamaica throughout the hotel suite. He lowered one of his hands and rubbed it over his throbbing bulge.

"'Scream if you like it, bitch,' he said. And I did, especially when he..."

Nelson realized he hadn't been breathing as he listened. "When he what?"

"He used my juices to coat his dick when he put it in my ass."

"Wait. What?" He almost choked on the whiskey. "You let him…"

"With the way he fucked my pussy, I couldn't deny myself the pleasure. He was so big and skilled. I needed him to stretch me out in a way I hadn't been in a long time. Plus he promised to be gentle with my tight little asshole."

Nelson leaned forward and whispered. "Was he?"

"Hell no."

The waiter returned with their meals. He refilled their whiskey glasses and vanished.

"Did you come?"

"Did I?" Jamaica grabbed at one of her breasts. "Repeatedly."

"Did he?"

Jamaica nodded. "All inside me."

Nelson wiped his forehead, wet with sweat, with the back of his hand.

"If you behave for the rest of dinner, I may allow you a slice of my Jamaican cream pie."

"Please don't tease me like that." The thought of tasting Jamaica, and the conquest who had ravished her both anally and vaginally, excited Nelson beyond words. He would obey each directive of hers for the remainder of the meal…but first he needed a release. He couldn't contain himself any longer.

"May I please be excused?"

A smirk appeared on Jamaica's face. "You may, but hurry back. There's so much more to tell."

PLAYING WITH A BEAST

Salome Wilde

Lee narrows his eyes, hardly blinking now. He knows how hard I'm reaching for it and that I won't shift my gaze from his until I come. Maybe not until after Jeff does.

I feel the butterfly humming away on my clit, pressed in by Jeff's body on top of mine. His cock fits me as perfectly as we fit each other. I know, as I always do, that the hubs will last only a bit longer than I do. I'll wrap my legs around him and hold him tight and feel his muscles lock and then release. Even with Lee watching, Jeff is Jeff and we are us. I love that.

I also love the sounds of Jeff's panting as he pounds away inside me and Lee's groaning from across the room as he doesn't. Lee is tied tightly to the armchair in the corner, ornate with pretty knots that crafty Jeff has had to get so good at recently. Jeff's always liked rope play, but he's had to up his game since Lee moved in next door and then into our sex life. Lee's so buff, he quickly busted out of our first efforts to tie him down so he could—at his request—"watch you fuck without being able to do a damn thing about it." We tinkered with swinging in the first bloom of our marriage, but now—a few gray hairs and kids finally off to college—we've suddenly returned to youthful kinks and added new ones to the list, thanks to Lee.

His thick dishwater hair, slightly damp at his temples, falls into his face as he watches us. He doesn't try to flip it back, and his hands aren't free to let him do anything else with it. We call him a "hair farmer" because he loves his locks almost as much as his body, but I personally call him my "Beast." To his face, I use his name, though he rarely uses ours. When he comes for one of his late-night visits, he says something like, "How're my favorite nerds?" (which we are, but the sexy kind). Then he kisses us, usually Jeff first. He gets so intense so fast that he leaves us breathless before we can even guide him to a beer and the bedroom.

As Jeff's panting turns to grunts, I know Lee's big dick must be achingly hard, straining against the rope that binds it to his thigh. I don't know if he's wishing he were fucking me or Jeff or someone else or no one at all. But I hold those rich brown eyes, and I feel as pinned by them as by Jeff's pistoning cock. I feel flushed and dizzy at the combined sensations of the familiar and the new, bound together as closely as Lee's thighs are bound apart, ankles held neatly to the heavy round feet of our sage-green armchair. It's the one I usually read in. Now, before I sit in it, I smell it. I'd bet money Jeff does, too, but I don't ask.

Suddenly, I'm there: trapped beneath the man I love, held by the gaze of a man I crave, connected by the fiery thread of desire to both. I'm soaring through and away from them at the same time, coming so hard I have to howl it out until Jeff can't help but hit it, too, yelling, "Yeahhhh!" like a sports fan, cheering me and himself on at our moment of shared ecstasy. "Fuck yeah," I echo, throat dry and a little sore.

After my breathing slows, I switch off the vibe and disentangle myself from it and sweet, sweaty Jeff. I'm only aware I've looked away from Lee when I hear him suddenly hiss through his teeth.

"Beast!" I snap, so upset that I've failed to keep him on task that I let my pet name slip out. I sit up and look over at him, feigning outrage to cover my embarrassment. "You came on my favorite chair!"

Lee nods his shaggy head, letting more hair fall across his beautiful eyes. "Gonna untie me and make me clean it up?" he asks, voice menacingly low. He runs his tongue across his teeth. He's fucking hot, and he knows it. It's why, tied up or not, he dominates our relationship.

Life is short. I take a risk. "Maybe," I answer. I lick my lips, hoping I match an iota of his oomph while I look at his half-erect cock, still wrapped up but, for the moment, spent. "But first Jeff and I are gonna clean *you* up."

Lee's eyes sparkle as he makes his prick jump and leak a little more. Jeff chuckles as we make our way off the bed together. I may be the happiest nerd in the world.

WE ARE
MAGIC

Giselle Renarde

B ody parts gleamed like polished bone as Parker lifted
them from their cardboard crates.

"I love hanging out with you," Nabila said. She
picked up a sheet of Bubble Wrap and draped it around
her waist like a miniskirt. "What do you think of my
new look?"

He handed her a legless torso. "Here, hold this for
a sec."

She dropped the Bubble Wrap before hugging Parker's mannequin to her chest. The plastic was so slippery
she had to squeeze it hard. "You've got the coolest job."

He snorted, laughing. "If you say so."

"You get to be alone in the store after dark, when the
mall is closed. It's so exclusive."

Parker's smile fell as he flicked his bangs out of his

eyes. "It's not like I went to design school to become a window dresser."

"Nobody ends up doing what they went to school for. I didn't get my masters so I could sell cheap denim to teens."

His gaze bore into her, like he was seeing something internal, something private. "You'll find a better job."

"I'm not even looking anymore."

"Yeah. Me neither."

Parker popped in one leg while Nabila gripped the body.

"What do you think of the new mannequins?" he asked.

"They sure are white. Did you order them?"

"No. Corporate picks the dolls."

"I wonder if there are any brown ones." Her skin looked darker than usual against the mannequin's shiny plastic whiteness. "When I was a kid, I watched a children's show set in a department store after hours. Ever see that?"

Parker found another leg and worked it into the empty socket. "Doesn't ring any bells."

"One character was a window dresser. She always wore a pink and red jumpsuit. Then there was a guy who was a mannequin. He came to life when you put on his magic hat. That's what I think of every time I stay after hours with you."

"I'm sure we could find you an ugly-ass jumpsuit," he said.

Nabila let go of the mannequin once it could stand on its own two feet. Grabbing a sunhat off the rack, she set it on Parker's head. "There's your magic hat."

"Am I supposed to come to life?" Parker asked. "Because I'll need a serious dose of coffee before that happens."

Nabila watched Parker sort through packing peanuts until he found a head. "What about the arms?"

He said, "It's easier to put them on after she's dressed."

Nabila played with the new summer stock while Parker flipped through his sketchbook. The mall was on a conservation kick, which meant most lights were turned off. Fortunately the place was built with so many sunroofs and windows that the moon and parking-lot lights kept their shop front pretty bright.

"You'd look great in this," Nabila said, holding up a sundress.

He barely looked up from his sketchbook before saying, "Not all fairies prance around in florals."

"But if you've got the body for it…"

"Who says I do?"

There wasn't exactly a glint in his eye, but she saw something impish in him.

"Do you believe in magic?" she asked.

Before he could answer, she sang Olivia Newton-John at him, dancing with the dress, hopping over scattered body parts.

"Well," he said, "I didn't believe in magic before, but that performance convinced me."

"Then you believe me when I say your hat's magic? And if you take it off you won't be able to move?"

His brow furrowed. "Nabila, I've got work to do."

He set down his sketchbook and started across the window riser. When he arrived center stage, Nabila plucked the sunhat from his head. "Abracadabra! Without your magic hat, you can no longer move!"

She expected him to either yell at her or ignore the gag, but he didn't say a word.

Nabila moved around front to get a look at his expression. It read blank, even when she waved a hand in front of his face.

"Haha, Parker. Very convincing."

He didn't even twitch.

"Okay, then." She tossed the sundress over one shoulder and took hold of his top button. "Time to dress my mannequin for summer."

She slowly unbuttoned his shirt. She figured he'd knock her hand away before she got all the way to the bottom, but his body remained stiff even as she pulled out his tucked hem.

She'd undone his shirt and he hadn't reacted in the slightest, not even to the cool mall air creeping inside his shirt, tickling his sides.

"Time to take off your top," Nabila said, hoping he'd break. "Here I go…"

When he didn't respond, she felt challenged to follow through. She took hold of his collar and pushed his shirt across his shoulders, then pulled it down. His arms were like tree branches hanging at his sides. He was right—this process would be easier without the arms.

His chest was lean, white. Tight pink nipples. Sparse golden hairs leading to his belt.

"Next I take off your pants. And without your magic hat, you can't stop me."

She expected him to laugh and say, "Okay, enough of this."

But he didn't say a word. Eyes forward, two glass beads.

"Here I go." She took hold of his belt, slowly slipped leather across leather. Unbuttoned his jeans. They were loose-fitting enough that they started sliding down his narrow hips even with the fly done up. She wasn't prepared for that to happen. She almost pulled them back up as they travelled the length of his shorts. The weight of his belt carried them down his legs.

No, not leg*s*. *Leg*. One leg. And one prosthesis.

Nabila would never have guessed. "I didn't know you were bionic! So that's why you walk with a limp."

He didn't laugh, didn't even flinch.

"Parker?" she asked. "You're scaring me. Say something."

She watched his slender body for signs of life. His chest didn't expand. His eyes didn't blink.

Cupping his cheeks in her hands, she said, "Breathe! Why aren't you breathing?"

She stood just a whisper away. If he'd breathed, she'd have felt warmth on her lips. But she didn't feel a thing.

She pressed her mouth to his and breathed into him. Her breath disappeared inside his body.

"Stop screwing with me, Parker! Breathe!"

But no matter how many times she planted the kiss of life on his parted lips, he remained stiff and still.

Tears welled in Nabila's eyes as she spotted the sunhat discarded on the riser. She scooped it up and placed it on his head and his whole body jolted.

"Oh thank goodness," Nabila cried, wrapping her arms around his nearly naked body.

"Did you strip me?" He stepped out of his pants, then plucked the sundress from Nabila's shoulder and put it on. It clung to his skin with sweet insouciance. "There. Satisfied? It even matches my hat."

"Good," Nabila said, panic stricken, amazed by the powers she apparently possessed. "Because you can never take off that hat. It's *magic*."

"Magic is just another word for obedience," Parker said, flinging the sunhat across the store. "Now help me with these mannequins. A window dresser's work is never done."

ROOM 253

Iris Ann Hunter

She knelt on the carpet, in position, naked except for the white silk scarf that hid her eyes. Her knees ached, but she didn't dare move. She knew He was watching her. He'd said as much in the note He'd left for her to find. It had been waiting for her on the bed, the scarf alongside.

Finally, a soft click at the door broke the silence. She heard the door open and close, followed by the sound of footfalls across the carpet. They stopped a short distance away.

She inhaled the air, seeking out the scent of her Master. A faint aroma welcomed her. It should've excited her, thrilled her, but it didn't. Instead, it terrified her, for one simple reason—it wasn't Him.

A small whimper left her lips.

"He said you were beautiful. He was right." The man's voice sliced through the air, cutting her deep. It was a compliment, but all she heard was confirmation that her owner had sent someone else in His place, something He'd never done before. In that moment, the fear blossomed, only to fall away like a spent flower, replaced by something else. Anger.

"Who are you?" she demanded.

The man chuckled softly. "He also said you were a handful."

She felt the air shift as he moved past her, ignoring her question. Off to the side she heard things being placed on the dresser—a wallet perhaps, and keys. He moved back and sat on the bed directly behind her, settling himself so she was nestled between his legs.

Her entire body trembled, but that didn't stop him from running his touch up her arm and along her shoulder. "Hair like the darkest night," he whispered. "Skin like newborn snow." She closed her eyes, recognizing the words that had first fallen from His lips. Now He had passed them on to another, just like her.

His hand fisted into her long waves and gently pulled her head back. "I wish I could gaze into those green eyes of yours—eyes he said were the color of wild emeralds. But it appears he has chosen to keep them hidden."

An abundance of warmth exploded within her core, a caress to go with the slap. She had assumed the blindfold was for her, but it wasn't. It was for Him. To keep something for Himself, despite giving the rest of her away.

A smile played along her lips.

"You think that's funny?" he asked, sounding slightly amused. "Shouldn't I tell you why I'm here? Shouldn't I tell you that you were the sweetener to a business transaction?"

The smile fell away. "If you're trying to hurt me," she snapped, "then you'll have to try harder than that."

She expected retaliation, but all she felt was a caress along her shoulder. "I don't want your pain. That is his, and his alone. He made that clear. But I will take your submission." His hand slid down between her legs and without warning, two fingers entered her, forcing a gasp from her lips. "You *will* obey me."

"And if I choose not to?"

She felt him smile against her cheek. "Then it won't be me you have to answer to, will it?" She didn't answer. She didn't need to. They both knew the answer. "He doesn't seem the type to take disobedience lightly. Aside from using your safeword, it would seem you have no choice in the matter." She groaned when a third finger slipped inside. "I am afraid that for now, until dawn takes back the sky, you are mine." A sound at the door drew her attention. "Or perhaps, I should say…ours."

Ours?

She heard a daunting click, followed by the low murmur of what sounded like two male voices—two unfamiliar male voices. Her heart leapt into her chest and she scrambled to flee, but a steel arm held her in place, as did the fingers still lodged deep inside her.

"Shhhh," he whispered. "I told you, we're not going to hurt you…at least, no more than can be helped."

"But—" Her voice cracked and a tear seeped into her blindfold. She froze when she heard the men approaching.

"Jesus, he wasn't kidding, was he?" a rough male voice asked, followed by the hiss of air through teeth that sounded like it came from someone else.

The man holding her placed a soft kiss on her hair. "No, he wasn't," he answered quietly, moving his fingers once again, drawing out her wetness. "She's the most beautiful thing we'll ever see."

She could already hear them shedding their clothes, already hear the growing eagerness in their breath. Only the man who held her remained steady and calm. In some ways, he reminded her of Him.

Him.

Her heart ached, despite the growing pleasure pulsing between her legs. But she knew that's what He wanted for her. Pain to go with the pleasure.

"I want her mouth," the rough voice said.

A moment later, hard flesh slipped between her lips. She choked back a sob, struggling to take him in.

"She's a petite little thing," came a voice she hadn't heard yet. "Think she'll be able to take us all?"

"Yes," the man behind her whispered, still fingering her. "She'll take us all. She's strong, this one." He swiped his thumb back and forth over her clitoris, and she could do nothing but let the dam break. She came hard on his fingers, arching in his arms, swallowing up flesh, consumed by hands, and fear, and pain, and lust. She came for Him, the one who watched her, the one who gave her away, the one who loved her.

"Master," she breathed, as the last of the wave receded. Around her, she heard the strains of control in the men who touched her, groped her. Her orgasm had enflamed their hunger, heated their desires. She shuddered at the knowledge that her time with them had only just begun. All she wanted to do was melt away, to have Him come and take her in His arms now, to say that was as far as He would let them go. But alas, such was not the case.

By the time dawn emerged, she lay facedown on the rumpled sheets, alone. They had finally left.

She couldn't move, couldn't do anything but lie there. The tears had dried on her face long ago.

Vaguely, she heard a click at the door. She tried to open her eyes, but couldn't. A moment later, she felt the dip of the bed and took in the familiar scent she'd been waiting for.

"Master," she murmured.

Strong hands took her aching body and gently pulled her into a cradle. "I'm here."

Fresh tears suddenly burst forth and she clung to Him. He offered no apology, no explanation, just simply held her. "Tell me something," He said, stroking her hair with the utmost tenderness, "did you like it?"

She swallowed down a sob, choking on the truth

she was too scared to reveal. But she sensed He knew already. "No," she whispered, more tears falling. "I loved it."

OKTOBERFEST ADDICTION

Roxanna Cross

O rder up," Sam yells from behind the pass. I grab the heavy tray with trepidation. This is one order I don't want to deliver. I don't know why it bothers me so much. No, that's not true. I know exactly why. Graham Stenson. The man sitting at my last table, waiting for the order on my tray. A beer-braised hot dog with braised sauerkraut with some spicy Guinness mustard on the side and a pint of Hacker-Pschorr Original Oktoberfest beer. The tray wobbles underneath my fingertips as I start to serve him his meal. The bastard doesn't even have the decency to look up. Still, I'm a professional. I plaster on my brightest smile. "Let me know if I can get you anything else," I say and twirl away.

I know my long legs look amazing in this Oktober-fest beer-wench uniform I'm rocking. The green grass with pink petticoat skirt hits me midthigh, the brown suede with blood-red corsage hugs my curves to a T, and the white scoop-neck top barely covers my overflowing chest. If he can resist that, then he can go to hell for all I care. The flutter of butterflies in the pit of my stomach when I feel his gaze on me as I walk through the festival crowd tells me I'm in big trouble.

"Thought I didn't recognize this sweet mouth of yours, didn't you?" He winks and rocks his pelvis forward, ramming his cock deeper down my throat. It's thick and hard and coated with a layer of the spicy Guinness mustard I served him earlier. I almost choke on it. My eyes water. By instinct my body fights against the restraints he's put me in. I try to free my arms that are now tied with my own ribbon corsage behind my back in the same chair he sat on. My feet attempt to kick out, but they're also firmly tied to said chair with the red ribbons he took from the ends of my alpine braids. The sick bastard. I hate him. I should bite his dick off. I know I'll do no such thing.

Ever since I walked away, nearly four years ago, I've been miserable. I didn't understand how much I need... *this*. As twisted and crazy as it is, I crave it. Like a drug. My pussy clenches in anticipation. I'm so wet I feel the moisture of my own juices against my panties. Graham slides his cock out of my mouth and lets a generous amount of spicy mustard dribble all over its bulging veins before inching it back in. "Lick me," he orders.

Aiming to please I run my tongue the length of his long shaft. The strong taste of Guinness and mustard seed greets my taste buds, as does the bitter one of red wine vinegar, before I'm hit with the spices: a pleasant mix of cinnamon, cloves, nutmeg, and allspice. When I reach his distended head, I suckle it deep, rolling my tongue under its sensitive skin.

"Fuck." He pinches my nipple, hard, and rocks his cock deep inside my throat. "Now look what you've made me do." He slaps my nipple and continues to fuck my mouth without any of his rigid control. His strokes are wild and frantic. Soon his hands are in my hair, his fingers pulling it at the roots until I'm sure I'll need a hair transplant because he's pulling so hard. Yet, I wouldn't ask him to stop for the world. I've missed this. Craved it. Jeez, he's like a drug to me. And I'm just like an addict who fell off the wagon and right into the arms of her favorite bouquet. I can't get enough of him.

I let his cock barrel into my swollen lips, graze my palate, and choke my vocal cords as it rams into my mouth deeper with each of his thrusts. Tears stream down my cheeks from the joy I feel to be *his* once more. I don't care that his fingers pulling my hair create fiery sparks in my skull. Or that my lips are going numb. It's worth it. He's worth it. The swelling of his cock against my tongue. His breath accelerating to a tempo a salsa dancer would envy. His precious control—gone. Because of little old me. I do this to *him*; I have this power over him. This revelation makes my heart swell and gives me the courage to endure the pain.

Graham's cock continues to rocket in and out of my mouth. The pressure of his fingers in my hair doesn't lessen and my pussy is now thoroughly drenched. I feel it. That ball of fire in the pit of my belly almost ready to explode. "Drink," he grunts and his cock shoots a load of hot come down my throat. As commanded, I drink and drink the hot salty liquid until there's none left. "Fuck, babe, I love that sweet mouth of yours," he growls before claiming my lips in a bruising kiss. His tongue demands everything of me. It doesn't dance or offer a sweet caress; no, it rolls with savage hunger as his teeth nip and bite. I fucking love it. His hands have released my hair. Thank the lord. But his long fingers are now busy circling my clit, making me squirm in my seat.

"Your turn to be my tasty treat." He dips his finger in what's left of the spicy mustard and spreads it on my clit and pink lips. He brings his nose close to my pussy to breathe me in. "You smell delicious." The tremors of his voice so close to my dripping core have me lifting my butt off of the chair, offering my pussy to him. With a wild appetite, he spears into me, mixing my natural cream with the mustard he spread on me. A deep moan escapes my lips. His mouth covers my clit. I melt. The ball of fire is nearing the combustion point. "I know, babe." He blows on my clit. I squirm. His tongue runs the length of my slit and then spears inside. Faster and faster he fucks me with his tongue. I'm panting. I can't control it; the ball of fire explodes and my pussy squirts and squirts, showering his tongue and chin in my juices. He laps it all up with glee. "Fuck, babe, I love that sweet pussy of yours too. Can't get enough of you. Do you understand?" he asks, eyes bright and a bit wild. I nod. As if my nod is not enough for him, he grabs my chin in his long fingers. "Say it," he commands. "I understand." I repeat it.

He makes quick work of my restraints, only to have me bent over the table, hands tied under it, legs spread wide apart, ankles tied to the table posts. Once satisfied with this new position, he places himself between my legs, leaving his thick erection resting on my lower back for a moment or two. "You're my addiction, my drug, babe. Don't you forget it." And he slams into me. In our mutual addiction, we've found—*home*.

THIS TIME

Jade A. Waters

I stand here, naked. Legs spread, arms at my side.

Rowan circles me slowly, quietly, appraising my body as if memorizing my every curve.

He knows all of them already, has for over a decade, but it's this game we like to play, sometimes. We are not fond of labels, but if I were to give him some, they would be *husband, father, entrepreneur, intuitive,* and *kind*. Sometimes, he is a sub. Sometimes, he is my Dom.

Today, he is my lover—which is all that really matters, to me.

So as he reaches out, trailing one finger around my waist, sending tingles up and down equally at the prospect of what will come, I am not surprised when he commands me this time, his voice calm but firm from behind.

"Lift up your arms."

I do, enjoying the sparkle in his eyes when he comes round to face me again. He takes two hands to me, one for each breast, molding them in his palms before making me jump with a pinch of my nipples.

"How do you want me?"

I am smiling, because we both love this question, posed in either direction—a challenge, a promise, an offer, all the same. *I will give you what you want,* it says, *but I will have you, too.* And so I raise my chin, keeping my arms aloft, feeling the sweep of lust that's already dampened the folds of my cunt. My heart pounds at the glide of Rowan's hands over my hips as he waits for me to speak.

"I want you deep," I say.

"And?"

"I want you hard."

He presses close, his bare chest electrifying my nipples, his cock straining inside his pants and rubbing, just so, against my sensitive clit. He shifts his hands around to my ass, cupping it before tugging me hard into him.

"And?" he asks.

I can feel his heart pounding in his chest, too.

"And I want you right here"—I pause—"now."

"Ah-ha…"

Now, I've caught him. I've turned it back on him, but the momentary surprise fades as he releases one side of my ass to unfasten his pants. They are open swiftly, down around his ankles, and I'm delighted to see he's caught me, too.

Today, he wears nothing beneath.

"Keep your hands up until I say," Rowan whispers, and so I stay spread, open, riled as he walks back around me. He nudges me forward just enough to guide his cock along my folds, then sinks inside.

"Fuck," I murmur.

"Oh, we will."

His words are a grumble on my back as he drives again. When he crushes me in his arms, I want to bring mine down to touch him, but I strive to keep them up, to move against him as he slams inside.

"Just like this?" he asks, and I know I don't need to answer. We move wildly, me bucking back, reaching up like I'm on the best ride of my life, his hold on my hips yanking me into him. It's hard to balance when he moves faster, but I dig my toes into the carpet, gritting my teeth as he pushes, and pushes again. He fills me hard and fast, lovingly yet rough, lips planting sporadic kisses on my back. With his next thrust I gasp, because he's caught me again, fingers reaching around, rubbing at my clit until I can hardly see. Heat rips through my body, shaking me completely as he fucks me with all he has. When he latches on to my shoulder with sharp teeth I cannot contain the cry that spills from my lips, can't stop my arms from falling down, the claw of my hands seeking his hips behind me as I come and he fills me with the hot burst of him inside.

"Oh my god," I moan. Rowan exhales shattered breaths against my back. Time moves slowly as we settle down. Once he releases me to draw his cock from inside and comes around to face me, he's got a grin on his mouth.

"You put your arms down," he says.

I wink, then shrug.

Rowan raises an eyebrow. He puts his finger on my belly, beginning to trace his slow circle around me again.

"Then, of course," he says, "we'll try this once more."

HIS WIFE'S WONDERFUL COCKS

Dahlia Lovejoy

Colin has sucked his wife's cock plenty of times—or rather, her cocks. Ananda has a whole collection of them in various sizes and shapes, in materials from glass to wood to silicone. He knows each one's unique taste, the weight of it on his tongue, how it bumps against the roof of his mouth as she slides in and out. Her biggest is about ten inches long and as wide as a dollar bill. Taking it feels like swallowing an apple whole.

He loves it.

Tonight, the cock she has chosen for him is different. It's one of flesh and blood, attached to the body of a naked twenty-seven-year-old named Ben with a blindfold around his eyes and a ball gag in his mouth. Colin isn't usually inclined toward men, but even he can see Ben is gorgeous. His chest and abs are perfectly cut, his legs long and sinewy. Despite the bindings, Ben stands proudly in front of the gauze curtains of the hotel room window, the filtered sunshine forming a halo. Cast in marble, he'd certainly be mistaken for a Greek god.

Well, if it wasn't for his huge erection. The Greeks tended to prefer their gods flaccid. Which is too bad, because Ben's hard-on—its thickness and weight—bring balance to his proportions and make him all the more ideal in Colin's sight. He can see why his wife likes this plaything.

Ananda motions for Colin to kneel in front of Ben. "Do you like the new dildo I brought for you?"

"Yes, Madam." Colin falls to his knees. He's been anticipating this moment ever since Ananda started to plan it a few weeks ago. He's long been curious about how her cock would feel covered by skin instead of silicone, and with a warm, beating pulse at its center.

But he's been dreading this moment too. He's never sucked a real live dick before. What if he doesn't like it? What if he does something wrong? What if he can't make Ben come? What if he doesn't *want* to make Ben come? Ben might be Ananda's plaything, but he isn't Ananda.

This is the moment of truth. Ben's cock stares Colin right in the face, growing harder, expanding like a lung, its veins twitching as blood pumps through them. The skin flushes the way Ananda's labia do when she's turned on.

Colin has the urge to lick it.

Huh. Maybe he didn't need to be so worried after all.

Ananda applies a clamp to Ben's left nipple and tightens the screw. The slightest moan escapes around the fabric in his mouth. In his blurry near vision, Colin sees the head of Ben's cock glisten. Colin can smell it, too—the sharp, masculine scent of precome. The scent makes him woozy.

"Are you ready to suck my flesh dildo, sweet? You're so good with your mouth."

Colin folds his hands primly behind his back and adjusts his knees on the Berber carpet. "Yes, Madam."

"Then open up." Ananda sidles up behind Ben, her pelvis snug to his ass but a little off-kilter so that her curvy hip peeks out past the straight lines of Ben's waist and thigh. Against the haze of sunlight, Ananda's and Ben's bodies blur together; if Colin squints, it looks almost as if Ben's cock is jutting from between her own thighs. "It's time for you to show me what you can take."

She nudges Ben forward and his swollen cockhead brushes against Colin's lips. The texture is silken and inviting, not so different from Ananda's mouth when they kiss. So Colin kisses back, closing his lips around Ben's foreskin, pushing it back gently as Ben begins the slow drive in. It's not too different from Ananda's other cocks, just warmer and...saltier. The foreskin feels different, too, in the way it clings to Colin's touch. It reminds him of the delicate folds of Ananda's labia. His own cock grows heavy.

Ben grunts something indecipherable but pleasured-sounding. Ananda reaches around Ben's hips to grab Colin's hair. "So pretty with your lips around my flesh-dildo, sweet. Ready to take more?"

Colin grunts his assent. She yanks him forward by his hair so the head of Ben's cock weighs solidly on the center of his tongue. Ananda's grip grows tighter, sending fine threads of pain through his scalp. "Open wider, sweet. I'm going to fuck your mouth."

With a quick thrust of her hips, she propels Ben's pelvis forward. Ben's crown bumps against Colin's soft palate, precome barely easing the friction. Ananda thrusts at just the right pace, which means it's faster than Colin would dare accomplish on his own. His chest prickles with sweat. His cock stands higher, bumping against Ben's calf.

Ben's moans become increasingly desperate with each thrust, and when Colin relaxes his throat to let more in, the sound that Ben makes is enough to shake the paint from the walls. Ananda moans too, a forceful, feminine grunt that makes Colin's cock ache.

There's an art to deep-throating. It requires intense concentration and complete absence of ego, the willingness to bend and mold one's muscles to an invading form. Colin must be alert for the smallest signs of resistance and quickly dismantle them. His wife's satisfaction is paramount.

Colin's nose is just an inch from Ben's curly pubes when a familiar scent jolts him from his meditative state.

Lilac. It's Ananda's favorite body wash, but it's on Ben's body, clinging faintly to his skin and hair.

Only it's not Ben's skin or Ben's hair, because Ben belongs to Ananda. Ben's body is Ananda's, and so is his cock. In this moment, in this scene, the cock in Colin's mouth is Ananda's. Each suck, each lick is for her pleasure.

Colin drives toward the scent, taking the cock's head deep into his throat until his nose buries in Ben's—Ananda's—soft cloud of hair. The lilac scent overwhelms the flavor of Ben's—Ananda's—leaking erection.

Ananda withdraws her hands from Colin's hair, but this alters neither his pace nor the depth to which he takes her cock. Her moans and whimpers are difficult to distinguish from Ben's.

"You're enjoying it, aren't you, my little cocksucker?" she taunts. "You like taking my dick, don't you?"

Colin's throat is too stuffed to answer with a moan, much less with a *yes*. All he can do is show her how much he likes it. He curls his fingers deeper into Ben's thighs—pulling and pushing, pulling and pushing—driving his wife closer to ecstasy.

The air is heavy with the scent of Ananda's arousal. She thrusts her hips against Ben's ass. Colin can feel the reverberations in his teeth.

"I'm going to come." She pronounces the words like a threat. "I'm going to come down your slutty little throat, and you're going to take it."

Ben's cockhead mushrooms deep in Colin's throat

and hot, slick come bursts forth. It's bitter and plentiful, and Colin wants to swallow every last drop—this gift from his wife, his Dom, the woman who knows him better than himself and gives him what he needs.

GOOD GIRL

Genevieve Ash

This is insane." Louise gathered her favorite tote bag, the one with the flowers cascading over a wall in Tuscany—or was it Greece? She just thought it was pretty and it made her feel better about never having the courage to travel there alone. Since her husband had passed, she kept pretty much to herself. Sometimes she was lonely, but she enjoyed the quiet. More time to read and knit and craft.

"Excuse me, is everything okay?" A voice sounding like melted chocolate trickled into her ear with a puff of warm air, making her shiver. She stopped, but as in a paralyzing dream, she could not turn to see from where it came. The heat from a warm body covered her back, taking the chill and replacing it with an odd sense of comfort.

"Yes, I have all the information I need. I'm not staying for the hands-on session."

"I assure you, what we do here is practically vanilla. And there is no pressure, no judgment. It is an opportunity to learn and share. You don't have to participate."

Louise had been a psychologist for many years and had heard many wild stories, but her most recent client had a penchant for control and his tales had piqued her curiosity. She had only attended the BDSM seminar in an effort to understand him better.

"I am a grandmother for god's sake. I don't belong with—" A warm reassuring hand squeezed her shoulder and she sighed. How long since she'd felt the gentle touch of another? It was a reminder that she was alive.

"Stay. Sit. You needn't worry, I will keep you safe."

Louise didn't want to create a scene. The lights dimmed and she took a seat while risking a glance at the man whose body warmth was now in her personal space. Dark suit, close-trimmed beard, strong features. Maybe he was handsome, she didn't really look, but his indomitable presence gave her a sense of security. His fresh scent drifted toward her nose and she inhaled: all male.

The stage now held a couple involved in a discipline scene. A skinny young man wept at the feet of the strong redheaded Mistress who wanted to make sure he'd learned how to listen. As she raised the paddle, Louise squeezed her eyes shut.

"Open your eyes," he commanded, as his large hand came down to rest on Louise's thigh. "They have rules.

Their lifestyle requires this type of punishment and they both enjoy it."

"But, I—oh!" She jerked as the paddle made contact with a resounding thwack. "I can't believe that anyone would enjoy this." She bent to gather her things once again, but he tightened his grip on her thigh.

"Are you not still safe?"

"Yes, of course."

"Then why are you leaving?"

His hand was caressing her thigh now, sliding the slippery fabric of her skirt over her flesh. She wanted to stop him, express her outrage, but somehow, between the pounding of blood in her ears and the shallow breaths that numbed her upper lip, she couldn't find the words.

His fingers found bare skin, and Louise panicked. The room was dark, silent, as the crowd focused on the couple on stage. Louise heard a few soft moans before she realized they were coming from her own lips. His fingers slipped and slid closer and closer to the now damp swatch of silk between her legs. Suddenly the years fell away and she was a young woman again. A woman with needs and desires. She wanted to feel again. The daily routine, the filling of time with busyness, was no longer enough. But she was in a public place; this was not what Louise would ever do. She knew it was wrong, but she didn't want to stop him.

"Now, close your eyes for me." Louise wished he'd make up his mind, but did not hesitate. "Good girl. Keep them closed."

She smiled despite herself at being called a girl, because that was exactly how she felt. Her world began to spin, the intensity of sensation increasing as her sight disappeared. She felt the pathways and diversions of her nerves as if it were a road map leading directly to her clit. *If only he would touch me, just once...*

She felt him lift the edge of her panties and push them to the side. She gasped, holding that breath in anticipation of his touch. But he stilled, and waited.

"Do you want me to touch you?"

Louise wanted to war with herself, but knew that she had already answered when she'd allowed his advancing caress.

"I asked you a question." His voice had a hard edge now and the gooseflesh rose on Louise's skin.

"Yes, Sir," she said, remembering her notes from the seminar. The simple act of using the words gave her a thrill and, swallowing hard, she tried to slow her racing heart.

The darkness, the silence, and the surreal reality all collided in a moment of waiting that seemed interminable. She thought she might literally explode; her need was front and center, any control she had left hanging by a thin thread.

Suddenly, his fingers slid through her wet folds and straight into her cunt. She gasped with shock, and relief, but when his slippery thumb began circling her clit, she forgot about everything except pleasure.

"Shh. You must not make any noise or I will stop, do

you understand?" His graveled whisper carried a threat, and Louise felt the panic rise inside.

"Yes," she whimpered. "I'm sorry."

"I beg your pardon?"

"Yes, I am sorry, *Sir*."

"Good girl." He began again immediately, the slow lazy circles pressing on her clit as his fingers once again began working their way in and out of her pussy.

Louise fought to stay quiet, but she was sure everyone could hear her screaming on the inside. The pressure was building, lifting her higher and higher. The wet sounds of his fingers inside her seemed to echo in her ears as she neared her breaking point, though it was the firm hand across her mouth as he whispered, "Come quietly for me," that sent her spiraling into the oblivion of pure bliss.

Her body splintered into fragments of color as the long-overdue release lighted every part of her body. Never-ending sensation seemed to roll on as wave after wave of pleasure filled all the empty places inside of her. Finally, she shuddered softly, complete.

"Well, I do hope you enjoyed our hands-on session. I have many more lessons for you. Here is my card. Call me tomorrow."

"Thank you," she mumbled, keeping her head bent like a small child to hide the heat in her cheeks, "but I think we both know that I won't do that."

"Oh, but you will. You know it and I know it, isn't that right?"

Louise sighed, the orgasm making her relaxed and happy. "Yes, Sir," she said, turning to him as the lights came up, but he had already gone. *Well, a little more research wouldn't hurt.*

KINTSUKUROI

Corrine A. Silver

Kintsukuroi: The Japanese art of repairing broken items, i.e., pottery, with precious metals or lacquers, in the belief that they are then more beautiful for having been broken. See also, *Kintsugi.*

I know when he finishes with me, I will be a heaving, flailing mess of limbs. A pile of rags. A sack made of skin, filled with flesh and the putty, the Jell-O he has made me. I will be tears and weeping, the dragging edge of being lost in my own mind, pulled down under the depth of giving to him.

I will be resplendent.

I will be carved from the earth, repaired with the gold of his words, of his work.

That is the way of it with him, and why he will only come to me once a month, sometimes not even that frequently. He doesn't have any interest in explaining himself to me, but I know it's because he likes to see me mended, threaded through with my strength. We that do this, that love like this, have the same vocabulary with alternative definitions. My beauty is in being broken and repairing. My strength is in my scars.

He traces old scars when he touches me. He traces the stains of his love. He licks the places where he has curetted away what I didn't need. And shivers run through me. Because his mouth is cold. His words are cold. The floor is cold under my knees.

He nudges them apart again until I'm spread the way he likes to see me.

"Eyes down." His fingers are warm as he tilts my face. "I think there may be a day when I don't have to remind you of that. Why do you want to look at me?"

I know I'm not meant to answer so I don't speak. But there's an answer on my lips. *I look because I can't look away. You're a maelstrom I can touch and not die. You are gravity.* I'm so glad I don't get the privilege of a voice because I would have felt so stupid if I had said that out loud. He doesn't appreciate childish flattery. He doesn't like me to idolize anyone. I shouldn't, but I do.

His cock is out, brushing my hair where it has fallen out of the braid, against the back of my neck. I want to look at it, touch it. I want it on my lips. Tears prick my eyes because I can't stop putting myself first, putting what I want first. The velvet head brushes my cheek.

I know the moment he sees my tears as he rounds my body, a small intake gasp. A murmured hum and his hand gripping his shaft. "Why are you crying? You know how much I like that."

His thumb collects a tear from the corner of my eye and circles around the head of his cock, mixing the salt of my tears with the salt of his skin and the salt of his precome. Three salts. My tears come harder and I don't know why. Only that this is all playing out in front of my face and I know it means he's not done with me yet. And that he is nearly done with me. I'm already aching and sore. I'm already empty. But I can't breathe for how much I want him. I want to be torn apart. I want to surrender more than I have. I don't know what I want and that's why I kneel. It's what he gives me.

His thumbs slip into my slack mouth, massaging my tongue and running along my teeth. His cock follows and his hand crowns me. I'm golden. Mouth open. Ears open to his murmurs. I want to move on him. I want to swallow and suck and massage, maybe nip at him. I want to get his scrotum in my mouth too. I want to hum and smile and drool all over him. I want to frenzy. All the tension, all the coiled energy of the day fills me.

"Pause, hold there, beloved."

I close my eyes and feel *beloved* trickle through me, finding the cracks. Each broken place. Each empty, achy spot. He feels like honeycomb dripping directly on my brain. Like summer sunshine heat on the back of my neck.

The tears leak around my lashes again because he heals me. Healing hurts. Repair is painful. The hot lacquer that will hold me together burns as it finds every defect.

He sets the pace of what he does with my mouth. But we both know it's because I want it like this. I want to be splintered apart and put back together. I want to hold him in my mouth, literally and metaphorically. I want the seat of my power, my words, my worth, to have been filled with him. I want the vessel that carries me through my life to be marked with him. I want it to last. I want him to king me. To let me worship him, serve him.

And because he knows it, he always makes it a challenge. Today he lashed my back till I bled, the deep scarlet splattering on the strands of his implements. My implements. I own them. I keep them, maintain them. But they're his. The way my skin is his. The way my mouth is his.

My throat is crowded now, the head of his cock filling me up, unapologetic. It could be so impersonal, but it isn't. This is art. This is holy. This is something I can't name.

My wrists are still tied to my ankles and another length of rope connects my elbows. He likes to contort me. My fatigue wrecks my posture. But these are the absent thoughts of a mind wandering from its task.

His cock in my mouth. His skin on my skin. I want it all. I want to give it all to him. I love that he gets naked with me. That he doesn't need to lead from a place of clothing while I'm nude. I love that I can see the hair on his legs, the twitch of the muscles in his thighs. He turns my head to the side, angling me for his pleasure or just to remind me that he can move me however he wants. I can see his feet, my initial tattooed over the top of his right foot. He told me he'd take pain for me too, that when I kiss his feet I am loving myself too.

I shudder as the familiar emotions run through me. The feeling of emptiness and the molten shock of being filled with love. The spasm of pain at bursting for him, exploding with his heat. The love of him.

I hate that it's this complicated. I hate that I can't just love like someone else. Like other people do. I hate that I need it to hurt so much in order to break me open so I can access this. But I'm so goddamn grateful that he understands.

BUILDING
SOMETHING
NEW

Xan West

Rickie wanted to approach this conversation with Jax's needs and desires in mind. He wasn't going to let Jax focus the negotiation on him. He needed Jax to name what he wanted, especially since this was the first time they were contemplating taking their D/s relationship out into the world, on their first romantic date. It wasn't just play anymore.

"When we spoke earlier, I got the impression that this party might be difficult for you."

"Yeah, that's true," Jax admitted.

"I'm going to the party to support you. Do you think being in dynamic would feel supportive? Or might it create more pressure, make things harder on you?"

"My gut says that it would feel supportive."

"And is it what you want? Do you want to stay in

dynamic with me tonight, throughout the night?"

"Yes. I want that. But only if you want it too."

"I think we should try out a discreet D/s dynamic. I don't want other people witnessing an obvious power dynamic. We don't have their consent. Something subtle. But where we know it's there; we can still feel it."

"That sounds good," Jax replied, his voice suddenly hoarse.

Rickie's heart was pounding. He reminded himself that they were trying this out. This was an experiment, not a commitment. It might not work out. This night might totally go down in flames. There was something comforting in that idea—that they were trying it on, and might totally fuck it up. He wasn't sure why it was comforting, but it was.

"It may be difficult not calling you Sir. It's how I think of you in my head."

Jax yanked him close and kissed him, fierce and trembling into his mouth. Rickie smiled at him, just let the smile take up his whole face.

"You like that, don't you, Sir?"

"Yes, boy. I like that very much." Jax's voice was all gravelly and serious, almost fervent. Well all right then. This was a whole bundle of new to hold. Wasn't that something?

"So," Jax said, "we should have a signal, for if you want to ease off a bit on the D/s."

"Okay. How about I reach for your hand, like this? Not grab for it, just offer mine. You take it, or not, either would be okay."

Jax took it and intertwined their fingers, his thumb tracing the inside of Rickie's wrist, making Rickie shudder, his breath shakily leaving his lungs. He was holding hands with Jax. He didn't want to let go. Didn't want that thumb to stop moving. They could just keep doing this, please.

Maybe this wasn't such a good signal after all. Except, it seemed right. Seemed like a *let's even out the power just a bit, but don't you go anywhere* kind of thing. Seemed like an offer of connection and comfort, too.

"We have our signal, then."

Rickie grinned. "I think we're going to be just fine, Sir."

"You know what? So do I. Thank you for agreeing to come to this party, boy. For wanting to support me."

"My pleasure, Sir. It is most definitely my pleasure. Thank you for trusting me to support you."

"I trust you a great deal, boy. We have built that, together. And we continue to build."

Yes, thought Rickie. *We are building something new tonight*. He hoped it would involve more kissing. More kissing would definitely be a good thing.

It didn't take long to get there, even with the transfer from one subway to the next. He'd gotten thrown off for a moment, because he always took the stairs. And Jax seemed to have a habit of taking the elevator. Rickie wasn't sure why. Was it about the crowd? Was it something physical about stairs? Maybe he could find a way to ask that, sometime.

It was this whole new thing, traveling through the world with Jax. They didn't have it down, were a bit awkward with it. It also felt like, whoa, this was a whole new set of information that he hadn't had before, about Jax, and how he moved through the world. It made it clear how Rickie had only seen a small sliver of him, even though in some ways he felt like he knew him really well. This was going to take adjustment.

There was also something so delicious about just following him. Letting him lead the way. He chose where they sat on the train, gesturing for Rickie to have the window seat, while he took the aisle, crowding Rickie just a bit against the window in this way that just flat did it for him. It was being cornered and being led and being protected all wrapped together and it filled Rickie with this electric pleasure.

That was even before Jax took his hand, holding it captive between his own, running his fingertips along every inch of it, before using his nails. Yum. Rickie held still, barely breathing, eyes intent on watching Jax play with his hand, teasing him with delicious pain, intertwining firm grip and gentle strokes until he was all shivery everywhere.

They were just two trans queers holding hands on the subway on a Saturday night. It would take a particular vantage point to pick out the way D/s was flowing between them, the way Jax was playing with him. This was so damn new in so many ways and he might not be able to breathe for the rest of the night.

Then Jax stood and drew him to his feet. They were at their stop. No elevator at this station, so they moved toward the stairs. Jax backed him into a pillar and kissed him thoroughly, his hands gripping Rickie's hair in these glorious pulses of pain. Rickie was shuddering against him. It was so much, and he wanted to soak it all in, all this newness and desire and expansion and nervousness and wow, we are doing this in public exhilaration. He held on tight to Jax and opened, taking it all in, grounding it through his boots on the platform. Yes, this, he wanted this, he could hold all of this.

Then Jax lifted his head and smiled down at him, his hand stroking Rickie's cheek all tender, not in a cruel way but in this almost reverent way, and Rickie just fucking melted. He could feel himself go all gooey inside. Like he could actually take that in, right now, could hold it, tolerate it. Believe it.

Rickie blinked, because it had gotten inside, and he had held it, and that was okay for just a moment, and then right away it was too much again. He had held it, and Jax had seen that, he could tell. Just as Jax had seen it become too much, because he answered by leaning in and biting down on Rickie's neck, giving him the perfect, invasive, burning pain that Rickie needed to move through the moment to the other side.

"Thank you," Jax whispered in Rickie's ear, before taking his hand and leading him up the stairs at a leisurely pace, and out into the night.

PLUG PLAY

Dorothy Freed

P lease, Richard, tell me you're not serious," I say, when he shows me the plug he has in mind. "That thing is enormous. It's *not* going to fit in my ass."

"Really, Kira," he asks, with that crooked grin of his, "that remains to be seen, doesn't it? Kneel on the edge of the bed, facedown and ass up."

Richard, an ass man from way back, has been training mine since I became his sex slave six months ago—moving gradually from the finger-sized plug he started with, to the big bruiser he's selected for today. We both know I'm okay with it—we have safewords for serious objections and I'm not saying them. Richard, looking amused, arches his brow and waits for me to comply. I huff with indignation, but I do.

"That's it. Higher even. Legs farther apart. Good

girl," he croons, stroking my asscheeks, spreading them wide, exposing me completely. I flush with embarrassment, imagining how I look with my face pressed into my pillow and my ass thrusting obscenely into the air.

My back arches. I shudder as Richard massages the nerve-rich flesh around my anus. Delight races through me as he teases my small puckered opening. I've been holding my breath and now release it, moaning, feeling my muscles relax as I do. Seizing his opportunity, Richard slides a well-lubed finger up my ass, while rubbing my swollen pussy lips with his other hand.

"You like this," he comments, feigning surprise. "Your clit's brick hard and you're dripping wet." He's right; although no way will I admit it, I'm aglow from the inside out and hungry for more. I moan again as the finger withdraws and the tip of the plug seeks admittance.

"Open," he orders when my muscles clench, involuntarily.

I take slow, deep breaths, willing myself to relax.

"Good girl," he purrs, rubbing my engorged clit— and I open. The plug enters with a sharp burst of sensation and to my surprise slides in like a launched torpedo. I yelp as the widest part enters.

My sphincter clutches the plug, with its flat base jammed up against my expanded opening. It hurts at first but hurt soon turns to waves of pleasure. I'm panting now, cunt clenching, clit throbbing, ass contracting around the turgid rubber invader. I could come in few swipes of my engorged clit, but Richard grins and orders me to blow him.

I obey, unhinging my jaw, snake-like, to accommodate his girth. I lose myself in his pleasure, sucking and licking until he tells me to stop.

"Slip on that little black dress and the red boots I like—and nothing else," he orders, stuffing his cock back in his pants. "We're going out for a night on the town."

"You're not serious?" The idea turns me on, but I'm too embarrassed to admit it.

"Ready, Kira?" he inquires when I'm dressed.

"Yes, Richard," I say, blushing. He rewards me with a kiss and throws a coat over my shoulders. We head out for cocktails. One of us is bottom heavy and takes slow, *very* careful steps.

Richard watches me ease myself onto the passenger seat where I list to one side and breathe deeply. He grins at me during the three-mile ride from our house, knowing that every bump and pothole in the road accentuates the throbbing in my ass.

The Harborview Bar is dimly lit and decorated in a seaside motif, with mermaids, fishnets, and anchors displayed on the walls. Richard leads me inside. We sit at a small table near the bar. I fidget and he grins again, enjoying my discomfort. The place is lively, with a mostly young, single clientele crowded around the bar, looking to hook up. A sprinkling of couples sit pressed close together.

I barely notice. My world is made up of Richard, me, and my electrified ass, clenching and contracting around that plug.

"What'll you have tonight?" the perky waitress inquires. I'm hoping Richard will order for me because I'm not sure I can speak, but he turns to me and waits for me to respond. I shoot him an indignant look, which he ignores—and choke out a request for dry white wine. Richard doesn't drink when he's topping, and he orders iced tea.

Our order arrives. Richard's feeling chatty, whispering in my ear, "Imagine, if that cute little waitress or maybe those super-straight office girls at the next table knew your secret. What if I told them that *my* girl has a big fat plug up her ass? Would they be shocked—or envious…?"

I smile, in spite of myself, at the thought of people around us knowing my predicament. Richard slips a possessive arm around me as we sip our drinks. As though we are alone, he gives each of my nipples a sharp pinch through the thin material of my dress, which sends a fresh rush of excitement coursing through me. I'm leaning forward in my chair, nipples puckering, clit tingling, ass throbbing. My breathing has quickened. I'm making little mewling sounds under my breath.

"Please Richard, may we go home?" I say urgently. He tilts my chin up with his hand and gazes into my eyes.

"Ready to go home and have me unplug you, Kira?" His grin is demonic.

"Yes, Richard," I whisper, feeling my face flush at the image *that* presents.

He signals the waitress. She brings the check. Richard takes my hand. We walk slowly to the car.

Back home, I'm allowed to pee. Then we head for the bedroom where I undress and await instructions.

"You know the drill, baby. Kneel on the bed again, facedown, ass up."

I obey. Electric sparks shoot through me as my nipples rub against the smoothness of the bedspread. The air in the room feels cool against my skin.

Richard strokes and pulls at my pussy lips; he sticks in one finger, then two. "You're soaking wet," he observes. "Too bad you don't like this."

I moan in response and hold my position as he massages my clit with fingers slick from my juices, while grasping the base of the plug with his other hand. "Okay, baby, relax your ass, and I'll ease this sucker out, real slow."

I writhe in delight when he begins to pull, but expelling the wide part makes me pant and moan. The sensation is so intense it's like giving birth to something. I scream as Richard pulls it from me, and erupt into the longest, most powerful orgasm of my life.

Afterward, I lie panting on the bed, overcome with sensation and gratitude for my relationship with Richard, who always knows when and how far to push my limits—and how I'll never go wrong by trusting my top.

"Forgive me for doubting you," I say when I can speak again. "That enormous thing *did* fit in my ass."

Richard grins and kisses me. "Speaking of fitting enormous things inside you, baby, get back on all fours again and stick your ass up high." He rolls on a condom and lubes it up. "There's an orgasm I'm about ready to have."

SIDETRACKED

VK Foxe

The action was automatic, thoughtless. Lewis followed the beautiful blonde running past him with his eyes, his head, and finally a twist of his upper body. The tight-knit fabric of her hot-pink leggings was somehow as alluring as bare skin, and the way her ponytail swung had a hypnotic quality to it. She hadn't even noticed him, alas.

With a heavy sigh, he turned back around, only to discover another attractive trail runner, who wasn't running. When had she come around the bend? How long had she watched him ogling the other girl—how long *had* he stood there stupidly? She had the radiant, light-brown skin of a mixed heritage and wore only skimpy, powder-blue running shorts and a purple sports bra, though she'd crossed her arms in front of her chest.

Her legs and abdomen were tight and toned, but her glare was pure disdain.

Lewis opened his mouth to explain, but what was there to say? He felt his cheeks reddening, and he tried not to make it any worse by staring at this beauty with the same wanting gaze. Too late already.

"Oh? You want some, then?"

How was he supposed to answer that? The woman took two swift steps forward and reached a hand around to grab a handful of his hair, but didn't stop walking. Lewis gasped, speech centers blown out. Sure, he'd been starved for contact, but he'd never expected to be turned on by being hurt—or maybe how she'd taken such a firm, possessive grasp explained his rush of excitement. He stumbled along as she led them off the trail for maybe thirty feet, then shoved him down to his knees behind a large oak.

What was it about being on his knees that made his heart race? Even if she hated him, he relished the focused attention. Did it make him a pervert that he wanted to volunteer to be hurt more, if that's what she wanted? She'd watched his eyes, and she nodded as if recognizing his thoughts having come to where she desired: *penance*.

The nameless goddess hooked her thumbs into her shorts and drove down in a single, violent motion. He'd been expecting her to grab a sharp stick and poke at him in some symbolic reenactment of the male gaze. Instead, Lewis found himself at eye level to her moistened pudenda as she stepped out of her shorts without bothering to remove her running shoes.

With a dancer's grace, she suddenly skipped forward, bounding to catch hold of a branch above them. As she pulled up, her perfect legs wrapped around his head, her sneakers catching him below the shoulder blades, Lewis found himself yanked forward and buried in her thighs. His goddess had been running a while, and she was slick with sweat. "Lick, boy," she said, breathless and excited.

He focused on pleasing her, as she shifted and tightened around him like a serpent. He breathed her in and obeyed, savoring the pungent sweetness and overjoyed at living the difference between penance and punishment. The danger of potential exposure, his bended-knee subservience, and her rough, inconsiderate handling combined to make his chest buzz with excitement. But when she began correcting him, Lewis felt the true sting of humiliation.

"Lower." His inexperience necessitated this. Lewis resolved to thank her for the tutorial by learning so fast for her. "Slower." Her scent was all over his face, all he knew, and he felt drugged by it, but he needed to obey, to focus on that, even as he relished being on his knees serving her. "None of that flicky shit," she snapped. "Savor that clit!"

Once he'd managed a full minute without correction, she dropped back off, shoved him backward, and settled down onto his face. He licked and lapped and zigzagged and sucked with increasing fervor. He would be so good, earn her praise—and maybe her name.

At last her thighs tightened, squeezing out sound, and Lewis worked his frantic tongue inside her while trying to tease her clit with his nose. He felt a sudden splash and drank deep, because there was nothing else to do. After a breath he resumed licking, with a more desperate need to prove he could serve her, making certain to swivel and slide and *appreciate* just as she preferred. He was throbbing and heavy in his jeans, making him wonder if he could climax from pleasing her.

As she'd relaxed in the wake of climax, her thighs came off his ears, and Lewis heard footsteps approaching, crunching too loudly to be on the main trail.

"Eyes," his goddess corrected, and he looked up to meet hers. Sounds weren't his concern. She smiled down at him, lacing fingers into his hair, then pulled him tight against her, breaking his rhythm. She'd taken charge of motion now, rocking a little, so all he could do was stiffen his tongue; he couldn't even breathe, he was too tightly pulled against her! Her sliding across his face lacked even the slightest lifting. Lewis watched her smile widen, wolfish, as she read the recognition of his utter helplessness. She began working herself more roughly against his face as he tried to gasp, receiving only a grinding mask of taut, wet skin.

"Keep that tongue out," she whispered. "Don't falter if you *ever* want to breathe again." Something cold touched his straining erection, though he didn't even remember his pants being undone. Then came a strange pressure, warm hands using a heavy object to work against him, to compress and confine him. Everything felt dreamlike and disjointed, difficult to track as his goddess ruthlessly rode him. Just as he felt himself slipping altogether, she reached a gushing climax that stung his open eyes and forced him to swallow.

As she rose to stand on trembling legs, Lewis was surprised to discover the blonde kneeling behind her. She pierced him with a mischievous glance as something she did made an audible, metallic *snick*. Their laughter made his cock pulse, and only then did he feel, with an intense rush of desire and need, how awkward and trapped his manhood had become. They had locked it into an impossibly confining metal prison. The blonde stood, picking up a tiny pink purse she hadn't had with her when she'd jogged past him. She removed a little note card and dropped it in his general direction as the nameless goddess pulled her running shorts back on.

"We own you now," his goddess said. "But you like that, don't you, pet?"

His face felt hot as he nodded, with both of them staring down at him.

The blonde said, "Wait one week before you call. The cage will make you properly pliant, ready for further training." They laughed again, and then began jogging back toward the trail, away.

Lewis hadn't just been used; he'd been tricked.

Somehow it only made him more desperately hungry
for them, and grateful, as his aching cock strained hope-
lessly against the metal.

MY GEMINI TWIN

Randi Miller

I'm celebrating the twenty-year anniversary of the night two men spanked me. I can remember as if it were yesterday: lying facedown across the white cushioned bench in the living room. Checkered white-and-black linen skirt pulled up around my waist, no panties. My naked breasts swung freely over the edge. My right wrist was handcuffed to the table leg.

My husband, Malik, and I had always experimented in bed. After taking an erotic, soapy shower together, he pounced on the bed, got on his hands and knees, and commanded: "Give me a rim job."

He wagged his big brown booty and spread his cheeks apart. I followed orders. My tongue tickled the soft, sensitive skin outside his asshole. He purred as I licked. His cock extended past his navel as he wedged his butt against my mouth.

"I have an idea," Malik said. "I'm going to spank you."

I pulled away in surprise. We hadn't done this before.

He walked over to his favorite leather chair.

"Angie. Be a good girl. Crawl to me and lie across my lap."

My swollen vulva came to rest on his naked thigh, dousing him with fragrant juices. He reached between my legs and slid a finger into my cunt.

"You're soaking wet! Let's see what happens when I tan your hide."

He pulled his finger out and then slammed my ass. My pussy streamed liquid.

He moved me so my mound pressed against his dick. Then he smacked my ass again. Hard.

"Ouch!" I squirmed. My dark nipples turned to stone as he spanked. And spanked me. He spread my pussy lips apart and stroked my clit. I begged him to let me come.

"No. Turn back over."

I heard a female voice screaming, "More, more," as I hovered above my body, watching myself. What was going on?

"I'm Nikki," she whispered. Who was Nikki?

She's my Gemini twin. When Nikki comes to life, she begs Malik for all the pain and pleasure we can stand. I watch her in awe—I'm there but not there. I can see what's happening, but I don't feel the pain until afterward.

"Get a hairbrush," Nikki said. "I need to be spanked harder."

Malik happily obliged. Her caramel ass turned black and blue. I could see it from my surveillance point.

"Angie. I need to fuck you now."

He carried Nikki to bed and laid her down. He caressed her ass with his stiff cock.

"Oh baby! That made me so hot. I'll probably come the minute I get inside you."

"I'm on the edge myself, honey, so let 'er rip!" Nikki giggled.

He dove into her like a diver searching for a precious pearl. Her inner seas welcomed him as his tool reached its depths. His cock resurfaced to take a breath, then charged again into her dark crevasse. Her pussy gripped him like a black velvet wet suit. She spread her legs wider and he pushed deeper, in and out, growing bigger with every thrust. She wrapped her legs around him as their rivers merged.

When her breathing returned to normal, Nikki disappeared.

Malik said, "Angie, you liked that a lot. I hope it doesn't hurt too bad."

"I'm okay," I said. I didn't tell him about Nikki.

A few nights later, after my bruises had faded, Malik said, "Todd wants to spank you."

"Huh? How does Todd know about that?" I growled.

"It slipped out at happy hour tonight. Just say yes. Try it once."

"Yes."

"He's waiting outside. I'll call him in. Take the drinks and wait in the living room."

I chose a spot on the comfy couch. Malik sat on my left and Todd on my right. Todd watched intensely as Malik kissed me and fondled my breasts through my blouse. He took off my shirt and my bra.

"Go ahead and cop a feel, man. It's okay, right, honey?"

I nodded.

Todd put both hands on my boobs, kneading them and brushing his hands against my nipples. He kissed me. I moaned. Malik twisted my left nipple. Todd bit the right. I had two handsome men sucking my breasts and the promise of a spanking. Todd reached down to play with my clit. My pussy juices flowed.

Malik unzipped his pants. Todd did too.

"Suck Todd's dick, Angie. Show him your skills."

Malik stroked himself and I lapped at Todd's hard white cock like a thirsty cat. I swirled my tongue around the tip and inside the hole. I sucked him. I licked his balls. Malik pointed to the bench in front of the fireplace.

"Go lie across the bench. Now!" Malik demanded.

He pulled my skirt up around my waist, the checkered white-and-black linen one. He removed my panties. He scooted me forward until my breasts hung down, ripe to be plucked. He asked if I wanted the handcuffs. My legs dangled.

"Go ahead, Todd. Spank her."

A couple of hard thwacks and Nikki showed up. I tried to talk but couldn't. My role became voyeur.

"Let's get her ass on fire. She loves it."

Each hand smack left an imprint on Nikki's burnt-sugar ass.

"Can I lick her pussy?" Todd asked.

"Of course," Malik said. He peppered her reddened bottom with kisses while Todd dined on her pussy.

"Do you want to come in Todd's mouth?" Nikki nodded. Malik punished her again.

"No. You don't come until Todd does. He spanked your ass like a pro and you need to give him a reward. Suck him off and swallow. I'm going to fuck your brains out."

Todd took the hint and stuck his cock in Nikki's mouth. She opened her lips wide. Malik pushed his long, dark cock into her sex.

"Baby. Your ass is a mess! You won't be able to sit down tomorrow."

Nikki didn't care about that. She drank Todd's come and shrieked like a banshee when she and Malik exploded. She waved good-bye when she left.

In the morning, my ass looked like Jackson Pollock had flung pots of purple, red, and blue on it. I admired it in the mirror and smiled.

Why am I celebrating this day? Because nothing like that ever happened again. I got divorced, and these days I'm dating.

I can still get myself off thinking about it though! And if I'm lucky, I'll find another man who likes to spank. Nikki and my ass are ready!

CHOKER

Rachel Kramer Bussel

One of the reasons I love Raul so much is that he knows exactly how to push my buttons, and doesn't mind that one of the best ways of doing so is stuffing my mouth full of cock. He gets that I don't just love *giving* blow jobs—to him and occasionally other men—but that I love being *made to give* them, the rougher, the better. Before him, I'd been with more than a few who just couldn't take my cravings, who found them unseemly or over the top—but not Raul.

The first time I went down on him, I wasn't sure how to convey this predilection. But the way I started moaning and opening my throat the moment he tugged my hair and stroked my cheek, then got louder when he pressed my head down so the head hit the back of my throat, clued him in. It was glorious to simply become a vessel for his passion. When he held me tight as he came, I loved every gagging second—not to mention the delightful spanking he delivered afterward as my reward.

Now, we've got things down almost to a routine. Blow jobs aren't just foreplay for us, they're often the main event, though he usually lets me use a vibrator or wear a butt plug while I'm giving one. But last night, he surprised me. No, it wasn't an anniversary or birthday, just a regular old Tuesday night, but it felt like a celebration of everything good in this world.

First, he made dinner: a delicious Cobb salad, served with champagne. They may not seem like they go together, but with Raul, they certainly did. He made me walk around the table to him to get the champagne, which he poured directly from the flute into my mouth. Sometimes it dribbled down my chin, but that was okay—did I mention I was naked? He licked up every spilled drop, giving my nipples a pinch whenever that happened.

When dinner was over, he said, "Get in position." I knew what that meant, of course. He'd pulled his chair out from the table, turned it around, and taken out his cock. I crawled around the table this time, my hard nipples hanging low. When I got there, he tied my hands behind my back and guided my tongue up and down his length. He knows I both love this act of tender licking and that it drives me mad—because I want the whole thing down my throat, as soon as humanly possible.

"Oh, don't worry, Colleen, you're going to get everything you want and more," he said with a wicked, beautiful laugh while I could do nothing more but press my tongue against his hot, hard skin. Mewling sounds of desire started in my throat, but I only made the merest of sounds, knowing that not only was he aware of exactly what I wanted, but he'd make me wait the more I begged. Some tops love the act of begging, but my Raul simply likes to know that I'm begging on the inside.

When I thought I'd just about collapse with my need, my pussy clenched so tight I wasn't even sure if his cock could fit there should he change course, he guided me up for a deep kiss, his lips bruising mine before he gave me a slap across the face that made tears and a smile leap to my face.

Raul untied my wrists, and then made me crawl ahead of him up the stairs, until I was once again kneeling, this time on the bed, blindfolded. Having won back the use of my hands, I wrapped them around his shaft, guiding them up and down. But within a few minutes, he'd instructed me to squeeze his balls, and was slamming his dick in and out of my mouth, the way we both like it.

That's when I felt it—fingers probing my pussy. I held back my startled reaction, because an even more urgent one was rushing on its heels—sheer arousal. The other times we'd played with other people, it had always been prearranged by both of us. Clearly, this was a special treat for me. "I didn't tell you to stop," Raul growled, giving my hair an extra-hard tug as he pulled me up, while the unknown person's fingers not only plunged deeper, but also played with my clit.

I didn't try to figure out who it was by sound cues, I simply let myself choke on Raul's dick. I can't truly say I was "swallowing" it because that would involve far more agency than my husband was giving me. He was fucking my mouth, plain and simple, while his accomplice tried to either distract me or enhance the experience.

No sooner was I grooving to this new triple play than Raul lifted me up, and then said, "Since you like dick so much, I brought you another one—and he's bigger than me." I lost it then, coming against the fat fingers that were deep inside my pussy.

"And no, don't even ask, because I'm not going to tell you whose cock you're about to suck. All you need to know is that I want to watch." Then I was turned around and given a pillow for my knees, as a hand I was pretty sure wasn't Raul's gripped my long hair this time.

"I was told you're the best," a voice I didn't recognize said. Then all of a sudden the biggest cock my mouth had ever met was probing my lips. I struggled to open wide enough, all too aware by now that there was no way on earth even a blow-job queen like me could swallow it all. Those familiar tears—of pleasure, of want, of challenge—rose up as I did manage to get some of it inside. "That's it, that's what I want," the man said as he pushed himself just a little bit deeper.

I took intense breaths through my nose, heady with

the high of having two men at once, when I felt something I'd know anytime, anywhere—Raul's cock, this time at the entrance to my pussy. I'd been wet as could be since dinner, so he slid right in.

This was another first. Sure, we'd had threesomes with both men and women, but I'd never gotten fucked while having a cock in my mouth. Having Raul inside me unlocked something for me. I was able to take more of the stranger than before, even before he pressed my head down.

No, I never managed to have the head hit the back of my throat as I do with Raul, but I got pretty darn close. I knew it was safe to swallow his come, so I did, also taking Raul's warm burst. I was placed on my back on the bed, but I never got to say thank you. When Raul finally took the blindfold off, the stranger was gone. But that was okay—my mouth was very happy, and I made sure Raul knew it all night long.

THE
FRAMEWORK
OF FANTASY

Sonni de Soto

Are you ready?"

Nerves churn in my stomach but my gaze never falters.

"Ready."

I tell you no; you do it anyway.

I shove you; you push back.

I try to scream; you seal my lips with yours, swallowing the sound.

Your fingers are unrelenting inside me. Each thrust of your rough hand pounds against my soft sex, reverberating through my whole body.

I raise my leg to strike, power surging as I bend my knee. But, when I kick, you catch my sole in your palm.

My body jerks. I bite back a shrieking laugh.

"Yellow." The sound squeaks out as my ticklish foot, trapped by your fingers, recoils.

"Sorry." You let go, wincing at the break in scene.

I give a small shake of my head, hoping to hold it together. "Green."

You nod, a relieved smile flashing before it's replaced by yet another finger driving deeper within me. Stretching me farther, you claim more space as your own, leaving me gasping at the loss of my body, bit by bit, to you.

"So, even though you'll tell me to stop, I *shouldn't* stop." You look at me like my words—like I—don't make sense. Like I'm crazy.

I know.

I'm sorry.

Sitting next to you on the couch, I shake my head. "If I say 'stop,' it's just part of the scene."

Frustrated, you shake your head. "Then how will I know if you, you know, *actually* want me to stop?"

I touch your knee. "That's what the safewords are for." I know this is hard for you. That I'm asking a lot of you.

I bet, when you'd asked me about my greatest fantasy, you were hoping it was anal or swinging or exhibitionism.

Sometimes, I wish it were too.

My voice cracks as I say, "Stop."

I feel your hand against my face. "Color?" Your voice is quiet, unsure.

I turn my face with a slight shake, my scent still strong as it clings to your fingers. "Green." I struggle beneath you while your semi-hard length smacks limply against my thighs. I push you; I don't need your softness. "Green."

Nostrils flaring, you grunt and nod. Your hand snakes around my wrist, my arousal slicking the twist of skin.

I sink my teeth into my lips, biting back the urge to beg you to stop. I want to scream it, but the muffled sound groans low in my throat.

You won't stop.

My mind centers on that thought, my other hand straining against the hard plane of your chest.

I just know it.

"I don't think I can do this." You pace our kitchen, from silverware to canned goods. "I've been thinking about it, and I just don't see how this is going to work." Pausing, you lean against the sink. "One of the best parts of sex is watching you get off."

I turn the stove down to a low simmer before facing you. "I'll still be getting off." That's the point.

"But it won't look like it." You shift your weight from foot to foot. "Will it?"

I purse my lips thoughtfully before sitting us down at the dinner table. "That depends." We've been together for a year and a half now. "You know my body." Better than anyone else. "You know, without words, how my breath hitches and my toes curl when I'm about to come. You know how my hands clench and my hips hitch. You know how hot—how wet—I can get at your touch."

Your gaze traces my body, remembering every hint and sign of my arousal. Desire sparks in your eyes before you shut them and shake your head. "I'm just not sure."

I cover your hand with mine. "So, we'll wait until you are."

My fantasy is to feel the force of your body on mine, but I never want to force that on you. "We'll wait."

I choke on a breath. The scent of your sweat, your skin, mixes with mine, infusing the room. It fills my nose, my lungs. I feel you in my pores, seeping into my blood.

Your thick length grinds along the lips of my sex, hardening with each pressing pass. You grip your shaft between us to plant it at my opening. I inhale sharply and wait for your thrust.

"Green?"

"Green."

My breath heaves out at your fullness surging into me, the sound helpless and inevitable in my ears. With each buck, you overtake me. My body. My senses. My thoughts. You plunge and push until I'm more aware of you than me, my receptive body a ripple raging against the brunt of yours. Lost to instinct, I cling to you and cry out, losing myself in the crashing swell of you.

* * *

You've been staring at me through the bathroom door while I floss my teeth. "Why this?"

Sighing, I toss the string in the trash. We've been having this conversation for weeks now.

Not that I mind, I remind myself.

Of course I don't.

This is how fantasy becomes reality. As awkward and uncomfortable as this is, it's what will make the experience, when it finally happens—*if* it happens—all the better.

So, I join you on the edge of our bed.

Look, I *know* I shouldn't like this.

Consensual non-consent.

Rape play.

It's so wrong. Disturbing and probably disrespectful. God knows I would never actually want to be raped. Would never wish that kind of violation on anyone.

Yet.

I frown, shaking my head and shrugging. "There's something about someone taking control of me, taking control *from* me. Someone forcing me out of myself and making me feel." I close my eyes and let the words I've guarded inside pour out. "I want someone's desire to overpower me, to be so big it consumes me. I want it to be so strong it reaches inside me and forces some unseen side of my desire out."

"And our regular sex doesn't do that for you?"

My eyes open at the sad tone in your voice. No.

That's not what I mean. "Our sex is wonderful." Always. "This is just…" I shrug. "A fantasy." One I would only trust to someone like you. Someone who loves me and understands that, even within a fantasy that plays with erasing my pleasure, this is all about my desire. All about transcendentally finding myself by getting lost in you.

But, at the end of the day… "I don't need this." Not if you don't want it. "I need you."

"But you want this?" You say it as if the words are an endless echo in your brain. "You want this."

I shrug. "I'd like to see what this fantasy is like. With you."

Furrowing your brow, you look down at the bed. You're so quiet, but I can almost hear every conversation we've ever had about this replay in your head. Our whole history spreads out silently between us.

Under the weight of all those words, I worry.

Then you look up, your face set. "Are you ready?"

I blink blankly. Slowly, almost disbelieving, I grin and nod. Even though nerves churn in my stomach, my gaze never falters. "Ready."

MORE

Michael in Texas

'll give you a while to think about that," he says. "Think about where I'll spank next." Then he drapes the tawse across the bench in front of my right hand and walks away behind me. The carpet muffles his footsteps; I can't tell where he is. Is he standing there looking at me?

I'm on the rails—that's our name for it. The first time we tried this elevated elbows-and-knees position, the benches were crossways to my body—both elbows on the same bench, and the same for my knees. It was uncomfortable, even though he padded the wood benches with folded bath towels, but I felt secure.

But the next time we tried it, he turned the benches so my left elbow and knee were on one bench, right elbow and knee on the other. Same position—entirely different effect. I felt vulnerable. And he could tell. Was my breathing faster? He knew somehow. We've done it that way ever since. Soft cotton ropes at wrists, elbows, knees, and ankles hold me in place. Each time, he moves the benches slightly farther apart—my thighs are at almost a right angle to each other tonight.

We use other positions—spread-eagle on the bed, faceup or facedown; bent over a chair—but this is our favorite. I'm almost always tied up nowadays—my struggles to stay in position are over, and I don't miss them or the extra swats I received for moving.

Where will he spank next? Oddly, that's not what I think about. Is it a form of defiance not to think about what he intended me to? At the thought of this inward rebellion, I feel the corners of my lips curl up.

I think about how we got here. He introduced me to spanking playfully, almost a year ago. I discovered I was into it. Gradually, I realized he was all the way into it. But at first it was all implicit. Except for telling me my safeword and how to use it—which he whispered in my ear, as if reluctant to break the spell of our unacknowledged role-play—we never discussed what we were doing explicitly. He gave orders or made requests; I complied or I didn't. I always got spanked either way, though the spankings for which I gave him excuses were harder. We never discussed the why.

Then one night four months ago he asked me to dinner, rather than over to his place to play. Partway through the meal, he said, "I love playing with you," and for a split second, I thought he was breaking up with me. I even had time to wonder how I'd find another playmate like him, because I did *not* want to give up spanking. It's amazing how fast the mind works, because he hadn't paused, and when he continued, "and I want to keep doing it," I felt a jolt of relief in my chest. I hadn't realized how much I'd come to need him until that moment. "We can go on just as we have if that's what you want," he said. "But there's more."

More. I felt the horizon expand and the earth drop from under my feet in the same moment, with the possibility of an undefined more. And then I was back in the restaurant, and I smiled and said, "I'd like to discuss more."

So now here I am, sweating, struggling to support myself on these damned benches that I love so much, stomach heaving as I try to catch my breath and stop crying, because he's been whipping my ass with that damned tawse that I love so much—and now I'm supposed to wonder where he'll spank next.

He showed me a photo once of what I look like in this position—well, not quite this spread, but about the same. I had no idea I could look that sexy. Ass in the air, asscheeks spread—hell, *I'd* fuck me, and I'm not a lesbian. I made sure he deleted the photo.

That was another thing that changed after that night in the restaurant. Until then, he'd fingered me and made me climax, but he'd never fucked me.

Marking me was my idea. He prides himself on being

able to leave my ass sore without marking it. But we talk about things more openly now, so I asked him for marks. He caned me, lovely railroad tracks all over my ass, perfect parallel welts. I asked if I could fellate him to thank him, and he accepted. Now I have welts on my body half the time.

It was a big deal six months ago when he asked me to take off my panties before I came from the office to his house. I haven't worn panties at all the last three months.

And earlier tonight, for the first time, he told me to undress outside. It was on his back porch; no one could see. But I removed my dress and bra (he let me keep my shoes—this time) and handed them through the doorway, and he left me on the porch. Through the storm door I watched him carefully fold my clothes and set them aside before letting me indoors. It was only twenty or thirty seconds; no one saw. But I almost climaxed just from standing there.

More. How much more is there? There's nothing vicious in him; I know I have nothing to fear. This is a journey we're taking together. But how much more?

"Had enough rest, little one?" he asks as he comes up behind me.

I'm an assistant manager. I have four clerks under me. If anyone else called me "little one" my reply would burn his eyebrows off. When he says it, it makes me weak. And wet.

Then he picks up the tawse, and I see the vibrator

in his hand. Oh, dammit, not that again. He's going to whip my pussy and vibrate it. I never know how much of each. He'll whip me four or five times, barely touch it with the vibe, then whip it four or five more times. Or he'll give me one hard swat, vibrate me for thirty seconds, one hard swat, then a minute of vibe. I'm going to be bawling and climaxing until I can't hold myself up anymore, and then he'll take mercy on me and fuck me till neither of us can do *that* anymore.

I hear the swish of leather through air and then a loud slap. Fuck, that hurts.

More. I want more. I don't know what it is, but I want it.

CINNAMON

Lazuli Jones

S it on the bed. No, not like that. Sit on the other side. Excellent, Miranda. Good girl."

I slid along the bedspread until my body faced the object resting on that side of the bed. The long silk negligee, on loan from Lady Grey, was cool and slippery against my skin. I squirmed, avoiding the object, craning my neck to keep my eyes on Lady Grey.

She was tall, taller than I'd thought, and gorgeous. Mocha skin, curly hair, her eyes smoky and her lips garnet red. A confident figure in her lace and corset. She held a small riding crop in her gloved hand and pointed it at me.

"Don't look at me. Look over there. *Now*."

I gulped and not for the first time tonight, the word *cinnamon* formed in my mouth. Lady Grey had let me choose the safeword and I'd chosen something cute and safe. I could end this at any time. She'd promised me. I'd promised myself.

I looked. In front of me was a wide, full-length mirror. My eyes landed on the negligee draped across my lap and skirted past my face to find Lady Grey's eyes. My heart pounded. She looked pleased.

"You're doing great, pet," she purred. She knelt on the bed. The warm leather of the riding crop tapped my shoulder. "Take this off. Don't stop until you're tits-out, or you'll be punished."

I could do this. I pulled the straps from my shoulders, letting the negligee fall, baring my chest. It was off-putting, but I could handle this part. Lady Grey had done me a great service earlier: while discussing what I wanted from tonight, while letting me sip some tea and choose my safeword, she'd done something she rarely did for clients, and unlaced her corset.

When I looked in the mirror now, I saw my breasts, the dusky nipples, and the fading scars from my augmentation. Hers had looked the same.

"Touch them," she commanded. *Cinnamon* wandered in my head before I obeyed and cupped my breasts, brushed my nipples. A flicker of arousal ignited between my legs and I squirmed on the bed, wanting more, wanting less.

As though sensing the crucial window of opportunity, Lady Grey tapped the riding crop against my hair. My eyes followed the movement, caught her eyes, caught her deliberate pause. "Now strip. Don't make me punish you, Miranda. Do as I say."

My hands shook. My fingers sweated against the fabric of the negligee. I hiked it up instead of pulling it down, technically disobeying Lady Grey's command to strip, but still in the spirit of what she wanted. I pulled the fabric up my thighs, up my hips, shimmying on the bed until the silk was pooled around my waist.

Lady Grey lightly smacked my left thigh. "Spread them. Foot on the bed."

Cinnamon...

I planted my left heel on the bed, my eyes always on the Dominatrix behind me. She placed the riding crop against the black curls of my hair and sternly said, "Don't you look at *me*, Miranda. Do you need to be spanked to obey me? Look at that gorgeous pussy of yours."

My eyes flickered across the mirror, half-focusing on the dark points of my nipples as they bounced up and down under my heaving breaths. The cool air hit my pussy and I was warm and aroused but *the pain* and *the stitches* and I *knew* it wasn't going to look perfect right after the surgery but I wasn't expecting so much swelling and it felt numb and the skin didn't look right and the stitches and *no one* told me I'd feel like this and—

"Cinna—"

The riding crop lifted from my hair. In the mirror I saw Lady Grey's body language shift, waiting for me to finish the word, ready to end everything. The negligee was sweaty in my palm.

"Breathe, Miranda. Good girl."

The game was still on as long as the word didn't spill from my lips, and as a Dominatrix commanded me to breathe with her honey-warm voice, I did. I relaxed. Lady Grey had opened more than her corset earlier. We were the same.

I looked.

She followed my gaze and smiled. My pussy looked small, the curls tight and tiny. It wasn't swollen anymore. The stitches were gone. I could barely see any scars. I was looking at it.

"Touch your gorgeous pussy," Lady Grey whispered in my ear. I jumped, almost forgetting her presence, feeling guilty at the thought. I wouldn't have gotten this far without her ordering me to do it. "Touch it until you come."

I'd barely looked at it in the last year, let alone touched it. *Cinnamon* tickled my tongue but I swallowed it, letting the tapping of Lady Grey's riding crop on my wrist goad me to action. I put my palm flat against my pussy, releasing a small sigh. It felt good. I'd read some books and some forum posts about how to go about masturbating now, but none of that mattered at this moment. I touched myself, slid my fingers along the folds, the numbness gone—I hadn't even realized it was gone—and found what had become my clit. Touching it sent little electric tingles up my pelvis. My chest heaved, not with panic this time, but with passion. I barely noticed when Lady Grey took my hand for a brief moment, rubbed a sweet-smelling lube on my fingers, and let me go back to myself.

I touched and rubbed, my wrist moving quickly in a motion I was learning for the first time, my fingers a blur, feeling myself swell, warm and wet, the tingles growing until the heat of unfamiliar orgasm bubbled between my legs. I panted, shivered, pushed out an expletive or two, and when the delicious pleasure faded, Lady Grey was there behind me, supporting my back, supporting me.

"Good girl, Miranda," she purred. "Good girl…"

1,000 WORDS

LN Bey

*D*ear Ellen—

Thank you for submitting "1,000 Words" for consideration for my anthology. However, it is not quite what I am looking for at this time. While your narrative is interesting and even hot, I am currently looking for fictional stories rather than memoir or nonfiction.

Best regards,
Editor

And P.S.—So sorry! ;)

Dear Editor:

This is not so much a story as a confession. I know that
sounds like one of those "Forum" letters, but allow me
to explain, and please, know that it is imperative that
you publish this.

I'll start from the beginning:

When Stephen and I first realized we were both kinky,
he told me that he wasn't the gruff, whiskery, alpha-
male type Dom that so many women fantasize about;
he was more the strict-music-teacher type, which certain
other women fantasize about. Women like me, who have
always been in thrall to meticulous—not "fussy"—men
with exacting erotic standards.

When we play, he is (or pretends to be) cold, analyt-
ical—yet he pays extremely close attention to me, eval-
uating my posture while naked, my politeness when
serving him, my enthusiasm while sucking his cock. He
assesses every detail of my body, behavior, and performance as he puts me through my paces, then tallies up
the day before he rewards me for my successes—and
Jesus, does he—or punishes me for failures. (And Jesus,
does he.)

Of course, even the punishments end with a solid
fucking, me bound, beaten, and begging for more until I
am so wrecked and exhausted I fall asleep in his arms—
but that's beside the point right now.

Where was I? Oh yes. My reason for writing this.

One of his strictest rules, and mine as well, is that *no*

one can know. We both live in conservative neighbor-hoods, have conservative jobs. What we do—the cuffs, the whips, the discipline—stays between *us*. On that we've completely agreed, from day one.

Until we didn't. *I* didn't.

If only he hadn't told me to wear my collar to that office holiday party, underneath my turtleneck.

Damn that Sheila for asking. No, damn *me* for answering. She was noticing the subtlest things (and how did she know to look? I should have asked myself)—that I was walking just slightly behind him at the party, that I kept my hands demurely clasped. My posture.

"Okay, what's up with you two?" she asked me in the ladies' room. She was leaning against the washbasin, lighting a cigarette against company rules. Of course, her husband owned the company. There was a gleam in her eye—she knew; she also likely knew I was half-drunk.

"You can't tell *anyone*," I said.

She crossed her heart.

I turned down the collar of my turtleneck and showed her the collar he had me wear to remind me that I was his—black leather with a symbolic silver loop.

I expected a giggle, a jaw dropped in amazement.

Instead she gave me a very...*knowing* look, one that only Stephen had ever given me.

"Well now, isn't that an interesting thing," she said, put out her cigarette under the faucet, and walked out.

Fuck.

"Anything you'd like to add?" Stephen said, back at his house. As we did every Friday night, I stood before his desk like a recalcitrant schoolgirl, only naked. And, as always, he sat behind the desk, his ledger book in front of him. This was part of our game that I found so oddly cold and hot at the same time—he saw it as his duty to tabulate the blows that would shortly be applied to my bare ass by either the flogger, if my transgressions were minor, or the cane, if they were major.

I really, really hate the cane.

"No, Stephen."

"How *could* you?" he said, angry.

Did I mention I hate the cane?

"I'm sorry!" I said. "She *knew*. She could tell. I thought she was...a soul mate." I was still a little drunk; I really didn't want to have to go through all this. Couldn't we just commence with the caning and fucking?

"She's my boss's soul mate!"

"I'm sorry." I went ahead and bent over the desk, pressed my breasts against its hard surface; my nipples hardened against the cool varnished wood. I stepped up on my toes, as he expected—my ass was presented high, ready for the beating. I gripped the edge of the desktop and waited.

"This is bigger than the cane, Ellen. You broke *the* rule."

"I know."

He walked around the desk, ran his hand down my back to my hip.

"Do you know what they want to do?"

"Who?" I asked.

"Ron and Sheila, who else?" He squeezed my ass, hard.

"No."

"They are very intrigued. They would like to see you in action, in the playroom, since I pretty much had to admit I have one. You hanging by your wrists seems to be Ron's preoccupation. How many whips I have, is Sheila's."

"What? No! Stephen, please. We have a *rule*."

"Yes we did, didn't we…"

Shit.

"I'm so sorry!"

"Yes, I know you are. And you'll be even more so, receiving your caning in front of two strangers, won't you? Well, almost strangers, anyway."

"Stephen…"

"Lessons must be learned, my dear, you know how things work."

"You're enjoying the idea!"

He shrugged.

He was still caressing my presented behind. The thought of being whipped—*caned*—in front of his boss and Sheila…

I lowered my face in embarrassment. His ledger was still open on the desk, just inches away. I looked at the columns of numbers, the neatly written words, all charges against me.

"Mr. Landon?" I said, much more formal. Perhaps if I could keep steering him into schoolteacher mode.

"Yes, Ellen?"

"Isn't there...some other way, for me to learn my lesson?"

He sat down on the desktop.

"Such as?"

"Maybe...I could write an essay, a paper. You know, like 'What I Did This Summer.' Only...what I did wrong tonight, and how sorry I am."

He looked up, deep in thought.

"Hm. That's an interesting suggestion. One thousand words, perhaps? On how very, very sorry you are."

"Yes! And of course, I'd still accept the cane, if you want." Better now, than in front of anyone else.

He nodded absentmindedly.

"Mm-hm. I like this idea. Yes. You'll write it right now, bent over the desk. No cane will be necessary, tonight, but I'm adding a little incentive to make sure you take it seriously."

"Anything! Anything but a public whipping."

Even if "public" meant two.

"Ah. Well, that's the incentive, my dear. You'll write it, and be as truthful as possible."

"Of course."

"And you'll publish it."

"What?"

"We'll find an anthology of those filthy stories you like, and you'll send it in."

"Oh. Okay. I'll have to think of a pen name…"

"No. You broke our rule and exposed me. Now you'll expose yourself, one way or another. Sounds fair, doesn't it?"

"I guess it does." *One way or—?*

"Because here's the thing: if it *doesn't* get accepted and published…"

"Yes?"

"Then Ron and Sheila will get that show they're requesting."

THE SOUND OF SILENCE

Lucy Felthouse

Yvette!" Jack snapped. "Are you even listening to what I'm saying?"

"Yes, Sir!" I'd only missed a bit. Maybe a couple of words. And it wasn't my fault.

"So what's the problem? Are you uncomfortable? Would you like a cushion?"

"No, Sir. I'm fine, thank you. It's just…" As another noise filtered in through the double glazing, I was unable to stop my gaze slipping in that direction.

"What—?" Jack strode past me, all stompy and masterful.

I allowed myself a shiver of pleasure at his demeanor. He was sexy when he was grumpy, though naturally I didn't enjoy it when he was grumpy with *me*.

He peered out the window to see what had distracted

me. "Neighbor is mowing his lawn, that's all. Can't very well go round there and complain about that, can I?" he muttered.

Jack stepped back in front of me. "The window is closed, Yvette. I can't really do any more than that." He shrugged.

"It's okay, Sir. He'll be done soon. I can ignore it. It's not that loud." Ever since he'd given me that *look* and ordered me into the bedroom, my pussy had ached, and I had yearned for his orders, to do his bidding. To please him. I certainly didn't want to *dis*please him by allowing the next-door bloody neighbor's garden maintenance to get in the way of our scene, but it'd be tough to remain entirely focused with that racket going on.

"Hmm. All right, then. Let's continue. So, where were we?"

I hoped like hell that was a rhetorical question, because I'd been distracted enough by the noise outside that I hadn't, in fact, heard all of what he'd said. I bowed my head and waited, mentally keeping my fingers crossed that Jack would answer his own question. Luckily for me, he did.

"Come here, take out my cock, and suck it."

"Yes, Sir!" I almost got carpet burns on my knees as I eagerly shuffled forward. I reached out and undid his zipper. Slipping my right hand through the gap, I maneuvered until my fingers closed around his shaft— which was rigid, red-hot, and irresistible.

Carefully, I popped his cock out through the

opening in his boxers and trousers, where it stood proudly, looking just as tempting as it felt. All purple and swollen, raring to go. Licking my lips, I pumped my fist up and down his length a couple of times, before closing my mouth around his glans. Immediately, the delicious, musky, salty taste of him hit my taste buds. I hummed happily and prepared to start sinking farther onto him.

Just then, a high-pitched roaring sound reached my ears.

Jack picked up on my flinch. Stepping back—and slipping his dick out of my mouth in the process—he exclaimed, "Oh, for heaven's sake! It's really distracting you, isn't it?"

I sat back on my heels and pouted. "I'm sorry, Sir! I can't not hear. If I could switch my ears off, trust me, I would."

Jack's expression softened. "Hey, it's okay. It's not your fault. It's just…kinda ruining what we've got going on here."

I bit my lip. "Yeah, I know. But what are we supposed to do about it?"

Jack opened his mouth to reply, then closed it again. I could almost see the lightbulb appear above his head. Quickly, he tucked himself away, then turned and headed for the door, throwing over his shoulder, "Back in a minute."

I frowned, wondering what the hell he was up to.

Fortunately, I didn't have to wonder for long. Jack

soon returned, grinning broadly. "I've got the solution to our problem, my love."

"Y—you have?" He didn't seem to have anything with him—but wait, maybe he did. His right hand was closed, as though holding something.

"Yep. *Voila!*" He lowered his hand to my eye level, then opened it. Sitting on his palm were two tiny metal things, with black rubbery-looking ends.

"Wha—are they earplugs?"

"In a manner of speaking, yes. But they're so much better than the regular kind. Put these in and you won't hear a thing."

Tentatively, I scooped them off of his hand. "But that means I won't be able to hear you speak. I won't know what you want me to do."

Jack's grin widened. "I'm sure I can make myself understood. Shall we give it a go?"

"Yeah…all right."

He explained how to fit the plugs, then waited while I did so.

One ear done; already the world's volume had been turned down. When I popped in the second, it was indeed as though my ears had been switched off. It was bizarre—I could hear myself breathing and swallowing, but otherwise…nothing.

Jack waved, drawing my attention. He put up his thumbs and arranged his face into a question.

I nodded.

He gave a curt nod back, and smiled. Then he

gestured toward his crotch, raised an eyebrow. He'd been right—he could make himself understood.

I soon had my husband's shaft in my mouth once more. This time, though, there were no distractions. I poured my entire being into sucking and stroking Jack's luscious dick. He was my only focus—nothing else mattered. Nothing else *existed*. The downside was that I couldn't hear any sounds he made, any moans, groans, expletives.

But that made me all the more aware of his other reactions: the tensing of his thighs, the jerk of his hips, the hands he'd fisted in my hair. Each subtle twitch, the increase of precome seeping onto my tongue, told me he was growing ever closer to climax. And I was ready.

Suddenly, as I bobbed up and down on his saliva-slick shaft, Jack froze. His hands tightened in my hair, sending sparks of pain dancing across my scalp. Then his cock twitched between my lips, and juices flooded my mouth. I swallowed them down happily, eagerly, buzzing with delight and arousal at his climax, secretly hoping I might soon be allowed one of my own.

I carried on swallowing and gently sucking until Jack's climax abated, then let his cock slip from my mouth. Looking up at him, I pointed to my ears, raising my eyebrows in query.

He nodded.

Carefully, I removed the plugs, immediately missing the quiet.

Jack asked, "How was it for you?"

"Totally amazing! I missed not being able to hear you, but I was so aware of everything else, how you moved, how you felt—"

"Good. But you can't keep them. I need them for work." He held out his hand.

I narrowed my eyes. "Well, then, you'd better order me some, hadn't you?"

"Consider it done. And just think what it'll be like if I spank, whip, or flog you while you're wearing them." He gave me a wicked grin. "You won't be able to hear what's coming, or when."

The thought made my heart race, and my mouth went dry. Clumsily, I pushed the plugs into Jack's outstretched hand. "Go. Now," I said, not even caring that I wasn't supposed to be the one giving orders. "And for god's sake, pay the extra for express delivery."

WARNING

Valerie Alexander

This is how it starts. It's just the two of you—in your bedroom, in the dead of night. All those exciting new toys are there, the leather cuffs and leash and collar, the state-of-the-art thigh restraints, maybe even bondage furniture if you've splurged. But those other comforts are there too: your pillows, your bedside clock, and the button-down you wore to work that day. Signifiers of a banality that you can step back into at any moment, if you need to.

But of course you don't need that, you're on fire for each other. You slap his face, pull on his leash until you're trembling as hard as he is. It's no longer a game. He's lost in submissive euphoria as soon as the spreader bar locks around his ankles. Kissing him, you bite his lips until pain shoots to his cock and stiffens it. *I'm not taking anything up my ass,* he announces early on and you respect that limit until you notice over the summer how his ass keeps rising up like an offer at certain moments. So you present a ridiculous ultimatum: if he fails to obey, his beautiful ass is yours for the plundering. He agrees, then fails to obey. And presents himself for defilement.

You're the only ones who know. There's a wall between your scenes and your daily life. But the wall starts to disintegrate on the day you force him to wear your black underwear to work, or maybe it breaks through with a crash when the neighbors watch from their upstairs window as you order him to crawl around your backyard. He keeps his eyes downcast when you run into them at the neighborhood block party, the humiliation making him hard right there—harder, after you casually insult him—and then you hustle him back home, where you bind his hands and tell him how the neighbors are laughing at him, mocking what a weak and desperate slave he is. And he comes without being touched.

"You're a joke," you tell him as you strip off his jeans in the laundry room. "A pathetic spectacle." But what you're really thinking is that this is getting out of control.

You can't stop fucking him in the shower, up against the tiles with a knife at his throat. He's so luscious to behold when he's tied to a chair, gagged and hard as you rumple his hair. You like the captive stoicism of him in chains, silent and pouting beautifully. You like the reddish marks imprinted on his skin. You love the way his eyes go dreamy when you take out the black rubber slapper. The way he grunts with relief the first time it cracks against his skin.

He doesn't know who he is anymore. You don't know who you're becoming.

Autumn arrives in a shower of scarlet leaves. In the firelight, him painting your toenails or serving as your footstool, there begin to be things unsaid. *Are you mine? How far would you go for me? How much can I hurt you?* His thigh muscles look more sculpted when he rakes your front yard. Maybe he's working out for you, you don't know, but you do know you love the uxorious votary he is becoming: bringing you gifts, pouring your iced chai, rubbing your feet. This wasn't part of the map you thought you were following as a couple but it's rising up in both of you like a fever. His devotion, your expectations.

You walk toward him naked in spike heels. An uncertain smile; your favorite kind. You kiss him. He knows enough by now not to kiss you back, that his mouth is yours to command. You're so tender with him. Then you push him to his knees and fuck his mouth, his fingers moving inside you until that feral hunger in your blood goes electric and you ejaculate into his mouth. "Hold it," you command—and he does. You leave him like that, with a hard dick and a mouth full of your come.

Because his happiness is yours to dispense and dismiss, and you want him to remember that.

But later you give him everything, because he is so very beautiful and obedient after all. "My lovestruck little bitch," you say, tracing the imprint of your teeth on the back of his neck, where earlier you bit him like a mother wolf disciplining her cub. The next day, you order the barber to cut the soft curls hiding his nape so your ownership can be seen.

His hair is still short for his office Christmas party, which is at a fancy hotel downtown. Dancing in the bluish lights while an orchestra plays, his body shakes as he holds you tight and his cock presses against you. It's been months now since you fell together down the rabbit hole into this dark wonderland and nothing will be stable again, everyone else shrinking as the two of you grow more enormous in each other's eyes. Blotting out the world until all that's left is a private temple of beautiful cruelty.

Up to the room where you order him to strip and get on the hotel bed on all fours. His body looks like marble in the diffuse city lights. He looks so trusting that you don't quite know how to be worthy of him. You don't know how to deserve this invitation to subjugate him, own him, control his worship. That's the night you bind his wrists to his ankles so he's on his knees facing the hotel room mirror while you slowly fuck his ass from behind. He stares at his reflection as if he's in a white-hot dream of degradation, as if the naked boy in the mirror is his beautiful and carnal hero. You want to tell him that you're in love with everything someone else might recoil from in him, so you say it wordlessly with a hand on his cock and your eyes on his in the mirror, fucking him faster until he cries out and comes on his stomach. Afterward you press his feverish body against the cold windows and say, pointing to the city lights beyond the falling snow, "I'm the one who gives you everything and the one who takes it away." And he looks back at you with a gratitude that says he will follow you long after you've both gone blind with this need.

At least, that's how it started for us.

POWER SURGE

A. Zimmerman

I first saw him manning the public pool lifeguard station. His back was to me. Half a forearm, one hand, a section of back, a shaved head, the occasional glimpse of leg—parts, not a person—yet I was riveted. Slouching low in a chair, I left my sunglasses on to hide my staring.

When his shift ended he swung to the ground, his lanky stride carrying him rapidly past me. Both nipples were pierced and a brilliant collage of tattoos scrolled down his arms, the artwork as impressive as the man.

Through the grapevine I learned he was engaged and so ignored him with mild success. I had shelved the idea of "Mr. Right," focusing on "Right Now," sometimes even "You'll Do." I was not going to contemplate "Already Taken."

The end of his engagement started our friendship. We fell into long, intimate phone conversations and platonic weekends away, weeks turning into month and months into years. At one point I found myself explaining power relationships and me being submissive. In turn, he admitted lovers of both sexes had mentioned finding him naturally dominant. I silently agreed; more than once over the years I had caught myself automatically doing his bidding.

A few months after our initial power conversation, the topic came up again at my house. This time I leaned toward him in a way I had never allowed before. He angled to me while explaining he found BDSM interesting and felt he needed to experience power to properly wield it. On a fact-finding mission to learn by doing, he would put himself in my more experienced, albeit submissive, hands.

Although caught by surprise, there was no question I would do it. How could I not? Using my favorite memories as guides, I sent him to my room with instructions, then wandered the house collecting a range of objects. My mind filled with plans, I entered the bedroom with a question.

"Scale of one to ten. Anxiety?"

"Five."

As instructed, he was lying on the bed wearing the blindfold from the nightstand drawer and had stripped to briefs. The array of bedside candles was lit. One lavender, for relaxation. One apple, to release anxiety.

And a scent-free paraffin taper, in case things got interesting. Dropping my armload of stuff, I watched him
fidget, lacing and unlacing his fingers while crossing
and uncrossing his ankles. Knowing this was a mind
game, I waited for him to break the silence. It didn't
take long.

"Do you like looking at me?"

"Why?"

"I like knowing people like my body. Do you—"

"Not relevant."

Sure, I liked looking. End of discussion. This was
about him, not me. I focused on the situation at hand
and facts to be established.

"Safewords?" I inquired.

"Yellow and red."

"Meaning?"

"Yellow slow down, red stop."

Okay. He understood. A pair of tights was wrapped
around the leg of the headboard, slipknot loops tied
into the ends to create soft restraints. Showing him how
to get himself free of the light bondage, I took a deep
breath and secured his arms over his head.

He woofed in surprise as a bed pillow landed on his
head. I dropped another on his chest, followed by several
smaller pillows on his arms and groin. I randomly hit
him with pillows, making him flinch repeatedly as blows
landed from different directions with varying force,
creating a mild sensory overload.

"Why pillows?"

"No talking," I reminded him. "Brief answers or safewords only."

"Can I ask what's next?"

He was pushing my authority exactly the way I pushed people. What went around was coming around. How annoying.

"No."

"Will you talk me through—"

"No talking."

"But—"

"Are you talking?"

"Sorry, no."

His hands clenched. I tossed a pillow over them, acknowledging I had seen his reaction but was ignoring it. I continued bludgeoning him, being careful not to create a rhythm.

"My fingers are cold," he announced, startling me.

It had been twenty-five minutes. I had been in his position with those restraints for upward of four hours before becoming uncomfortable. Checking, I discovered his hands were icy. He must have been channeling tension up through his arms, flexing and making the slipknots tighten.

Inexperienced, I had missed it. Clearly the power of bondage was balanced perfectly by the risks. I had to focus. Power wasn't as much about being in charge as it was about caring for someone else. I had to be more careful.

"Shake it out," I advised, releasing him. "When you feel warm, arms to your sides."

I fluffed a nylon feather duster until he let his arms fall to the mattress. His hands twitched as I danced the duster over him.

"You can hold on to the bed," I offered.

His arms shot out, his fingers curling around the edges of the mattress until his knuckles went white. Both his nipples were hard enough to lift the rings off his chest and there was a definite bulge between his legs. I tapped his erection, then tapped between his tense thighs. He ignored the nonverbal cues, forcing me to speak.

"Spread."

As he settled into the more vulnerable spread-eagled position, I tried to slide his briefs lower using the duster and failed.

"Count to fifty. By forty-nine, briefs are gone."

His lips moved as he counted under his breath.

"...Twenty-eight...twenty-nine..."

He pulled his briefs off and flopped back, displaying a porn-star worthy erection. Of course. If we weren't having a platonic relationship he would have had a pencil dick. So not fair.

Abandoning the duster, I hooked one of the tines of a serving fork through a nipple ring, tugging to make him moan. Doing the same to the other ring made his cock jerk. Tracing loops down his stomach made his head tip back. His spine arched and he dug his heels into the mattress. A guttural groan rumbled his chest as goose bumps danced over his skin. When I reached the base of his cock, his erection jumped and he groaned again, thrusting toward the kitchen-utensil-turned-sex-toy.

"Harder," he murmured. "Please…"

Adrenaline surged through me. Sex was fun. But this? This was wildly different. This wasn't about me; this was about what I could do, about him begging for me to do it. The power was impressive, more enticing than I anticipated. My hands started shaking.

Selecting a spatula, I used the flat surface to knock his cock downward. A smack to the underside drove it against his stomach. A few more strikes had it swaying. He thrust his hips up for more. I flattened his balls with a snap of the spatula.

"Damn!" he cursed, his ass crashing to the bed in self-defense.

Then he smiled.

My attraction roared, heart pounding, body flushing, palms sweating; I wanted to kiss him, to taste him, to have him inside me. We hadn't talked about sex, only the foreplay of bondage and toys. I had to stop.

"Should you come?" I wondered.

"Please," came his strangled response.

Lifting his hand, I kissed the palm, then wrapped his fingers around his cock.

"For me," I instructed, and his hand began to move.

KIMONO

Tess Danesi

I've always thought of myself, affectionately, as a slut. At least I did before the big, life-altering move from New York City to the Eastern Shore of Maryland. Somehow, small-town life won me over. Instead of enjoying my big-city ways, with my beloved rotation of always younger, always dominant partners, I now spend my time creating art, cooking, walking country roads, and gazing at the spectacular skies. It might not sound exciting, but it suits this stage of my life.

The art part is how I met Sam and, as the saying goes, "got my groove back." Right around the holidays, I found myself trying to sell my creations at a local art fair. Amid all the beautiful art, I was struck by the collection of vintage kimonos just a table away from mine. Between sales, my eye kept wandering back to the silky fabrics. They tempted me with both muted and vibrant tones, lush floral patterns, scenarios of nature—and the irresistible, to my magpie self, glint of metallic threads. I vowed, if I made enough money, one would be mine before the night was done.

Sam, though, was a complete surprise. Since I'd traded men in custom suits for those clad in camo or overalls, the entrance of Sam was reason for, if not celebration, salivation. This dark-haired, dark-eyed miracle brought his six-foot-two, trim and toned, late-twenties self into view as he casually strolled into the fair and headed for the kimonos.

He seemed to know Swallow, the kimono vendor, as they engaged in animated conversation while he removed his leather jacket, revealing a snug-fitting simple white T-shirt that hinted at six-pack abs beneath. I must have been staring; after all, I hadn't seen a man this fine since I left New York three years ago. And, of course, he caught me, no doubt wide-eyed and slack jawed, mid-stare. Surprisingly, he turned on that brilliant smile and I, remembering who I used to be, smiled right back.

I got busy with a customer, and when I was done he was gone. Sighing, I went over to Swallow and decided to console myself with the purchase of a kimono. I fell in love with one made of somber black fabric woven with gold thread on the outside and a colorful nature scene inside. While Swallow packed my purchase, I asked her, "Who was that young guy and wherever did he come from?"

"That's Sam, and, yes, he's something of an oddity around here. I know him from when he was younger and used to babysit my sons. Now, he models on and off."

"It's not often that you see a man have the confidence to wear a kimono, is it?" I queried.

"That's for sure," said Swallow. "In all the time I've been doing this, I think it's the third one I've sold to a man for himself. And I've been doing this for years."

I sighed again. "Oh well, a girl can dream, can't she?"

Back at my booth, I promptly got busy again, remaining cognizant of the tingle that had begun to awaken my somewhat dormant sexuality.

The night drew to a close and I began packing up and carrying boxes to my car. As I made my way out the door, burdened with too many boxes to see over, I was startled by a deep voice saying, "Here, let me help with that." Never being one to turn down an offer for help with manual labor, I quickly peered over the tops of the boxes to see Sam and allowed him to take them from my suddenly sweaty little hands. We made a few trips, Sam carrying the heavy stuff and me schlepping a bag or two while I watched his butt.

"Thanks so much for helping me, by the way. I'm Regan."

"Nice to meet you, Regan. I'm Sam. And you're very welcome."

In the crisp, cold moonlit night, his smile illuminated his face, one so strong and chiseled and everything that made my panties wet.

"Did you buy a kimono, Sam? I noticed you trying them on. I bought one." I started to ramble like I often do when sexual tension with a stranger makes itself known.

"In fact, I did," replied Sam. "I'll show you mine if you show me yours. Come on; let's take a walk. The grounds here are really beautiful, especially by the river. Grab your bag; I really do want to see your kimono."

And just like that, I let him take the lead. We walked down the path lit only by the moon and the stars, until we got to a weeping willow tree by the water.

"I'm going to kiss you now," he said, grabbing my shoulders and pushing me back until the tree stopped me. I think I nodded or mumbled; whatever I did it was clear I was in agreement. His lips were firm and demanding and when he took my bottom lip between his teeth and bit down hard, I knew we were kindred spirits. I groaned and pressed my pelvis into his leg, reveling in the sensation that had started in my clit and was now lighting even my toes on fire.

Still kissing me, his hands slid my coat off my shoulders. I heard it softly hit the frigid ground. He pulled off my top and my bra and slid off my skirt as I shivered.

"I'm freezing, Sam, I can't…"

He cut me off with another kiss, then removed his own jacket and T-shirt and brought my kimono out of the bag and helped me into it. The silken fabric rubbed erotically against my already hardened nipples, making them that much more erect. Then he slipped off his pants and shrugged into his kimono.

"I fully intend to keep you very warm tonight, beautiful Regan, especially if you're a good girl and do exactly as I say. Now, feel what you do to me," he said, guiding my hand to his erection. His cock felt rigid, pulsing, so alive and hungry that I sighed audibly at the thought of it sliding into my cunt and filling me.

After he'd spread his discarded jacket on the ground between us, his words weren't necessary to convey his next desire, but he spoke them anyway. "I want to feel your lips on my cock now, Regan. On your knees, pretty little bitch."

I must have tried not to seem as eager as I felt or maybe my bratty sub-slut self was returning; whichever, I wanted the electricity created by his hands as he gripped my head by the roots of my long hair, guiding me to that perfect cock.

Lifting me up from my kneeling position, he pushed my breasts into the rough bark of the willow tree, his chest hard against my back as the wind fluttered the soft silken fabric of our kimonos. His hands found my wetness, pinching my clit to the point of painful pleasure, as his erection teased at my cunt.

Even before his cock entered me, I knew my life had once again changed for the best.

THE EUNUCH

Regina Kammer

R elinquishing his body in service to the king had not
been his choice.

Arashis tugged on the twisted silk that slid across his
palms, the slick, soft cords wrapped around his wrists
binding him to the carved and gilded ebony bedposts.
Holding him securely.

No. Relinquishing his body in service to the king had
been necessary for survival.

He relaxed his eyelids under the velvety lambskin
blindfold, giving in to the quietude of the dark and the
euphoria of anticipation.

Chaos had reigned after the legions of Rome had
invaded Parthia. He had been but a boy, the third son
of wealthy merchants. Expendable—an offering to the
new client king.

Submission meant surrendering his body to royal butchers. They spared his manhood.

Arashis shuddered at the memory, his unbound legs squirming against the feather mattress.

Yet such submission and mutilation meant freedom. A freedom most did not enjoy.

Through the occupation, Arashis had made himself indispensable to the royal household. He walked the halls of power, administering counsel. He guarded the women's domain where scarred men such as he and the prepubescent sons of princesses were the only males allowed.

By the time Parthia had won back its independence, Arashis had achieved a measure of power.

What had he given up? Leading caravans along the Silk Route. Marriage to one in the merchant class. Children. His stones.

He filled his lungs with the sultry air and let out a sigh.

But what had a life of submission opened up to him?

Power in the throne room as an advisor to kings.

Power in the bedroom as the lover of a princess.

The pop and sputter of a candle signaled movement in the air. Someone had entered the bedchamber.

He chuckled. Not someone. *Her*. The princess. *His* princess.

Relinquishing his body in service to the king had not been his choice. But giving his body in service to the princess had been very much his choice.

The honeyed scent of burning wax mingled with the delicate fragrance of exotic floral perfume. She was watching him from the other side of the sheer draperies separating her bedchamber from her dressing room.

Her unmet gaze lay heavy and wanton across his flesh, prickling his nipples. She would be smiling at his nude body stretched against the fine linen sheets, at the effects of the magus's elixir on his male potency.

She loved to observe him like this, his vulnerable state a reflection of her own helplessness. By outward appearances, his princess commanded a bevy of attendants and lesser royals. But at any moment, her maidservants could be sent away to the bed of a prince. Or a rival king could descend upon the palace and slaughter her children.

Her hold on her power was tenuous. And she clung to a memory of when she held sway over the world.

A balmy breeze from an open window danced over him. The freshness of spring was fading on the cusp of summer.

Rome had invaded when her father was king, her mother queen, she a young girl. She had hid in the tower as her family was seized by the Roman guard, and reemerged to an empty palace. She sat upon the throne, holding the seat for her father. For one glorious moment, this little princess had been Shah of the Parthian Empire.

The moment had been too brief.

She endured captivity in Rome for a dozen years, then was returned to Parthia and married to a neglectful prince. She performed her duty as wife and mother while her husband dallied with concubines.

Never once did the princess reclaim her moment of glory. Until she and Arashis became lovers.

As they explored the possibilities of lovemaking, she discovered she craved the heady experience of taking control, of dominating another.

He discovered he did not mind being dominated by her. In fact, he found it quite thrilling.

His submission to the princess brought them both great joy.

A flowery scent flared his nostrils, swirling arousal to the root of his cock. She had finally entered the bedchamber. She glided softly along the mosaic floor, tugging carelessly on the bedsheet, the soft linen suddenly abrasive under his flushed skin.

She grazed a fingernail down his arm, eliciting tingling shivers across his flesh. When she scratched the hollow under his shoulder, he flinched with a gasp.

"You will pleasure me." Her command was edged with agitation.

"Yes, my queen."

She always smiled when he called her that.

The mattress dipped as she clambered up to straddle his head, her calves at his ears. No hem fluttered around his face. His princess was nude.

He breathed her in, his mouth watering. He clenched his fists against the silk and swallowed.

She brushed her depilated quim over his nose down

to his chin. Then she settled herself, his lips her throne.

He tasted slowly, tantalizing her with mouth and tongue, pleasuring her. Or was it himself he pleasured as he savored her?

He teased the pearl with the tip of his tongue, flicking gently, steadily.

She leaned over, her tremulous breaths hot and moist on the tip of his shaft. "More."

She gripped his hips, her nails digging into the sides of his buttocks, her ragged moans limned with despair. Droplets of warm water slithered onto his legs, tickling his inner thighs.

Sweat?

No.

Tears.

He sucked her pearl into his mouth, working it relentlessly, cruelly, her calves squeezing his cheeks as her purring moans crumbled into clipped yelps.

She tensed, muscles taut and strained, and let out a mournful wail.

She came, drenching him with her sweet essence, until the acrid taste of male emission slid over his tongue, filling his mouth. And then he understood the source of her anguish.

Her husband had demanded her presence in his bed. She had no choice but to comply.

She slumped over, shaking, sobbing, rolling onto the mattress. She curled up against him. "Hold me."

"Release me."

She loosened the silk cords, relief easing his muscles as he bent and flexed his arms, then removed his blindfold and slid to his side.

The gold of lamplight and candles burnished the dusky ivory of her skin. He traced her luscious saffron-red lips with a fingertip, then tucked a strand of hair black as obsidian behind her ear.

She lowered her lashes. "I fear I did not act the queen tonight."

Arashis offered a consoling smile and kissed her damp cheek. He pulled the sheet over them and enveloped her in his arms. He nuzzled his nose in her tresses, his unsatisfied erection prodding her cleft.

"I will always be here for you, my princess."

Giving his body in service to the princess had granted Arashis more power and pleasure than any king could have bestowed.

GOOMBAY LOVER

Zodian Gray

I lit a cigarette and stood naked in front of the large windows of my luxurious bedroom on the fifth floor of the most expensive condo complex on the island. The sun was just creeping across the sky like a lazy bitch nursing a hangover.

I watched the spectacle of colors and forced my body to wait, prolonging the sweet agony of hunger for my baby in the other bedroom. All I had to do was walk across the hall, dick swinging like it didn't have a care in the world. My baby had come to my little island in the sun for me to take care of him, like he usually did about once or twice a month when running his multi-billion-dollar portfolio of companies became too over-whelming.

I knew he'd had his shower, and had washed away

the person he was to become the person he could be only
with me. I wanted to rush over and tell him how much
I loved and missed him. I wanted to kiss him and hold
him like I would never let him go. But he didn't want
my tenderness or my love. He wanted—no, *needed*—me
to fuck him like he was a whore in purgatory in need of
repentance.

My dick twitched at the thought of that beautiful
part of him, doing time in the little silver cage. He
always waited for me in my music room, which was
soundproof, so no one would hear him scream.

I walked into the adjoining bath and washed away
the night's funk from playing at the jazz club. My baby
had come straight from the airport to the club to watch
me perform. He'd watched me with hungry eyes; the rest
of my audience had faded away and I'd sung only to him.

I heard my voice when I entered the room carrying a
bottle of lube and the key to the cage. I'd recorded the
songs just for him; nasty songs about fucking him deep
and tender songs about loving him just as profoundly.
The room vibrated with music. He had his back to the
door, but I knew he sensed my presence when his head
snapped up. I imagined his pale-blue eyes danced with
excitement and his pale skin looked flushed. He had a
beautiful ass and nice long legs. I loved him, not just
because he afforded me a lifestyle where I spent my
days making music with my band. I loved him because
I knew he was more than the hard-nosed businessman
everyone thought he was. I knew he'd had to take care

of six younger brothers and sisters after his parents died. I knew his unrelenting drive to succeed came from his need to take care of the people he loved. But sometimes it became too much and he had to let go of that damn control. I would do anything for him, including beat his ass until he went crazy.

"Hello, Carl," I said, even though I knew he couldn't hear me. I just had to say his name.

As if he heard me, my Carl fell to his knees. I walked around in front of him and cupped my dick. Yes, when it was this big it had to be called dick, because cock was far too tame. Carl called it his Mandingo dick.

He lifted his head and took that dick into his mouth.

"Welcome home, baby," I purred.

I grabbed Carl's ponytail. Some people thought it obnoxious that a man in his forties should still have a ponytail but Carl kept it for one reason only. I wound his beautiful brown hair around my hand and shoved his mouth farther down my dick. I used that ponytail to dictate how fast he should suck. I liked it wet and slow, while he suffered silently.

"Yeah, it hurts to keep him confined, doesn't it? Maybe if you're a good boy and take your punishment, I'll let him come out to play."

Carl looked up at me with glazed eyes. He was so happy to have my dick in his mouth. He already looked better than he had last night. The stress lines looked softer in the morning light when his only thought was to please me.

I yanked his head away from my dick and threw him over my piano.

"You came to my room last night, after I told you you'd have to wait until morning."

"I just wanted to see you, Reggie," Carl confessed.

"Did you touch yourself?" I asked.

"No, you locked him away, remember?"

"Did you touch any other part of yourself?"

When he didn't answer, I know that he had. He had been in an intense state of pleasure for hours now. Carl liked pushing himself to his limits, edging himself toward pleasure but never going over. And I was about to take him further.

"I have to punish you for your disobedience."

"Yes, Sir."

His voice trembled with excitement.

Carl liked for me to use my hands to spank him because when we'd first met, I was beating a goatskin drum at a local Goombay festival. He said he'd known then that I would be a good spanker. I brought my hands down on his ass in time to the music.

"Yes, my Goombay lover."

Carl liked to call me his Bahamian Goombay lover. *Goombay* was an African Bantu word for rhythm, and I had rhythm on that ass, wildly beating him red. When my final symphony ended, I lubed up and shoved my dick into Carl's ass and he groaned like an animal. It had been too long for both of us.

I fucked him hard and fast. The little cock cage

banged against the piano and Carl begged me to release him. I grabbed his hair and shoved his head down.

"You don't get to come until I tell you to," I growled. I increased that sweet, punishing rhythm he liked, and pretty soon he was sobbing for release. He'd reached his limits. I pulled out and spun him around. Carl had that crazed look in his eyes, like he was about to die if he didn't come. His cock was red from straining against steel for so many hours.

Still I lingered before kneeling in front of him and unlocking the little latch. I carefully removed the cage. I swear I kissed his cock maybe three times, and just that easily he came, beautifully and gloriously loud, spewing his pent-up come right into my face. His beautiful face scrunched up in pure sweet agony was the most amazing thing I'd ever seen, and I beat my dick to an explosive finish as I watched him come a second time.

I looked up at Carl, and he looked down at me. He seemed so at peace. Our world consisted of just the two of us; all of his stress was on my face and dripping down my body. I stood up. Now I could kiss him and tell him how much I loved him. Now I could hold him and feel the rhythm of his heart next to mine.

DIXIE CUP

Anastacia Lucretia

Warm. The air-conditioning was doing its best to cool us down. But with the temps in the nineties outside, the room was still warm. The fucking probably didn't help things either. Sweat covered both of us as we lay side by side, eyes closed, random body parts touching each other.

She and me. My Domme and I. It was a Saturday afternoon; we had both gotten up, had our caffeine together, and then went our separate ways to deal with the things in life that most people push off until the weekend. I brought home lunch, and afterward we decided to nap. The truth in the previous statement was this: there was in fact a bedroom involved, and we both did go in there to sleep. But so far, little sleeping was being done. It wasn't my fault. I couldn't stop touching her.

Touching led to kissing. Kissing led to groping. Groping led to more and once you added nipples into the mix, napping wasn't going to happen. She ended up face-sitting me, grinding her pussy onto my mouth, lips, and tongue until she reached down and pulled herself as tightly as possibly against my face and came. So very Domme.

With her come drying on my face, we lie there, her hand slowly playing with my nipples. That's a good sign for me because if she stops touching me, we're done and I don't get a chance to make my own mess. But she's still using a finger, flicking it up and down across my nipples. I make a low sound and turn toward her, kissing her.

"Please," I say. Nothing else is necessary. I don't need to ask for something specific. I don't get to choose. My Domme will decide if I should mess and, if yes, how I should do it. And while that unequal power seems unthinkable to your average vanilla guy, it's how we both prefer it. My sexuality is Femdom. It's the only way I fuck these days.

Her eyes are still shut when I lever myself up to an elbow and kiss her stomach. I say a little prayer to the fertility gods of old, asking them for help. I want to mess. I want to come. She opens her eyes and turns her head to look at me. Her eyes lock on to mine. "Up. Off the bed. On the floor."

I kneel. She rolls and sits on the bed, bending to reach for the second drawer from the top and coming out with a seven-inch latex dildo. Kneeling between her legs, I kiss her knee. She reaches down and plays with a nipple. "You better start," she says.

I'm already half-hard as I begin to jerk my cock. I close my eyes and feel myself get fully hard. I still smell her pussy on me. I'm kneeling in front of my Domme, and I know she's watching me. She's always watching me.

I hear her say, "Open." I open my mouth and narrow my eyes a bit. I see the cock in her hand begin to slide past my lips. I feel her begin to use little fucking motions, in and out of my mouth. My hand on my cock begins to work faster. I try and keep my mouth closed tight around her cock.

"Cocksucker," I hear her say. She knows that doing this for her makes me feel dirty. She knows that having me suck "cock" makes me feel more than a little humiliated. With my mouth around one of her dicks, I feel like I'm being used. I feel very much not like a guy, but more like a slave whose purpose at this moment is to just be a thing—a sucking thing.

"You look so good, sucking my dick. Bitch." Faster now. I make a noise, then another. I hear her say, "In the cup."

I look. She's handing me one of the little Dixie cups from the dispenser she keeps on her nightstand. When she put them there I didn't understand. But she told me that nothing breaks a vanilla guy faster of his old life than cleaning up after himself. That a guy who will clean up and eat his own mess begins to leave vanilla fucking behind. That the taste of his own come, time after time after time, ingrains submission into him like nothing else. So for weeks now when I've been allowed to mess, she has me finish in her little Dixie cup, then holds it to my lips and pours the salty come into my mouth to swallow.

She bought a package of one hundred cups. She said when I've used all of them and her dispenser is empty, after I've swallowed one hundred of my own loads, she was going to take me to get a small Dixie cup tattooed on me. On the front of the cup will be a big letter C, indicating the Roman numeral for one hundred, or *come eater*. She said I would find greater submission in this. That I would be far from vanilla. I believe her.

I take the cup, glance down, and put the head of my cock in it. She pulls my nipple while pushing her cock farther into my mouth. I close my eyes and take a breath, hoping that my aim is true. I hear, "Don't you fucking stop, bitch," and I feel the rise and know I've made some kind of noise. I'm dimly aware that I can't breathe very well from the amount of cock that's in my mouth. She pulls again on my nipple and fuck, I just do that thing where I try and hold back for a half-second because I know it will make that first spurt harder. I feel myself go. I begin to mess, my hand jerking very fast. I feel the sides of the cup on either side of my cockhead and hope I'm where I need to be because she's watching.

I slow down. I bend forward and rest my head on one of her knees as I milk the last bit of come out of me and into the cup. I open my eyes to look. Nothing on the floor.

I straighten up in time to see her put the cock down. She leans over and kisses me on the lips. "Good boy." I wordlessly hand her the little cup but she doesn't look in it; she knows what was done. She was watching. Her other hand pushes my bottom lip down and open. I close my eyes and feel the liquid move past my lips onto my tongue. I swallow. They say it's a tablespoon, but trust me, it feels like more.

I swallow again and hear her pitch the used cup into the trash. I rest my head again on her knee. We stay like that for a few moments, letting that energy swirl between us. I will eventually use that one-hundredth cup, and I have no doubt she'll have some other challenge ready for me so I can continue to be and become what we both need me to be: Hers.

MUM

Charlie Powell

Before the baby, she'd worried about having to deal with all the sick and shit, but it's the endless saliva that's been the greatest shock. Now the gifts from people who'd been there already make sense. She'd expected stuffed toys, cute sleepers, nappies, but instead there was just an endless stack of muslin cloths. They're six months in now, and the appearance of teeth has only made things worse. Not only is she constantly covered in drool, she's up half the night trying to pacify a fretful child with sore gums.

It's killed her sex drive.

Friends talk about the way motherhood makes them feel their body—their tits especially—is no longer their own, and while she sees what they mean (her nipples are dry and cracked from all the feeding), it bothers her less than the way that tiredness and lack of time have led to a sex life that's distinctly vanilla.

She misses kink.

"I've booked a hotel," Mike tells her, as he paces up and down the bedroom, rubbing Jessica's back and wincing at her furious tears.

"Why? Oh god, have I forgotten our anniversary?"

"No! You need a break. *We* need a break. My mum said she'd look after Jess."

It's true; they do need a break. She feels like motherhood has become her whole identity in a way she never would have predicted. Pre-Jess, she'd have gone all soft and gooey at the thought of her baby saying "mama" or people referring to her as "Jessica's mum." Now that it's reality, sure, it provokes love like she's never felt before, but it also makes her slightly wistful for the days when she was just "Susie." Not to mention the days when she was "slut," or "bitch," or "whore."

"Do you think we should stop calling each other 'Mummy' and 'Daddy' in front of the baby?" she asks Mike. "After all, she's too young to understand. Perhaps we should start using our real names again?"

"I don't mind 'Daddy,' actually," Mike says, winking at her. "Though I'm happy to answer to 'Sir' if you'd prefer?"

"I've never called you Sir!"

"It's not too late to start!"

* * *

The hotel is stunning, an old country house with a huge four-poster bed, a roll-top bath, and a bottle of champagne on ice.

"For now or for aftercare?" Mike asks, gesturing at it, and she knows this is his way of asking if she wants to submit or if she'd prefer to go vanilla.

"For aftercare."

"Sure?"

"Dead sure."

"Lie on the bed."

She reaches for the zip on her dress, but he stops her. "Clothes on, please."

Susie does as she's told.

The weight of his body and the feeling of his lips on hers bring her back to herself. Her breasts may still be heavy with milk but right now, her body is hers and hers alone. He takes his time unbuttoning her plaid shirt but then he sinks his thumbs into her soft, pale flesh and she mewls with delight.

"Look at me," he says, and she opens her eyes to meet his gaze, hoping that he'll hit her. She's always loved the feel of his palm connecting with her cheek, the shock of it, the way it leaves her with no choice but to be utterly present in the moment.

He doesn't slap her. Instead, he spits, fiercely, right into her open mouth.

It's the hottest thing she's ever experienced. Somewhere at the back of her mind, clouded by lust, she remembers a friend complaining that her husband never actually listened to the things that bothered her, he just pretended to listen until she calmed down.

Mike has been listening.

Every time she's wondered aloud at the fact that she used to get off on fluids—spit, semen, tears—whereas now she spends most of her day mopping them up, he's heard her.

"I love you," she says.

"I love you, too," he replies, and spits again. The warm, wet blob of saliva hits her squarely on the forehead.

"More," she begs.

"Ask nicely."

"Please."

"Please what?"

"Please, Sir."

All the things the baby has tried to claim as her own, Mike takes back for the two of them. He pulls Susie's hair in thick, grasping handfuls until she yelps in pain. He bites her, leaving marks on her neck that she knows will turn purple before the morning. She knows too that she'll gaze at these bruises in the mirror once she's back to her normal routine, reliving her sexuality between night feedings and nappy changes.

Then, once he's reduced her to her old, submissive self, he makes her suck his cock, pushing his length deep into her mouth until her own saliva runs down her chin.

He scoops it up and wipes it across her cheeks, mixing it with his.

He pushes her skirt out of the way, her knickers to one side, and with a single thrust, he's inside her, thick and long and oh so good. They've had sex since Jess was born, of course—often, in fact—but this is the first time since the baby arrived that it's been like this. She comes hard, and quickly, and he does too, filling her with semen, so that she is soaked with him from top to bottom.

There's saliva in her fringe, on her face, dripping down between her breasts. Her mascara is smudged beyond repair. She's a mess, but she feels wonderful.

"I'm not sure we have time to shower before dinner," he says. "Not if you also want to drink that champagne."

"Shouldn't be a problem," she says, digging deep in her handbag. "I'm sure I have something in here I can clean up with." And as she pulls out a muslin cloth, one of the million spares she carries everywhere, both she and Mike dissolve into laughter.

TWENTY-NINE

Rose de Fer

Lara braces herself. She stands on tiptoe and bends forward over the padded armchair, gripping the seat. The leather creaks beneath her hands. She can feel Michael behind her, the displacement of air as he positions himself at an angle to her.

He lifts her skirt and she closes her eyes, her heart beginning to race with anticipation. Then his fingers are inside the waistband of her panties. He pulls them to her knees.

Lara takes a deep breath, preparing herself. She wants to make him proud.

Michael doesn't speak and neither does she. She knows both what to expect, and what is expected of her.

After a few moments she feels the cool caress of the little leather whip. It's disarmingly small and inoffensive to look at, but she knows its kiss can be vicious. Michael trails it over her bottom, teasing her for a moment. The calm before the storm.

Then he brings it down and the room rings out with the sharp crack of leather against bare skin. It doesn't hurt much, but as always, it takes a moment for the sensation to fully blossom. Lara gasps and waits until it has reached its peak before she counts.

"Two."

"Good girl."

The next stroke falls and again she waits for the stinging warmth to spread before she counts.

"Three."

The whip lands again, harder this time.

"Five."

And again.

"Seven."

Michael pauses to stroke her, running his fingers over her cheeks. Right now her bottom is only slightly warm. She knows it will be burning before he is finished.

The next strokes come in a brisk volley, one right after another. She gasps, trying to keep track. There are four in all.

She calms herself and then speaks the numbers. "Eleven. Thirteen. Seventeen. Nineteen."

"Very good." Michael is smiling behind her. She can tell. It makes her smile too.

But her smile vanishes instantly as the next stroke falls. This one is much harder, and begins to challenge her composure. She yelps, kicking her leg up as the sting washes over her. Then she counts.

"Twenty-three."

Another stroke, this one even harder.

"Twenty-nine."

Michael stops, once more caressing her tender bottom. Lara relaxes, sagging over the armchair. Her punished skin is tingling, the pleasure and pain producing a heady cocktail of sensation. She waits for him to tell her she can get up.

And waits.

When she feels the tails of the whip tickling her bottom again, she gives a little whimper of confusion and protest. They've already reached her age. Is he planning to give her one to grow on?

He answers her silent question with another volley of strokes, and her disorientation makes it difficult to keep track. Four. No, five. She counts them aloud.

"Thirty-one. Thirty-seven. Forty-one. Forty-three. Forty-seven."

Behind her, Michael chuckles softly. And suddenly she catches on. Yes, she is twenty-nine today. That means twenty-nine *strokes*. Quickly she performs the calculation. She's had fifteen already. But she can't factor far enough ahead to know when he'll stop. All she can do is keep count and try not to lose her place.

The whip falls again, harder. The stinging leather tails elicit little cries and gasps from her and she wriggles over the chair. It is all she can do not to reach back and rub the burn out of her cheeks. But she stays focused.

Another three strokes. Fifty-three, fifty-nine, and sixty-one. Another four. Sixty-seven, seventy-one, seventy-three, and seventy-nine.

For a moment she loses count. Was it twenty-one or twenty-two? Another stroke falls as she decides it's the latter.

"Eighty..." She hesitates. Oh god, is it eighty-one or eighty-three?

She hears Michael pulling the tails of the whip through his fingers, slapping it against his palm, prompting her. Twenty-three is eighty...

"Eighty-three!"

He laughs softly and pats her bottom. "Very good," he says.

The numbers are getting harder now. And so are the strokes.

Eighty-nine wrenches a cry from her and it takes her some time to compose herself enough to speak. She pants out the number for him, and when the whip lands again, she realizes she has lost count.

She freezes in horror, staring wide-eyed at the blank wall before her as her mind spins its gears frantically.

This time he has to prompt her. His deep voice says her name, a low sultry warning tone.

"Eighty-seven," she ventures uncertainly.

She can tell by his silence that it's wrong. Blushing to the roots of her hair, she hangs her head in disgrace, her entire body burning with the shame.

"Lara," he says gently, "what is three times twenty-nine?"

She visualizes the numbers in a dance, circling and combining like cells. And she groans as she sees the divisors neatly carving up the number. "Eighty-seven," she says with a groan.

"We'll try that one again, shall we?"

She grips the seat, knowing it will hurt. He doesn't disappoint. The leather tails spread sweet fire through her flesh and she cries out, writhing and kicking her feet as it washes over her and through her.

When she finally gets control of herself, she concentrates. "Eighty-nine," she says. And they're at twenty-four. Only five more to go. She is determined to make him proud.

Ninety-seven makes her gasp, but doesn't shake her concentration. With renewed focus, she counts the pair that follow it, twin primes as it happens.

"One hundred and one, one hundred and three."

Only two more. And she smiles to herself as she realizes that they are twins also.

The whip falls, ringing out in the little room. Lara gasps and whimpers, panting as she gathers herself.

"One hundred and seven."

She knows the next one is the twenty-ninth. A prime itself, and her age. She holds her breath as she waits for the stroke to fall. And Michael makes it count. Her bottom is alive with stinging pain as the whip falls, its tails splaying over her already sore and reddened cheeks.

It is all she can do to stay in position, but she refuses to disgrace herself again.

She takes a deep breath and speaks in a loud, clear voice. "One hundred and nine."

Michael doesn't speak. The room is nerve-wrackingly silent. But he doesn't rattle her this time. She knows that was the final stroke, number twenty-nine. But before there can be any question of it, she lifts her head proudly.

"Thank you, Sir," she says.

The next thing she feels is his hand, warm and smooth, stroking her bottom. His touch intensifies the burn, but the sensation is wonderful too. He guides her up and gathers her in his arms.

"Happy birthday, Lara," he says.

She curls into his embrace, feeling light-headed and slightly dizzy from the endorphins pinging around in her brain.

Michael smiles, gazing into her eyes. "I'm so proud of you," he says.

She blushes and lowers her head.

"I think next year we'll have you count in binary."

SING

J.C. Parker

I cannot live without Tasha's music. I'd do anything to hear her play, it doesn't matter what instrument. That's why I'm onstage in an empty theater disrobing. My cheeks feel warm as I step out of my panties. The darkness of the auditorium feels as if hundreds of unseen eyes are on me. I'm aware of sweat forming on my body once the breeze in the room blows against my backside. Tasha circles the stage, scanning me with her brown eyes. She's dressed to perform, wearing a long black gown that touches the floor. Her jet-black braids are tied in a ponytail. Most important to me are her elbow-length black Lycra opera gloves she wears when she plays piano.

I love the contrast of her elegant look to my shameful state. My brown hair extends to the middle of my back.

I normally cover my hourglass figure in long dresses to hide my curvy hips. Without my clothes, I feel disrespectful standing before such a talented woman, unworthy to be in her presence. Her hand touches my chin and she says, "Sing for me."

My lips tighten. I don't sing, especially not onstage. The pressure to perform makes me more self-conscious over every uncovered inch of skin. I turn my head to hide my blushing face as I try to cover myself.

"No. Display it," Tasha says, grabbing my wrists and holding my arms behind my back. My knees buckle as I feel the heat from the stage lights touch my breasts. Sweat accumulates, as the open feeling of being exposed sends a warm current from between my legs to my chest. Despite my embarrassment, I'm flattered Tasha sees the beauty in my curves that I often hide.

From behind, Tasha grabs my right breast, squeezing hard enough to make me grunt. My nipple stiffens as the pain signals travel straight to my heart. Even though her grip is hard, the gloves feel like a soft caress, making my toes curl the more her hands leave their red marks over me. I don't expect her other hand to slide over the dark-brown hair covering my mons. Her fingers brush against the small curls and push against my outer labia. A small pulse grows from within my lower abdomen the more she pets me. A soft rumble travels up my throat and passes through my trachea, muted by my exhales, all giving Tasha's trained ear data on how she'll play me tonight.

My tuning is interrupted when her arm wraps around my waist to pull me closer. I feel her hot breath against my collarbone before both hands pinch my nipples, twisting them until I grunt. My throat tightens, doing its best to stifle my desire to squeal.

"What's that? I can't hear you," Tasha muses before chuckling. I growl as the pressure on my breasts feels as if she's breaking the skin. Her fingers are precise, applying the right pressure to get a specific sound out of me, as if she knows my body more than I do. By now the pulse becomes a rippling wave of pressure that spreads to my thighs.

"Almost," she says once she releases my breasts, giving me time to take a deep breath of fresh air. My break is short lived. When she raises a hand to slap my pussy, I double forward as the pain explodes throughout my pelvis. I bite my lip to silence my cry. I'm afraid my scream will echo throughout the building and draw the attention of the night staff. My revealed weakness makes Tasha laugh, and now I feel sweat on my brow.

"Stubborn, are we?" Tasha asks, finally letting go. I sigh as my muscles relax. My breast feels like it was bitten, but now it's hard as a rock, excited from Tasha's cruelty. "Fine, I don't need your voice. On your knees."

I don't even lower my legs before Tasha grabs my hair, pulling my head back before guiding me toward the ground, not hard, but with enough force that I barely break my fall with my hands. I stare at the ground that is inches from my face. The amount of disregard to my person sends more adrenaline through me as I anticipate what she'll do to get sound out of me. I lower my head to stick my backside up, my face turning crimson as I think about how foolish I must look.

Tasha runs both gloved hands over my shoulders and down my back, taking her time to give me a soft massage. The Lycra acts like a conductor, sending a current up my spine before she raises both hands and claps down on my ass. The sharp sting travels to my thighs as I wince. My heart stops when I hear the percussive noise my ass makes. It's a dull echo that bounces off of the walls. The flesh of my rear cheeks ripples after each spank; I'm so mortified I cover my face. Snickering, Tasha raises her hands and swings so hard I lean forward. This time the sound is so loud I look at her with indignity, biting my lip as I pray no one is nearby to hear my ass being spanked. Tasha's dark-brown lips spread into a wide grin aimed at me. Her hands rise, this time swinging down in beats of four. Every strike seems to make a louder pop; butterflies are in my stomach now that my ass is a drum. By the time she stops, my posterior is so raw, the air in the room feels like needles. My thighs squeeze together and I feel a dampness between my legs. I should have known resisting her was pointless; she will always get a sound out of me.

"Now sing," Tasha says, right before sliding her fingers against my labia. My mouth opens as I bury my head in my hands, the soft fabric making my sex ache with every stroke. My voice cracks, trying to remain silent while also loving how my will is about to be broken just from my lover's fingertips. It's when she slips her index and middle fingers into my pussy that I squeeze my eyes shut and let out my first cry, a high-pitched noise that fills the auditorium. My lower belly tingles while Tasha plays me, hand turning counter-clockwise as it pushes in and out. My body has soaked her gloves so much the suction of air makes a percussive noise while she continues to fuck me.

The final straw is when she reaches around to lift my torso up, holding me tight against her body to grope my breast. Simultaneously, she begins to flick her fingers as fast as she can while twisting my nipples. The barrage of pain sends my pussy into spasms as I scream. My voice resonates throughout the building and I don't care. Let them see me, wet, naked, completely helpless against my Master, my owner, my musician.

A TESTING TIME

Suzanne Fox

Only the tension of the seat belt halted Cerys's sliding from the front seat as the Audi bumped its way across rough terrain and crunched to a halt. She guessed that they had been on the road for about an hour but she couldn't be sure, and she was clueless as to where they were. Her blindfold masked the outside world from view and she had heard no rumble of traffic for at least fifteen minutes. Apart from the car's engine, the only sound had been the whooshing of blood as it surged past her ears, pumped by her adrenaline-fueled heart.

They had met online a few weeks earlier and, through their chats, learned a little about the other's needs and desires, negotiating a fragile path through a maze of protocol and trust. They had met a couple of times in the anonymity of a cheap hotel chain and each time he had hurt her, leaving her purple with bruises and welts. Their play had been rough and exciting, but each time there had been the security of hotel staff and guests ready to raise the alarm if his games got out of hand. Now she was alone with a man who was little more than a stranger.

Cerys licked dry lips with a tongue that was just as parched. She was treading a dangerous path. Was consenting to be taken blindfolded to god knew where with this man, the most irresponsible and perilous thing she had ever done? The realization that she would soon find out excited and terrified her.

The engine cut out.

Silence.

A brush of leather scuffed her neck, sending frissons of tension trembling down her spine before the collar was tightened and buckled. A metallic snap alerted her to a leash attaching to the collar's ring, and unseen hands released her seat belt. It recoiled like a startled snake into its holster and Cerys flinched. His hands battled hers for control of her wrists before she surrendered to the grip of hard steel cuffs. Her sharpened hearing strained for the slightest of clues. The driver's door slammed shut and muffled steps circled the car.

Cerys jumped, a small yelp escaping her lips as the door beside her flew open and the leash snapped taut. She tumbled from the car, only stopping when she crashed into the broad torso of the man who currently had control of her. Regaining her balance and poise, she stood motionless, feet apart and head bowed.

Waiting.

Fingers tilted her chin, darkness disappeared and a landscape of stippled greenery saturated her vision as he removed her blindfold. Woodland stretched as far as she could see, broken only by a rough, beaten path. Her eyes questioned the man holding the leash but elicited only silence in response.

Hoisting a canvas backpack onto his shoulders, he yanked the leash, dragging Cerys toward the path. She struggled to keep pace with his long strides, picking her way past any roots and rocks waiting to snare her feet. She ducked beneath low branches and stepped over patches of stinging nettles, knowing that any trip or stumble would tighten the leather band around her neck, choking the breath from her. They marched in deliberate silence, which fueled her imagination into overdrive as scene after scene toyed with her mind, teasing and playing her doubts into a meticulous medley of anticipation and fear.

Cerys revered fear. The thrill of living on the edge breathed life into her existence. It ignited the fire that nourished her spirit. It enticed her along the path to pleasures most people never encountered, or only experienced vicariously as they surfed the Internet in shameful solitude or thumbed the pages of the latest socially acceptable BDSM paperback. That wasn't enough to sate the appetite of her inner submissive. Cerys knew she craved the sting of the whip, the bite of the rope, and the discipline of an alpha man to push her to the heights and depths of pain and pleasure.

Her neck extended and her body lurched behind it as the leash pulled taut. His pace quickened and Cerys matched it. The August sunlight streaming through the leafy canopy scorched her already perspiring skin as she felt the hot rays penetrate deeper, warming her muscles and bringing her blood to near-boiling point. The heat spread farther until she felt a familiar aching in her pussy as it swelled in response. Her inflamed flesh, now fully sensitized to the rub of the crotch rope he had tied beneath her clothing, began to get wetter as the friction increased. Cerys whimpered as the first stirrings of an orgasm blossomed. Imaginings of what would soon happen evicted all mundane thoughts and, for Cerys, the anticipation was almost as thrilling as the scene itself. But underscoring the exhilaration and the expectation ran a cold current of dread. Not the sense of controlled fear that usually accompanied her play, but a deeper, more primal terror that wormed deep into her psyche, urging her to snatch the leash from his grip and race for the security of a crowded space.

The trepidation that had simmered all day was now threatening to erupt. Her life was in the hands of a man intent on causing her pain. The contents of the backpack that weighed down his shoulders were a mystery. She hoped for rope, a flogger, a paddle, or maybe a whip. But what if there were other things—a knife, a hammer, or worse? A rat of dread that wouldn't be ignored chewed at her stomach.

Blinding sunlight dazzled her vision and she squinted as a clearing opened in the trees. Through the haze, Cerys saw the dark outline of an ancient oak near the center of the glade and she stumbled toward it following the pull of the leash.

In silence, he freed one of Cerys's wrists, spun her around, and cuffed her hands behind her. She realized she couldn't outrun him restrained in this way. He tipped open the backpack, spilling the contents onto the ground, and selected a length of hemp rope.

Cerys felt the chafe of rope as he secured it to the cuffs and she broke her silence. "What...what are you going to do?"

His answer was a huff of breath as he hurled the other end of the rope over one of the lower branches. It rasped against the gnarled bark. He pulled the rope down and Cerys's arms began to rise behind her. She bowed forward as her arms lifted higher, rotating her shoulder joints, displaying the curve of her bottom and tightening the thin rope that rubbed against her cunt. It was now or never. She prayed she would be proved right and drew in a deep breath.

"RED!"

The rope slipped free and her arms fell back down. Strong arms hugged her, pressing her body against his. Warm breath kissed the top of her head and a comforting voice whispered, "Tell me what's wrong, baby. We can stop if you're not ready."

Cerys looked at his face. It was scored with concern. Smiling, she realized she was going to be safe and treasured in his hands.

TRADING PLACES

Myra S. Hart

I watched in anticipation as Adrienne unlocked the door and entered the living room. I wondered how she'd felt, going out shopping dressed like she was dressed.

Her dark hair was short, as it had just started growing back, and was slicked down with gel. Black eyeliner followed the almond shape of her gray eyes. A black suit with severe lines was worn over a lacy corset, pushing up her new boobs so that a mound of cleavage could catch the eyes of onlookers. High-heeled black boots completed the look.

I also knew she wore no panties underneath. My cock was hard as hell thinking about her bare pussy, air rushing underneath that skirt to tickle it, reminding her she was still a sexual being.

I knew she hadn't been able to recapture that part

of herself since the breast cancer. The double mastectomy had stolen that from her. We barely had vanilla sex anymore, let alone any serious playtime.

So, I had an idea that we should try trading places. When I first gave her the flogger with a pink handle, she cried. At first I feared I'd offended her, but then she hugged me hard and said it was the most incredibly thoughtful thing I'd ever done.

Today was our first experiment.

"How was your day, Mistress?" We hadn't discussed any details of how the role-reversal was going to work. All we'd decided upon was that the safeword would be "enough." I had no idea what to expect, and it was terrifying and thrilling all at once—like when you reach the peak of a roller coaster.

Her eyes narrowed. "Only speak when spoken to, My Pet."

And so it had begun.

"Yes, Mistress."

She opened the buttons of her suit jacket, no longer appearing uncomfortable with her reconstructed body as she leaned over her shopping bags, flashing substantial cleavage. She pulled a few toys from her bag. I watched eagerly, wondering what Adrienne had planned.

Selecting a collar, she announced, "We are going for a walk, My Pet. Get undressed."

I raised an eyebrow.

"Do not look at me unless I allow it."

"Yes, Mistress."

I took my clothing off slowly, deliberately, and stood before her holding my hard dick, eyes cast downward. She walked over and said, "Get on all fours."

Hmm; I wondered how long she would have me stay like this. *Could get uncomfortable*, I mused. But thoughts of what I might get in return...

I'd tried on numerous occasions to reassure her that I found her just as desirable as I always had, but nothing worked. The closeness that had developed from our special playtime together was dissolving, causing a rift that I didn't want to keep widening.

I would do whatever it took. Over the long weeks of watching her suffer and our bond deteriorate, I decided I needed to do something to empower her. The cancer robbed her of control of her own sacred temple, so I was offering her mine.

Thinking about all the pain and agony she'd endured over those many months saddened me, but also made me admire her strength. Now, she was entitled to use that strength for her pleasure.

Adrienne fastened the black studded collar around my neck and hooked it to a chain leash. Then she turned around and walked back to the bags. Of course I had to look as she bent over, her skirt rising up enough for me to get a peek at her naked snatch. My whole body tightened with desire as she pulled something out of the bag.

"Come." She tugged the chain, and I followed on my hands and knees to the kitchen. She went to the kitchen sink and quickly washed whatever she was holding.

Then, she filled it with water. She placed a pet bowl near the kitchen door. I noticed the words MY PET were painted on it. "Drink," she instructed.

I had the audacity to glance up at her and received a flogging on my buttocks. It was fascinating how the pain created little tingles of pleasure. I put my head over the bowl and drank, slurping up as much water as I possibly could. Her fingers ran through my hair, the tips of her painted nails lightly scratching my scalp.

She continued down my neck and back, and when she reached my buttocks, gave me a good, hard slap.

"Time to go outside, My Pet."

What?

She opened the kitchen door and placed the heel of one boot on my backside, giving me a little push. We had a fenced-in yard, so I didn't think anyone could see… but on the other hand, the thought of a voyeur gave me a little thrill, just as the cool night air did, brushing against my naked body.

I let Adrienne lead me around the yard, in the direction of the trees.

"Now, be a good boy for Mistress, My Pet."

I remained still, uncertain what she was asking of me.

Her flogger with the pink handle whipped against my ass, and then she slowly ran it down my crack until it tickled my balls.

"Go pee-pee, like a good boy, or I will have to punish you."

I didn't want to urinate in the yard. I wanted to fuck the shit out of her in so many ways that she wouldn't be able to sit for a week.

"I don't have to take a piss, Adrienne."

Suddenly, I felt her boot on my neck, pushing my face into the grass. The outdoor scents of tree bark and greenery enhanced my senses and my desire.

"Don't call me *that!*"

"I'm sorry, Mistress." I added a bit of a whimper to emphasize the point.

"I believe I'll have to find an inventive way to punish you." She actually chuckled as she stood in front of me. "You may look at me from my knees down," she commanded. I raised my head and watched her jacket fall to the ground. Then her skirt dropped around her ankles. She stood like that for a minute, making me highly aware of the fact that she was standing above me in nothing but a corset and those shiny black boots, snatch exposed. She kicked off the skirt. "Lick," she instructed, sticking the toe of her boot under my chin.

I traced my tongue from her toe, traveling up the curve of her leg to the bare skin of her thigh. I was rewarded with the type of wanton moan I hadn't heard in quite some time. I was bursting with need for her. I moved my tongue to her other thigh, but instead of allowing it to travel down her other leg, she lowered herself onto her back and spread her legs wide for me. Her boots dug into my back as I brushed my lips against her throbbing clit, suckling it before sticking two long fingers inside her wet hole.

"Take me, My Pet," she commanded, flipping around onto all fours. I pushed my aching cock deep inside her snatch.

As we both climaxed violently, I thought, *I could get used to this, my pet...*

But let's keep that our little secret.

VISCERA

Emily Bingham

Knives have never turned me on before, so I think it surprises us both when I ask my lover, "Would you cut me?"

"Of course!" he says, smiling slyly, always game to explore new things. His eagerness almost makes me regret asking. Almost. But I trust him, knowing it's because he cares that he's able to dole out the pain I regularly solicit.

I watch nervously as he reaches to his back pocket where the knife sits, the clip of it always peeking out of his jeans. Until this moment, I've never considered it as anything other than a practical tool.

With a flick of his wrist, the blade clicks open. He draws out the moment, letting the light glint off the razor-thin blade with its intimidating point. My entire body thrums.

He keeps his distance, looking me over, savoring the tension and the tease. I take in the knife and his face, unsure when he'll make a move. My fear has nothing to do with him and everything to do with my own hunger. I'm wet simply from watching him.

Soon the fingers of his free hand tug at my dress. I pull it over my head as he takes a step back to watch, the open blade held casually at his side.

When I'm seated again he places the knife in my bare lap and says, "Hold this."

Paralyzed, I focus on the tip poking my thigh where it dimples the soft skin. He steps out of his clothes while I'm too distracted to enjoy the show, focusing instead on the dangerous promise of the knife. So it's a relief when he removes it from my lap, yanks off my underthings, and pushes me down on the bed.

My nudity feels especially vulnerable tonight, and he toys with that feeling by wordlessly walking away; I watch his delicious body round the corner into the bathroom. I hear water run and the medicinal scent of alcohol wafts through the room as I realize he's preparing himself for the minor surgery about to be performed.

When he returns his touch is a balm against anxiety. I smile and lean into him, my gaze pinned to the knife. He kisses along my neck, playing innocent, but I stiffen to watch him pull the blade between us.

Our eyes meet and I don't dare look elsewhere. He slides slowly down my body to kneel between my legs, denying me the contact with his skin I'm longing for, parting us to assure his concentration. The intensity of his gaze is intimidating.

He's silent as he raises the blade so I can watch the course he draws in the air between himself and the target he's decided upon—the crook of my thigh where leg meets hip, so close to crotch as to be nearly indistinguishable.

I gasp as the impersonal metal presses into my flesh. He grins wickedly. Again the blade only dimples my skin; no blood yet as he continues to tease me.

His grasp on the knife handle changes suddenly as the blade makes purchase with my flesh; the surprise is greater than the pain. The only sensation is cold metal and my heart racing in response. The cut is finished in an instant.

My brow furrows as I suck in a breath and look down, but the cut is so superficial that it barely bleeds. It's more of a scratch, which part of me is disappointed by.

"Ready?" he asks, bracing the dull side of the blade with his index finger, preparing for the next cut. This is so visceral, so intimate, that tears well in my eyes. I nod. Immediately he's in action, creating a second and third cut identical and parallel to the first. Endorphins and dopamine flood my body as I struggle to catch my breath.

Soon he adds a fourth cut, this one deeper, and now there's blood and a blaze of heat. Rivulets so red they're almost black dance down the curve of my thigh. My vision blurs and my body swims; I feel made entirely of liquid until his fingers replace the knife, bringing me back to earth.

Setting the blade aside, he cleans the wound with a stab of isopropyl alcohol. Though his blade felt like barely anything, this stings and causes me to cry out. I hiccup around a breath and he stops, allowing the blood to creep to the surface again. We observe this small red river traversing the whiteness of my leg.

His body language changes suddenly as he stands, his cock popping free and rising to full mast, a display of the pleasure he's taken in his work. I reach to touch him but he pins my arms above my head with a single hand. I was so sure the game of power given and taken was over that I gasp.

I kiss along his neck, and his stiffness resting on my belly jumps. He's so near and yet so far away from where I long for him. I nuzzle my face and crotch against his and he sighs. Rather than giving in to temptation, he lifts away, using his legs to force mine wide and bring his hips close. I could have him if I angle my body just so, but his stern expression suggests I not try.

The Rorschach blot of blood that's seeped from my body decorates his where our legs met. He glances at this messy design, then at me, predatorily. With his free hand he grasps his cock, stroking it; I lick my lips. On a downstroke he uses his hardness to slap the marks on my leg, reopening the wound. He slaps me again and again with his cock until the ache he's awakening in those cuts is enough that I try to wiggle away, but splayed open and pinned down, there isn't anywhere for me to go.

He's motionless, cock resting in the tiny puddle of blood on my leg. Chuckling, he uses his hips to trace circles in it, reddening the head. Blood is so easily spread that this looks more frightening than it really is and I'm surprised to find this titillating.

Suddenly he's inside me to the hilt, blood and all. When he releases my hands I pull him closer, with no concern for keeping away the stab of discomfort when my leg rubs against him. After the long anticipation, the pain doled out expertly, it isn't long before we're both on edge. I can't bear to wait, allowing myself to cross over into orgasm.

When his turn comes, he draws out, stroking himself at my thigh. I grin to watch him climax, his whole body goosefleshed and quivering in aftershocks.

He collapses onto me for a kiss and when he pulls away our fronts are smeared in stains of color, a mixture of blood and come, the vitality of our bodies intermingling. I twirl my finger through the vastly different textures, painting the creamy opal in with the slippery claret red to fashion a testament to what our dark desires have created.

APPRENDIMENTO

Kathleen Tudor

Gia shifted behind me, breaking my concentration, and I bit my lip as I struggled to tune out my awareness of her. A pointless task. Every nerve ending in my body seemed to twist toward her like a weather vane, all atingle with anticipation. "*Avete*," I finally said.

"No, *bella*, it's *avere*." She tsked as she stepped forward and lifted a clothespin from the bowl on the table. My breasts were already adorned with several pins, but she had no trouble finding a bare spot to pinch. I winced as the clothespin clamped down, but that little pinch was just the appetizer. Taking them *off* again was the tricky part.

"To run," Gia said.

"*Correre*." I tensed, nervous until I saw her little nod, almost subconscious. This had seemed like such a good idea last weekend, when I'd been listening to the buoyant words flow from Gia's lips. As soon as she'd hung up the phone, I'd blurted it out: "Would you teach me Italian?" Oooh, she would, all right, if it's the last thing I do.

"How do you say 'I want?'"

I swallowed. "*Viene?*"

The pinch was a bright spark of pain, but I was focused on Gia's lips as they formed the words before my face. "*Voglio.*" I should have remembered. Wanting... now that was something I understood.

Language, not so much. The words seemed so obvious when she said them, as if the answers had always been there, lurking in the back of my mind. I'd studied the pages she gave me—why wouldn't any of it stick?

By the time I was done with our little lesson, my breasts bristled with clothespins and my eyes were clouded with unshed tears. I couldn't do this. It was too hard! I took a shuddering breath and held it, trying to will the emotion down. Out.

I was still working on getting myself together when Gia yanked the first pin free. I screeched in surprise, and then moaned as blood rushed back into the half-numb bit of flesh. Amazing how much such a tiny spot could *ache*.

"*Mela,*" Gia whispered.

"A-apple." It had been one of the first words I'd forgotten today, but fuck if it didn't spring nicely to mind right then.

Gia pulled me to my feet and guided my hands up to the pull-up bar we kept over the door of the study. We... didn't use it for pull-ups.

I gripped hard and closed my eyes, waiting, and just when I had begun to think that the pain was never coming, she pulled another pin free. "*Zucchero,*" she whispered, so close I could feel her breath on my throat.

"That's sugar."

Another word, another pin, again and again until my breasts tingled and ached and throbbed and tears flowed freely from beneath my closed lids. I held tight to the pull-up bar and sobbed. I was no good at this! I was never going to learn, and she was never going to let me quit!

By the time only two pins remained—one on each nipple—my sobs had quieted to the occasional sniffle and I felt empty of the frustration and despair. It had all poured out of me, and now I was an empty vessel, a bundle of nerves, and every single one pointed, as usual, to my True North.

Gia kissed my damp cheek and pressed so close that her breasts brushed against the last two clothespins, making me whimper at the short bursts of pain. It was nothing to what was coming.

But before she pulled either of them free, her hand slid down my belly and beneath the elastic of my pajama bottoms. My whole body jolted as her fingers slid into the engorged heat of my pussy lips, and gave a little purr of pleasure as she slid her fingers inside me. "My goodness you're wet. I didn't know you were so excited by learning!"

"Please..."

"No, no my sweet. In Italian."

"I...I...*Per favore!*" Dear sweet baby Jesus, why hadn't she told me how to say "more" yet? She pulled her hand away and I sagged, limp with thwarted desire. Her hand closed on a clothespin and she toyed with it, sending shocks of pain straight to my clit. "*V-voglio...*"

"Oh, *molto bene*," she said, and without mercy she ripped the clothespin off my nipple.

Pain surged through me, crashing and melding with the pleasure that wound ever tighter in my belly, and they both throbbed through me until my mind was afloat on a sea of sensations that I couldn't begin to name in any language.

"One more pin, *mia bella*. One more word. Are you ready? This word means 'come,' and that's just what I want you to do." She flicked the pin and I moaned. "I want you to come when I say. Can you do that for me?"

I reached for the words to beg, but they were lost to me. I whimpered instead and tried to press my chest forward, inviting her without words to shred that final piece of my self-control. To tip me over the edge and watch me fall and shatter. *Now. Please. More.*

Gia ripped the pin away, and she spoke with a clear, strong voice. "*Venga.*" Come.

The pain and the pleasure arrowed through me, and where they met there was an explosion that drove the breath from my lungs. My clit and my nipples seemed to pulse in rhythm with each other, and I was helpless, riding the sensation until stars sparkled in my vision.

"Breathe, *bella*. That's my good girl."

I obeyed, and soon enough felt strong enough to open my eyes. I was on the ground, but Gia had been ready for me, and rather than letting me topple, she'd guided me down and into her lap. A tremor twitched through my legs in an aftershock of pleasure, and the smile she gave me said she'd be riding my face until sunrise.

"That was *perfetto*," she said, gathering me even closer. "Tell me when you feel strong enough to stand and we'll move to the bed."

"*Sì*, Gia." I snuggled close, every nerve attuned to her, my muscles lax with satisfaction. Somehow, I was already looking forward to our next lesson.

FIRST SLAP

T.C. Mill

As always, he walked her up to her door, and they kissed good night on the front step. Her arms squeezed tight around him. Lips parted, tongues brushed each other in question. Stroked more certainly in answer. When the kiss finally broke, she invited him inside.

They stretched out on the couch, where the kissing continued, along with his hands moving over her back and then around. Just as he cupped her breasts, her fingers started to slide over the crotch of his jeans.

Behind his closed lids, his eyes seemed to roll back at the rightness of the feeling. She understood exactly how and when to touch. His hips stuttered toward her, letting her know it. Her nipples hardened through her bra. The kiss slowed, broke apart for breath.

"Can I…" she started.

"What?" He almost told her, *Anything, just go ahead*.
"Can I slap you?"

He was struck by how she asked the question. Clearly, but softly, revealing not shyness but a sort of respect for the request's significance. It was the same way she had suggested their first kiss, resolving his private uncertainty over the nature of a conversation that had grown steadily warmer and more intimate. Then, in what seemed like a continuation of their exchange, the kisses had gone on, deepening until her lips turned red and his felt swollen and helpless but not numb, not exactly.

He wasn't sure if that had anything to do with the present discussion. "Have I, um, done anything to deserve it?"

"No..." She leaned back enough that he could see her smile, a small quirk pulling the side of her mouth. "Or *yes*..."

"Oh. Kinky."

"Obviously." Her smile bared teeth.

He was half-hard from making out with her and that didn't flag, but he couldn't help thinking of corporal punishment. His parents were believers in it, not harsh or anything but routine and inescapable if they caught him climbing the rain gutter or teasing the neighbor's dog. It was the indignity of spanking that he'd hated most, that had kept him in line as a kid. For some reason the idea of her slapping him didn't feel undignified. He wasn't ready to think about her spanking him.

She pulled back a little and smoothed her hand down

her skirt, over her thigh. He thought of her hands as small, but mostly in comparison to his own. Still, he remembered her tight squeeze when they held hands, the way she almost gleefully ripped a baguette into pieces at dinner, the way she cupped his chin as they kissed. Blood rushed at the idea. First under his face, and then lower, and then back to his head in an afterflow of embarrassment. He was getting dizzy. And his cock was pressing uncomfortably against his fly zipper. He knew she knew it and that just made his arousal stronger. Maybe indignity wasn't the problem, not exactly.

"Okay." The words sounded almost liquid in his mouth. "Go ahead."

Her smile became close-lipped, shyer. "Thank you."

She got up and flipped, straddling his leg. Her knee sank into the cushions right in front of his erection. He found himself shifting his hips closer. She caught him doing it, laughed, and wiggled enough to make him regret it. He bit his lip.

"Yeah?" she asked.

"Yeah." He settled his arm over the back of the couch and let his hand hang limp. Part of him wanted to grip the pillows like the armrests of a dentist's chair, like he had to brace himself. Not that he thought she was going to hurt him all that much. Maybe subconsciously he wanted her to, wanted to be tough enough to take her worst.

One of her hands settled just above his elbow. The other touched his cheek. She started by stroking, fingers sliding down to his jawline and back up, against the grain of his stubble. His hair began to stand on end. Her lips parted, her breathing growing deeper and brushing across the bridge of his nose.

After a few more strokes, she lifted her hand and swung gently. Her palm was soft, and she didn't land hard, but neither did she hesitate or pull back at the last instant. She delivered a quiet tap against his sensitized skin. It was a dull blow; it didn't sting at first. The impact ran to his ear, which he realized was ringing. Not from her strike, but because he wasn't breathing right. He pulled air in, let it out in a short moan.

"Yeah?" Her fingers rubbed again, making circles in the heat on his skin. Her knee pushed his cock and made him moan more. She grinned.

"Yeah," he said. Dumb with it. "You can try again."

This time she rocked into the strike, and he thrust back against her because the friction at his groin was too much to resist. That brought him in to meet her. Their collision traveled through him in a burst not of pain but of warmth. His head turned, not with the blow but toward it. He nuzzled her fingers. When she laughed, he smiled, too.

Her next slap made the smile drop. But the dizzy, happy feeling remained: the urge to throw himself against her, into her, to let her surround him and do what she pleased. The whole-body *yes*.

It felt like falling in love all over again.

"I like it," he gasped. "I didn't know—but I *like* it."

She'd bared her teeth again. Her bright eyes danced over him, his quivering shoulders, his face, his chest that wasn't lifting and falling fast enough, his hips that jerked against her. "Look at you." Her grip on his arm vanished; instead her fingers started unzipping his fly. "You've gone red—scarlet—and you're *trembling*." The word spoken with a reverent hush. "You're gorgeous."

"I am?"

"Oh yeah." She started to stroke his cock, and just as he sank into it her other hand slapped him. Still gentle. A hint of sting beneath the growing heat. A clap like distant thunder, a lightning strike, a line of fire racing toward his core.

Both her hands went to the waist of his jeans and started pulling them down. It was all he could do to lift his hips to help her. Then his briefs—she just tucked them back under his balls. It felt awkward with them wadded up, still partially imprisoning his hips and thighs. A little undignified. But he didn't care, and she wasn't making fun of him. She'd started to slide against his leg, her silky panties gliding over his skin.

"Kiss me?" he asked.

A gush of heat and wetness from her cunt as she pulled on his tongue, pushed her own into him, as they stroked each other. He fucked into her fist. She held the nape of his neck tightly, and then her fingers came around to grip his chin, cup his cheek—the heat from her slap still rising there, her touch like velvet—and he loved it; he loved it so much and he never would have known if she hadn't asked.

CONTINUING EDUCATION

Rachel Woe

Izumi found the lingerie on the bed beside a squat black box and a letter of instruction written in Miles's meticulous hand. She was to eat the soup he'd prepared, wash her dishes, then change into the lace bra and panties.

She crumpled the letter into a ball.

Food could not have been further from Izumi's mind. Miles—her Master—whom she hadn't seen in weeks, had promised to spend his first night back with her. Thanks to a snowstorm along the coast, his plane hadn't touched down until six that morning. His text arrived shortly thereafter: an invitation to have lunch at his house. After letting herself in and seeing the table set for one, Izumi had almost walked out.

She plucked the box from the duvet, and was about to open it when her phone pealed with Miles's designated ringtone. She swiped to accept. "Oh, good. You're alive."

"Just barely." He sounded tired. "Have you eaten?"

By then, the scent of tomato and basil had wafted into the bedroom. "Not yet."

"Not yet...*what*?"

She sighed. "Not yet, *Sir*."

"That's better." Miles chuckled, his mirth a thinly veiled portent. No doubt Izumi would pay for her insolence eventually—an extra-hard flogging, a denied orgasm, no Netflix for a month. She shuddered at the thought.

"I would've preferred to eat with you. Sir."

"Yes, well. Unfortunately, I had an eleven o'clock meeting I couldn't cancel. Believe me, I would rather have spent the afternoon inside you."

Her pelvic muscles clenched, like an empty fist, want assuaging her ire. Miles was busy; they both were. His brand of busy just happened to include extensive travel, while Izumi's kept her tethered to a nurse's station.

"Have you opened the box?"

"No, Sir."

"Open it."

She removed the lid. Inside, she found a silver bullet-shaped vibrator, surprisingly heavy for its size. "It's so small."

"It's meant to fit discreetly into the pocket inside the underwear. After you eat, I want you switch it on and make sure it's snug against your clit, then text me."

"Yes, Sir. Will I see you tonight?"

"Perhaps. Depending on how today goes."

Izumi frowned. Miles's flair for topping from afar had served them well in his absence, but as his submissive, she longed to anticipate and fulfill his desires. How could she reach him if she couldn't touch him? Or serve him in ways that made her feel of use? As long as her confidence was tied to service, she'd never measure up.

Izumi drank her soup from an oversized mug. Back in the bedroom, she stripped down, shimmied into the panties, and nestled the bullet against her clit. Unfortunately, the device didn't so much as hum when she switched it on. She dressed in the time it took Miles to respond to her message. He told her to keep the bullet where it was, then texted a university address and a time less than an hour from now.

Curiosity piqued, Izumi copied the info into Google Maps and set off on foot.

The app directed her to a lecture hall bustling with students, where a front-row seat had been taped off: RESERVED FOR I.A. Her initials? She pocketed the sign and sat down, avoiding eye contact with students, most of whom were young enough to be her children.

A moment later, the crowd hushed. She scanned the room until her gaze centered on the source of everyone's attention: Professor Miles Pinchot.

This had to be his two o'clock introductory physics class. He shed his bag, but not his suit coat, then logged on to the computer.

"Today," said Miles, "we're going to set aside Newton's celestial mechanics to touch on Einstein's Spooky Action at a Distance, better known as Quantum Entanglement."

The bullet inside Izumi's panties fluttered to life. She grabbed the armrest, startling the student beside her.

"Who can give us a basic definition?" He gestured to Izumi's neighbor.

"It's the idea that an object can exist in two places at once," said the girl.

Miles nodded, pacing the platform, spine straight and hands tucked into pockets. That was why the bullet seemed broken, Izumi realized; it was remote controlled. "Right now," he said, "at the University of Maryland, there's a group of scientists working to employ this concept in order to build a fully secure, quantum computer network."

The vibrations sped up. Not enough to get Izumi off, but enough to hold her attention hostage. She folded her legs.

"They have a table," he continued, "upon which sit two metal boxes, one on each end. Both containing a distinct, separate atom, pulsing and spinning at its own rate. Between them sits a contraption that can shoot a laser beam into both boxes at once."

Izumi held stock-still, torn between arching forward to increase her pleasure, and back to try and abate it.

"When the laser hits the atoms, they spin faster, until each emits a photon. These photons then crash into each other, entangling the atoms left behind. Now, if you were to do something to affect one, the other would be simultaneously and identically affected."

The throbbing deepened. Her legs twitched. Miles was about to make her come in front of all these people. She could leave. Safe out. He wouldn't hold it against her. But he wouldn't have brought her here if he didn't want her to stay.

"So far, scientists have managed to observe entanglement at a distance of about eighty-eight miles. Theoretically, you could fly these atoms to opposite ends of the universe, and they would still be connected."

Tension ratcheted up Izumi's spine, and the harder she fought to stay composed, the more her legs trembled. He was going to make her come without touching her.

"It's believed that this kind of linking occurs randomly in the natural world, all the time."

The vibrations dulled to a whisper.

Her muscles cramped. Panic set in. She could feel her clit pulsing in anticipation of the orgasm that now dangled out of reach. Perhaps if she were able to rock her hips, but not with all these people here, their knees and shoulders and stale coffee breath pressing in on her.

Miles flashed Izumi a knowing grin. "I hope you were taking notes."

She wanted to scream. This had to be her punishment for acting petulant over the phone.

He kept the bullet at a bare strum for the remainder of class.

By the time the door slammed shut behind the last student, Izumi could hardly think straight. Miles hopped down from the platform in front of her.

"I'll be home in an hour. And I want the bullet inside you when I get there."

"Yes, Sir."

Izumi could feel him inside her right now. It didn't matter that they weren't touching. He could've been across the room, the country, the universe; it made no difference. Miles didn't have to push in order to move her, or pin her down in order to keep her in place. She was his. Here, there, everywhere. On her back or on her knees or standing in a crowded room. They were two and one in the exact same moment. Together and apart. Entangled.

BECOMING

Violet R. Jones

S he wore nothing but the blindfold, tape, and ropes. The muscles in her arms and legs ached. The ropes that bound her arms over her head were just a little too short to let her feet rest fully on the floor, so Elizabeth had to stand on her tiptoes like a ballet dancer on point. She tried to stay calm and make her breath come slowly, but it wasn't easy. The heavy tape over her mouth was slightly damp near her lips, but still fully in place.

Mistress had blindfolded Elizabeth before they left home, but Elizabeth still knew where she was. She recognized the scent of dust, floor polish, and canvas. She thought she could even smell the oils. Before she met Mistress, Elizabeth had practically lived here for two months. The museum was the whole reason Elizabeth had left behind her university, her friends, and her family, and moved to Paris. She had stayed in a student hostel, spent her money on cheap food and expensive charcoals, and spent her days copying the works of the great masters into her sketchpad. Back then, she thought that if she was dedicated enough some great mystery of art would reveal itself to her. Then Elizabeth met Mistress, and found something else to be devoted to.

The memory came back to her all at once. The sketchbook was snatched out of her hands. Elizabeth stood up and started to protest. She found herself staring into the darkest eyes she had ever seen. The woman who Elizabeth would come to call Mistress had an amused smile on her red-painted lips as she said, "How are you going to make art if all you do is copy the work of others?"

Elizabeth had never been in the museum and not been able to see the art. She could feel the largeness, the emptiness of the room. The total darkness behind the blindfold made her feel cut off, trapped in her own head. At the same time, her other senses felt awake in ways they seldom were. She heard the click of air-conditioning as it came on. The fine hairs on her naked body raised as the room chilled. Her nipples hardened.

Elizabeth thought about the picture she would make with her long hair spilling down her back and stopping just above the curve of her ass. Posed as she was, her butt and breasts were thrust out to their best advantage. Restrained, she would look inviting. She wanted to be seen. She wanted to be touched. Elizabeth had had enough of being alone.

Something in the air changed. Elizabeth heard foot-steps—more than one set of footsteps—on the tile floor outside the room where she was being held. Elizabeth lifted her head, alert to the change. She twisted in the ropes, feeling sudden apprehension and at the same time trying to figure out the best way she could show herself to her impending audience. It only made the binds bite into her wrists. The pain was familiar. It reminded Elizabeth what Mistress had taught her, and Elizabeth relaxed. The pain ebbed. Elizabeth heard a crack as the heavy wooden doors were pushed open. Elizabeth heard a pleased sigh and a murmur of voices. She felt herself begin to blush. They spoke French. In spite of living in Paris for almost a year now, she still only had a basic understanding of the language, but she could decipher just enough.

The room was warmer with the people in it. She could feel their eyes on her. She could hear their voices coming from all around her. Elizabeth was wet. She ached. She wanted to see them. She wanted them to do more than look. She pressed her thighs together. The ropes were almost a blessing. Elizabeth wasn't sure that she could keep from touching herself, and Mistress would be unhappy if she did that without permission.

The first touch was to the small of her back. The fingers were like bone—a thin old woman's fingers. They glided down Elizabeth's back to the curve of her butt. The still strong hand grabbed a fistful of Elizabeth's flesh and kneaded it. She was so grateful for the touch, she moaned loudly into the gag. Elizabeth rocked her hips. There was nothing for her to rock against but air.

A quivering voice sighed, "Belle."

Elizabeth felt an arm wrap tightly around her hips. A strong arm—a man's arm, she could tell by the scent of him. Then she felt a large hot mouth fasten on to her breast. It was almost too hot after the coolness of the room. The man began to suck. It was perfect and not nearly enough at the same time.

A quick argument erupted at her side. Elizabeth's thoughts were so scattered that she would not have been able to follow the conversation even if she understood the words. The argument was brief and after the silence that followed, more hands were on her. There were fingers caressing her, spreading her, rubbing over her clit, sliding into her cunt and her ass. There were thin fingers, fat fingers, and bony fingers. Elizabeth could not be sure how many people were touching her. She couldn't stop herself from rocking into the fingers playing with her. She forgot there was a reason to try.

Elizabeth's feet were pulled out from underneath her. Voices erupted like a cacophony of irritated birds. The world spun and strong hands were pulling her legs apart and something much thicker than fingers was filling her. Fucking her. Everything was...more. The scent of his sweat. The murmurs of the crowd. The cock pounding inside her. Elizabeth moaned into the gag.

He finished before Elizabeth could. She slipped from his hold. Elizabeth didn't notice the way he had been holding her up until the pain in her arms returned. Someone knelt between her legs and someone's tongue traced along her thigh.

With all the people touching her, the one she didn't feel was her Mistress. She knew it. She knew her Mistress's touch. Elizabeth wanted…

…but it didn't matter what she wanted. She was there for her Mistress's pleasure. As the stranger's tongue ran up her thigh and into the folds of her inner lips, Elizabeth had to believe that this was what her Mistress wanted. Everything seemed easier after that. It was not so much that her arms stopped aching. The pain just stopped mattering.

Elizabeth felt her Mistress's body press against her. She felt her Mistress's breath tickle the small hairs on the back of Elizabeth's neck. "Finally, you're ready."

The blindfold was removed. Elizabeth found herself looking into an antique mirror. Hazy as her vision was, she could still see that what was reflected back at her was beautiful and wild and more of a masterpiece than anything hanging on the walls. Elizabeth had become the work of art she had always wanted to create.

SUBMISSIVE-IN-CHIEF

Kristi Hancock

I raise the zipper on the inside of my black thigh-high patent-leather boots. The pair I keep in my locker at the club. A trophy for pleasing myself. I don the matching bustier that pushes my nipples to peek from the top. They pucker in anticipation. My Master awaits. The memory of his blond spiked hair and indigo eyes scorches my mind. I know what I want tonight, but I don't know what he wants for me.

I step through the doors, strut forward on my stiletto heels, and drop before him. My eyes go to the polished cement floor between my knees. It grinds against my bones. His fingers on my head tell me that my endurance of the pain pleases him. Hopefully tonight he will see to my pleasure in return.

His rough hand beneath my chin lifts me with the

merest touch. Since I've chosen him as my Dom, he has trained my body to want him—and it always does.

"You're hot tonight. I love your tits in that thing."

He's crass, but I don't care. He embraces his role, and he meets my needs. For now, I am his—mind, body, and soul. I am accountable to him alone.

He takes my hand and leads me through the crowd to the voyeurs' room where he sits with legs splayed in an overstuffed chair. My eyes can't help but absorb the portrait of him as my gaze returns to the floor. His crisp white long-sleeve shirt is unbuttoned at the neck. His freshly pressed black wool suit will soon be rumpled if I have my way.

He removes and holds out his glossy leather belt with the tarnished silver buckle. I'm trained to fold and place it beside him in the chair, and I do. My heart pounds as I wonder if he'll use it on me later, and where. On my ass? On my breasts? On my pussy? Will it leave me a rosy pink for hours, or marked for days?

He delivers his initial command. "Pet, focus."

My eyes quickly dart to his, and I fight a smile. The game has begun. Sweet heaven awaits me. I've earned it.

"Do it."

I have no doubt of his meaning. I lean forward so my breath strokes his clothing. His trousers give way under my gentle fingers as I unhook and unzip them down over the hard-on that may or may not belong to me.

"Shall I, Master?"

"You know better than to speak, brat."

I smile to myself, proud to have provoked the words and freshly willing to embrace my submissive role.

I slide my arms behind me and manacle my right wrist with my left hand. I lean in to lick the underside of his ten-inch cock from root to tip. Center. Left. Right.

I haven't looked up—he won't allow it—but his breathing accelerates. I'm nothing if not attentive.

I awkwardly wrap my tongue around the head of his curved penis as it rests against his taut abdomen. My long black bangs tickle my eyelashes though my short bob remains tucked behind my ears. His muscles contract beneath me, taking my target farther away. That doesn't matter. Within three seconds I have five inches of him in my mouth. I turn my head back and forth, my tongue rubbing all sides of the beautiful monster. His salty precome coats my mouth, and I back off to play in his slit.

"Stop."

I freeze in place.

"Release."

I resume my earlier position, this time with my hands on my knees.

"Stand. Turn. Bend."

The orders are my favorites, and I execute them flawlessly.

His hands caress the fleshy globes of my ass, pulling them apart and bouncing them up and down. He exhales across my cheeks as he inspects the massive clear glass plug I inserted half an hour before.

"I'm not going to ask if you're ready."

I don't want you to.

He pulls the toy out slowly, fully aware of how I love the stretching of my anus as it exits. I hear the snap of latex, the squirt of lubricant. He enters me slowly, not because my body requires it but because he knows I relish it so. I groan in pleasure and my back arches. Then he's inside me and pushing balls deep into the lube I added in hope of this very moment.

My pussy clenches, and my juices slick my inner thighs in excitement.

"Don't come yet."

Shit. He felt it. He always feels it. That's why I chose him.

"Brace."

I move through an awkward version of downward dog as we both go to our knees. He places his legs outside of mine and pushes them together. I shove back to regain his full penetration.

"Stop."

Like a porn star, my Master has total control over his orgasms. We peak together without exception. Whatever he's doing now, he's doing for me.

I don't have to wonder long as a vibrating rubber bullet strokes my clit. And he wants me to withhold my orgasm? *Damn.* He's getting better all the time. Master settles the toy inside my soaking core and then places the belt between my teeth. The gag is a relief after speaking all day. "Quiet, Pet."

He clasps my left hip in his hand, pulls out to the head, then rails me. Over and over I fight to keep my pussy clenched, my body stiff as he repeatedly rams his massive cock into my ass.

I taste the leather as I count to keep my mind tethered to sanity...*eleven...twelve...Oh god!*

My jaw opens and the belt clinks as it hits the floor. "Purple," I moan. We have safewords—ones I've never used—but this is our *unsafe*word, the word that means I'm losing control.

"Give me three."

One, two, three strokes and his prick pumps semen in rhythm with my contractions.

I scream my pleasure while he groans his. I collapse to my forearms as he drapes across my back. Our chests heave from our exertions.

Minutes later, our muscles slack, we struggle to stand. I release a sigh. There's no point in trying to disguise my reaction to his power. I turn and face him so I can watch him pull off the condom before tucking his softening cock away. The ritualistic closure gives me peace.

"Excuse me, ma'am?" he blurts out as I begin to turn toward the locker room. "It's been over two years. Don't you want to know my name?"

I shake my head in response and smile. "I'll see you next Thursday night."

After all, a CEO should be relaxed for casual Friday, shouldn't she?

ABOUT
THE EDITOR

RACHEL KRAMER BUSSEL (rachelkramerbussel. com) is a New Jersey–based author, editor, blogger, and writing instructor. She has edited over sixty books of erotica, including *Best Women's Erotica of the Year, Volumes 1, 2 and 3; Best Bondage Erotica 2011-2015; Dirty Dates; On Fire; Come Again: Sex Toy Erotica; The Big Book of Orgasms; Begging For It; The Big Book of Submission; Lust in Latex; Anything for You; Baby Got Back: Anal Erotica; Suite Encounters; Going Down; Irresistible; Gotta Have It; Obsessed; Women in Lust; Surrender; Orgasmic; Cheeky Spanking Stories; Spanked; Fast Girls; Do Not Disturb; Suite Encounters; Tasting Him; Tasting Her; Please, Sir; Please, Ma'am; He's on Top; She's on Top;* and *Crossdressing.* Her anthologies have won eight IPPY (Independent

Publisher) Awards, and *Surrender* and *Dirty Dates* won the National Leather Association Samois Anthology Award.

Rachel has written for *AVN, Bust*, Cleansheets.com, *Cosmopolitan, Curve*, The Daily Beast, Elle.com, Fortune.com, TheFrisky.com, *Glamour*, Gothamist, *Harper's Bazaar*, Huffington Post, *Inked, Marie Claire, Newsday, New York Post, New York Observer, The New York Times, O: The Oprah Magazine, Penthouse*, Refinery29, Rollingstone.com, The Root, Salon, *San Francisco Chronicle*, Slate, Time.com, Time Out New York, and *Zink*, among others. She has appeared on *The Gayle King Show, The Martha Stewart Show, The Berman and Berman Show,* NY1, and Showtime's *Family Business*. She hosted the popular In the Flesh Erotic Reading Series, featuring readers from Susie Bright to Zane, speaks at conferences and does readings and teaches erotic writing workshops across the country and online. She Tweets @raquelita, blogs at lustylady.blogspot.com, and consults about erotica at eroticawriting101.com.